I0847274

Other books by Kim Yesis:

<u>Mayenne Bay Series Novels:</u>

Artifice

Brush with Fire

Coming next: **Not for Profit**

<u>Nonfiction:</u>

Side by Side Tales from Behind the Canvas, a memoir
Maine Literary Award and Indie Book Award finalist

Artist in the Allagash, a wilderness journal

Brush with Fire

Book 2 of the Mayenne Bay Series Novels

KIM YESIS

For Charity and Justin,
joys of my life

Map of Mayenne Bay

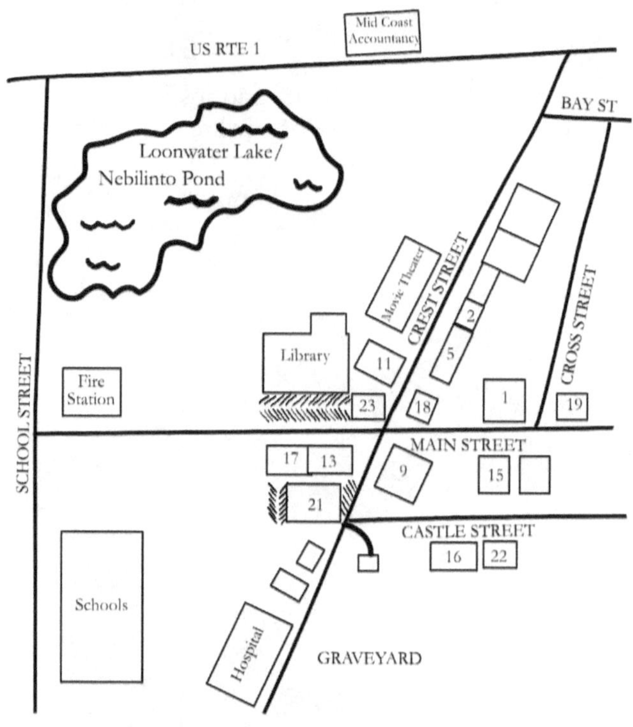

1-Bank
2- Bobby Tripp
3-Chamber of Commerce
4-Claire's Apartment
5-Consignment Shop
6-Creative Agenda
7-Fish House
8-Free Choice Hair Salon
9-Grace Grocery
10-Hardware Store
11-Historical Society
12-Main Street Coffee Bar
13-Mainsail Wine & Cheese
14-Mayor's House
15-Peabody Shoes
16-Police Station
17-Roxie's Frames
18-Salty Dog Toys
19-Seafoam Candy
20-Town Office
21-Unitarian Church
22-USPS
23-Vicki's Lingerie
24-Wharf Cafe

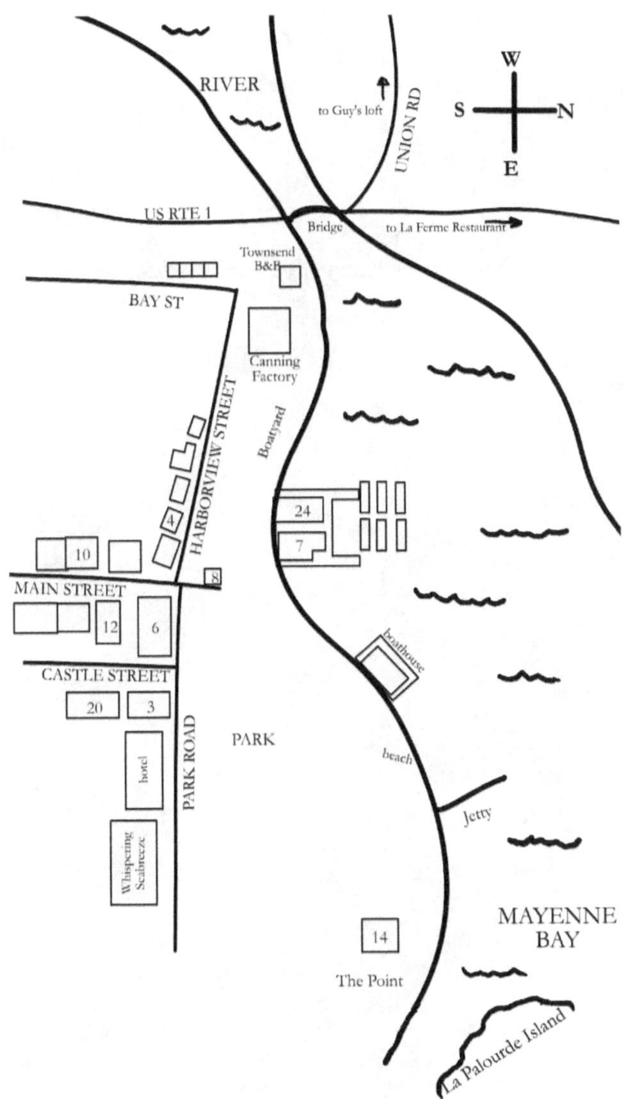

RIVER
UNION RD
to Guy's loft
W
S
N
E
US RTE 1
Bridge
to La Ferme Restaurant
Townsend B&B
BAY ST
Canning Factory
Boatyard
24
7
10
4
HARBORVIEW STREET
8
MAIN STREET
12
6
CASTLE STREET
20
3
hotel
PARK ROAD
PARK
Whispering Seabreeze
boathouse
beach
Jetty
MAYENNE BAY
14
The Point
La Palourde Island

"Nobody is ordinary if you know where to look."
\- Maeve Binchy

Bayside Squawker, November 1

Readers,

With all the foreigners in town, stores are stocking weird food. Japanese sweet potatoes. Vegan cheese. Purple carrots and yellow cucumbers. Falafels and curried chicken. Let's not crowd out traditional Maine food for tofurky on the Thanksgiving platter.

Captain Crabbish

Dear Captain Crabbish,

Regarding your October letter in favor of Columbus Day over Indigenous Peoples Day, I hope you won't repeat the same sentiment on Thanksgiving. Thanksgiving began as a celebration of a bountiful harvest made possible by the aid of our country's native people. Let's continue the tradition but with eyes open to the realities of the past.

Respectfully,
Louis Mac Rainwater

1

Smoldering

Claire Munro trudged down the empty hallway toward the ladies' room. The only sound in the building aside from the soft tap of her shoes against the polished floor was the occasional hum of the overhead HVAC system. She preferred the office this way. Alone, in the quiet, she could work without disruption. She had been deprived of that peace this evening, and her shoulders sagged with the weight of it.

Sweet, highly competent and good-looking, even in middle age, Ricky Diaz, the firm's lead IT systems engineer, was an office favorite who had come to Claire's rescue more than once when her computer malfunctioned. This evening, though it required him to remain after hours on a Friday night, he had arrived in characteristic good humor and set to work immediately to find the problem du jour.

"Nothing a system upgrade won't cure," he told Claire, "but I don't see that coming anytime soon. I'll have to patch it for now." He slid his short form—his head of curly black hair rose only slightly above Claire's own five feet, five inches—onto her desk chair, leaned into the computer screen and squinted his dark eyes.

While he worked, Ricky and Claire engaged in light-hearted chit-chat, which, tonight, featured Ricky's lament over the short supply of authentic Central American food in Maine.

"You read the Captain's letter last week. He's not a fan of weird food," she joked, hands gesturing as she spoke.

"Which means any food he doesn't happen to eat, I guess. Celia and I have begun lobbying Grace Grocery to expand its stock and we'd love to see a quality Latino restaurant in the area. Until then, we can only be thankful we're good cooks. One day I'll bring you one of her enchiladas with mole sauce. Heavenly."

When the conversation stalled, Claire used the interval to pack up her belongings for home. From the corner of her eye, she saw Ricky reach up to cover his eyes with one hand and then drop his head.

"Ricky, are you okay?" she asked urgently.

Without turning around to face her, he stammered an answer.

"Yes…no. Sorry. I'm struggling today. I…my…my daughter, Valentina, disappeared again this week. We can't find her. She's twenty-one, but bipolar, and has trouble staying on her meds without help. The last time she neglected her pills, it took us months to locate her. She was working the streets in Connecticut."

He choked on the last sentence, and his free hand flew up to cover the rest of his face.

Claire's intake of breath was audible. Ricky's shift from banter to heart-rending disclosure threw her off balance. She was accustomed to impromptu confessions from people, but this, his sunny disposition darkening before her eyes, pierced her soul. She cast a worried glance toward the door to make absolutely certain they were alone.

"I'm so sorry," she whispered.

The words seemed inadequate, but what else could she

say? She was just a work associate, an accountant, ill-equipped to deal with a mentally ill daughter gone rogue.

"Celia and I hoped relocation from the city to a small town would steady Valentina, but it hasn't changed a thing. All the professional help she's had, all the love and family support, all the intimacy of this place, have failed."

Ricky's story rang a familiar bell in Claire's ears. She, too, had come to Mayenne Bay for a change in circumstances though she hadn't trusted her transformation to the town's charms. She had seen from the start the same human struggles prevalent everywhere, scaled to size. Unemployment. A slow economy. A housing shortage. Competing interests. Ricky, it seemed, had relocated here with great faith in the powers of the place itself and had been sorely disillusioned.

"Ricky, I…if there is anything, anything at all, I can do, please tell me."

He wiped tears from his eyes before he turned to look at Claire.

"No." He shook his head, loosing his neatly arranged hair from its proper place. "Thank you. Sometimes, I feel so powerless and exhausted, it overwhelms me when I least expect it." He winced and added contritely, "I can't believe I just dumped all that on you."

"Don't give it another thought."

Claire had read the agony that lingered on his face. The lines around his eyes, usually traces of laughter, drooped in pain. She had reached out with one hand to squeeze his shoulder, then left her office to give him privacy to recover.

She had made her way down the hall and, for lack of a better idea, taken refuge in the ladies' restroom. For the first few moments, she had stood trance-like staring into her own hazel eyes in the large mirror, uncertain what to do next. Then, seized by the inevitable urge to move her body that always followed an emotional episode, she stroked back her auburn bob several times with her fingers, shook herself out and began to pace the floor, breathing out the tension.

Claire was troubled not only by Ricky's story but by the fact that it had taken her by surprise. She felt she should have detected such deep distress in her friend before now, before her longstanding and inexplicable magnetism for troubled souls had drawn him out. Since her adolescent years, strangers and friends alike had unloaded their hearts to her. It was rarely convenient and, at times, like this evening, almost more than she could bear. She stopped pacing, straightened her spine and threw off the sensation. How could she bemoan a little vicarious discomfort when Ricky lived with such pain first-hand?

By the time Claire returned to her office, Ricky had gone. A sticky note stuck to her screen read "Thanks for listening". She pulled it off and fingered the note thoughtfully. Tossing it felt cold-blooded. She stuffed it into her pants pocket and headed for her apartment on Harborview Street in the heart of downtown.

At home, Claire prepared a bath seasoned with lavender oil, turned on soothing music and set a glass of red Bordeaux on the corner of the bathtub. As she shed her slacks, she heard Ricky's note crinkle in the pocket and withdrew it. "Thanks for listening." She was glad she had been on hand for him in such a moment, but struggled to shake off his plight. Always quick to tap into feelings but slow to recover, the discomfort was still with her when she emerged from the tub, wine glass drained, fingers and toes pruney. She stuck the note to her bedroom mirror and stared at it before flipping off the light and slipping into bed.

Sleep eluded her for several hours and, even when she found it, her rest was fitful. To make matters worse, Claire awoke, dazed and grumpy, to the wail of Mayenne Bay's fire siren, one of the prices she paid for living in town. She glanced at the clock: 4:47 a.m. When the siren stopped, she burrowed deeper beneath the warm bedcovers listening to the wind and the muffled crinkle of snow as it struck her window, a stark contrast, she imagined, to the roar of a runaway fire.

"I hope no one's hurt," she said aloud, then caught herself and laughed. "You're going to have to change this habit of talking to yourself if Guy moves in, especially at this hour."

Claire had been seeing kind, blue-eyed Guy Gardiner, a graphics designer and fine artist, for just over six months now, if she didn't count the interval when they split after an explosive argument. A few weeks afterward, she had found him standing penitently by her car, a wet painting of a red rose in his hand and an apology on his lips. The raging headwind that had been her anger had ended in a gentle breath of forgiveness against his shoulder. They had been together ever since.

She shifted uncomfortably beneath the comforter, and her heartbeat quickened. Her own failed relationships had pushed her, and her mother's sad history with men had trained her, to a single life. Then, Guy had appeared on the scene and disrupted her well-laid plans. She had resisted him at first. Now, they were virtually inseparable and contemplating co-habitation. At least, that was what Guy wanted. A committed, live-in partnership. The idea scared Claire half to death. She pulled her pillow over her face, then sat up and leaned forward on bent knees as her head flooded with the recent counsel of her cousin and best friend, Daniel Munro.

"Look, Claire, I urged you to walk away from him after you two argued, but Guy has really come around since then. Even I can see that. You two get on like a house on fire. Take the man at his word. He wants to live with you. He loves you, for God's sake."

Daniel had plopped onto the couch after these opening remarks and run one hand through his wavy, ginger hair while the other slid the tissue box closer to his tearful cousin. Claire had answered through watery eyes and sniffs.

"Only until he meets my family."

"You can't believe your family could change his mind if he's that serious."

"Why would a man tolerate, let alone tie himself, to a family like mine? Remember when I brought Mick home to meet them?" Her face took on a faraway look, and her voice dropped. "It was excruciating, mortifying. Robert and Mark bickered. Mom bitched at Dad without drawing breath, then broke into sobs. Dad overdrank, then abandoned the dinner table for the bar. Mick might as well have been old wallpaper for all the attention they paid him."

"I think you mean 'prick', not 'Mick'," snorted Daniel, "and he was as good as wallpaper, a nonstarter and a far cry from the man Guy is. Your chosen lifestyle tells Guy all he needs to know about where you stand in relation to your family's behavior. Can you really believe he won't be able to put things into perspective and see your worth? Think of Darcy and Lizzy Bennet."

That last remark earned him a giggle. Claire was a Jane Austen fan, and *Pride and Prejudice* was her favorite. Even Guy, through her influence, had felt compelled to watch the movie just to understand the analogies Claire drew from it.

"That's just it. Why should he have to adapt? I don't want to condemn any man to a lifetime of insanity, of constantly dodging and checking, just to be with me. You know what it's like. Half a glass of gin and tonic, and Mom is out of control. If the boyfriend-of-the-month doesn't foul things up, then Dad shows up, and they tear each other to pieces. I'm not sure which is worse. My family knows no boundaries. How, in good conscience, can I invite a man like Guy, raised in a civil home in a close-knit family, to join that kind of bedlam?" She released a long breath and shook her head. Her voice quivered with her next words. "On the other hand, how can I fail to show him the truth and still claim to trust him?"

"Exactly," answered Daniel with a tone of finality, "You've hit the nail on the head."

Claire's gaze shifted to the window as she contemplated her dilemma. She had survived her nuclear family but never thrived. The day she had escaped to college had begun a long process of disentanglement from its influences. She knew then she would never return, not to live, anyway. In the years since, she had managed a precarious balance between attachment and detachment. How could she prepare Guy for this knife's edge?

Daniel regarded her with a knowing look.

"I can hear your wheels turning. The dutiful scout in you continues to believe you can head problems off through advance preparation. Claire, it's impossible to be ready for every contingency. Your family is too erratic. If you want to be honest, you're going to have to give Guy the full monty and deal with the fallout, like I did when I came out to my parents. How many times have you counseled me that I can't control anything but myself? Though, admittedly, self-control does elude me sometimes."

He ended with a laugh, and Claire laughed with him, in spite of herself. She had spent thirty years raising preparation to an art form in a quest for some semblance of order in her life. A little forethought, she maintained, could hobble the gods of chaos enough, at least, to survive the worst of the pandemonium. Daniel had witnessed these efforts, declared them futile, and persisted in the same opinion he repeated today. In her bones, Claire knew he was right. There was no way to prepare Guy for a visit to the Munro family. And even if she could control the situation, she would deprive him of the unfiltered truth he deserved.

The impotence she felt made her stomach so tight it hurt.

"I'll be there if you want me to," Daniel had offered gently.

"Count on it when it happens but don't expect it anytime soon."

She had reached over and hugged him in earnest.

Claire returned from this reminiscence to the present wintry morning with the same knotted gut. She pushed back the blankets, suddenly quite heavy, and set her feet on the cool carpet next to her bed. Her eyes landed first on the work bag she had dropped carelessly by her bedstand last night and then on Ricky's sticky note on the mirror. Instantly, her own troubles melted away, displaced by the agony of the Diaz family. It was just as well. Guy was taking her to breakfast this morning. If she didn't pull herself together, he would be reading her thoughts as easily as Daniel.

Bayside Squawker, November 8

Mayenne Bay Neighbors and Friends:

Houses burn hot and fast. Be sure all your holiday lighting is safely connected. Water your trees frequently. Have a working fire extinguisher handy.

Each Saturday from November 9 through December 21, 9 to noon, your volunteer firefighters will be at the station to provide free fire extinguisher inspections and fire prevention advice.

Roxanne Nadeau, Volunteer Fire Chief

Readers,

Please, let's enjoy the remains of leaf season and not rush Christmas. Leave trees and lights in the storage room until December.

Captain Crabbish

2

Brush with Fire

Louis Rainwater pressed his large foot hard on the accelerator, his usually patient nature overruled by imperative. He crossed shoreline Route 1 just outside of town and raced, to the extent one could race in blowing snow, west down Union Road, heart thumping. Sunrise was over an hour away, but at least the dark enabled him to keep one eye on the orange glow above the trees in the distance. He had purchased the neglected woodland acreage just west of Mayenne Bay meaning to preserve the stands of pine and hardwood and plentiful native vegetation. Barely a week after closing on the place, fire threatened to severely damage, if not fully consume, the expanse. If only the weather reports had been accurate, the night would have been drenched with heavy rain, rather than obscured by an early November snowstorm.

The wail of the fire station siren stopped, signaling his fellow firefighters were on their way. When it had first sounded, Louis had already been awake, intending early Saturday work hours at the engineering office, and had been first to respond to the call from dispatch. Once he had learned the fire's location, he had grabbed his gear and jumped behind the wheel of his own four-wheel-drive pick-up, knowing his fellow volunteers would be right on his heels. He grimaced. The team would not make good time on these treacherous roads. And then there would be the challenge of the unfamiliar and narrow access lane, obstructed by snow-laden tree branches, blowing flakes and darkness.

He was close enough now that the acrid smell of smoke struck his nostrils even through the closed window, thanks to the gusting wind. Louis steered the truck's off-road tires onto the access lane, the only existing inlet to the property aside from footpaths. The vehicle pushed and fish-tailed its way through eight inches of unplowed snow and bumped hard each time it made contact with the uneven ground beneath. Tree branches whacked the windshield and scraped the sides of the truck before popping back into the air, freed of their snowy burden. He kept pressure on the pedal, knowing full well that, though snow might slow a fire, it couldn't be counted on to suppress the flames, especially in this wind.

He slid into the turn onto the driveway that led to the only structures on the 200-acre property. The tires alternately gripped and spun him toward the bones of a dilapidated house that leaned precariously to one side as though it couldn't quite decide whether to live or die. Louis's expression tightened, and his stomach wrenched. The house itself was not on fire. Orange light radiated from behind it. His worst fear, that the very woods he had intended to save might perish, gripped him. Yet, the smoke didn't smell like fresh wood; it had a chemical odor that Louis could taste on his tongue.

He turned off the ignition but left the headlights on, then slipped from the truck cab to pull on his protective mask, suit, boots and goggles. He jogged toward the glow at the back of the house behind the meager beam of a flashlight, listening closely. His feet swooshed through the virgin snow cover. Wind sounded against his ears. Not once did he hear the tell-tale gunshot of frozen tree sap exploding or the distinct crack of a desiccated branch as it split or fell. The fire's smell, rush and crackle told him the source was more likely a structure than a stand of trees. The old shed, he thought. It must be the shed.

He checked his face mask before he approached the flaming shed, the only outbuilding on the place, about a hundred feet back from the tottering house. He stopped at a safe distance, his training reflexively kicking in. He needn't have worried. The structure was so far gone that anything explosive would have blown by now.

A truck siren sounded, telling Louis the fire brigade was almost at hand. Familiar red lights flashed across the tree tops along the access lane followed by a single, blinking blue light. It was probably a police SUV driven by the town's rookie cop, Officer Ben Tripp, who usually got the less palatable assignments, like leaving his warm bed to investigate a pre-dawn fire on a wintry morning.

The vehicles came to a stop next to the house. The firefighters sprang into action and efficiently unraveled hose along the tracks Louis had made. A torrent of water burst from the nozzle, arced through the air and landed on the shed. Bull's-eye. Within thirty minutes, the shed, still illuminated by vehicle headlights and portable flood lights, was a smoldering mat of debris out of which rose the remains of its blackened, stone foundation.

"This could have been so much worse, Louis, after such a dry fall."

The voice came from behind him and was louder than usual to compensate for the surrounding din. It was the smallest, but no less capable firefighter, Fire Chief Roxanne Nadeau, the 35-year-old owner of Roxie's Frames downtown. Louis, who stood over six feet tall, looked down at the muscular, five-foot-four woman who ran their unit. Roxie had overcome a great deal to qualify as a firefighter, including getting gear resized so it wouldn't hobble her and devising ways to perform the job despite lower height and weight than her fellow volunteers. She had proven exceptionally useful, too, by fitting into spaces larger firefighters could not. Roxie's determination, grit and heart had won the respect and trust of her team, resulting in her position as chief, though they affectionately nicknamed her "Cubby Rat" because she could fit into nooks and crannies.

Louis shone his flashlight at the nearby stand of unscathed trees.

"You guys were quick to get here. I think it made all the difference. Thanks. I'm really grateful."

Roxie nodded and returned to the firetruck to join the clean-up.

Louis had fought countless fires in his tenure with the rescue squad, but none before had struck so near to his own welfare. His own loss was, mercifully, negligible, a rickety, old shed he had intended for storage but hadn't yet had the chance to put to use. But this first-hand brush with fire gave him a small but humbling taste of the fear and loss felt by the victims he served.

He stepped gingerly around the ruins at a safe distance and continued to scan with his flashlight while the firefighters bustled around him double-checking the smolders and clearing equipment. Evidence of the shed's former contents, contents he hadn't had time to inspect prior to the fire, was visible amongst the remains on the cellar floor: sooty bowls, glass jars, a crumbled clay crock, pieces of metal and other objects he couldn't identify in the muck and the semi-darkness. It occurred to him that this charred clutter was all that remained of a bygone person; an entire history had been snuffed out this morning in a single blaze.

"I mean no offense for your loss," Louis said aloud, looking skyward to the ghosts of the shed's past, "but I'm thankful for the unspoiled land."

Another voice called from behind.

"Louis!"

It was Ben in his customary khaki uniform buried under a thick, black winter jacket, hood and boots. "The team tells me everything's under control here for the moment. I'll be back as soon as I can with the fire inspector after dawn, if you'd like to join us."

"I'll wait here."

Louis felt better watching over the place for the little time remaining until first light, just in case. As he began his lone vigil, the chill hung on, intensified by the wind. Hoping this early freeze wasn't a harbinger of an extreme winter to come, he settled into the shelter of his truck cab and blasted the heat to defrost his fingers and toes. For the next hour, he drifted in and out of sleep, then awoke fully to a hazy dawn glowing through the windshield. His lips curved in an involuntary smile. Sunrise was his favorite time, a case of both nature and nurture, belonging as he did to the Wabanaki People of the Dawn and being naturally a morning person. Louis sat back to enjoy the birth of the new day over these woods that had been spared this night by an inexplicable stroke of good fortune.

Back in town, Guy pulled into Claire's driveway just as she finished clearing it of snow. He slid a ski hat from his head and bent down for a kiss. Claire responded warmly. They hadn't seen each other all week.

"Did you hear the siren this morning?" she asked.

"My place is too far out, but I smelled the smoke when I drove down Union Road."

"You wouldn't think a fire could survive this."

She gestured toward the mounds of snow she had shoveled.

"I'm sure the wind offset whatever meager benefit the snow provided. Lots of drifts out there."

Claire grabbed her bag, flipped her hood over her head and headed hand in hand with Guy down Harborview Street to Main. They turned in the direction of the bay and trudged the remaining distance to the Fish House restaurant on the wharf, pushing snow with their feet and listening to the soft rustle made by their boots.

"I love the way snow muffles sound," Claire said.

"When there's a blanket of it, and the wind is calm, I can hear my paint brush against the canvas."

Claire stopped.

"It never occurred to me to listen for the sounds of a paint brush."

She started walking again.

"Think this snow will stick?"

It was Claire's first winter in Maine, and she was learning the ropes.

"No. Ground's not cold enough yet, and it's going to be sunny this afternoon."

They climbed the neatly swept and salted steps into the warmth of the Fish House, the place where they had first met, and stripped off their winter wrappings. The dining room was already almost full despite the weather or, perhaps, because of it. Chatter about the morning fire was in full swing. Guy and Claire looked around for Celeste Baptiste, the restaurant's most popular server and their friend, who delivered breaking headlines as generously as steaming brew.

"No Celeste today," remarked Claire.

She gave a final stomp of her snow boots on the floor mat.

"That's a first for me," Guy said. "I've never been served by anyone else here."

"Celeste is on vacation in Florida," Patty Libby informed them from the cashier's counter. Patty was owner of both the Fish House and the *Bayside Squawker* newspaper. "Kitty is handling Celeste's shifts this week."

"Should I have heard of Kitty before this?" Claire asked.

"I'm surprised you haven't," Patty answered as she led them to their favorite booth.

Behind her, Claire stared at the back of Patty's greying head, just an inch or two below her own, and observed the slight waddle in the gait of her overweight body. Patty's stoutness, it seemed to Claire, fitted the woman's jolly and generous nature. When they reached the booth, Patty dropped her voice to a whisper and leaned in.

"Kitty's a no-nonsense waitress, sometimes abrasive, but very efficient. Few can remember the Fish House without her. Owners have changed, but Kitty has remained the constant. I kept her on, help being so hard to find, but the surprise was mine. You wouldn't guess it from her age, but she can single-handedly manage a crush of customers for hours. She's a longstanding fixture in Mayenne Bay, though no one knows exactly how longstanding. People have placed bets on her age."

If the Fish House was the town's newsroom, Patty was the town's bookie, though always for a good cause. She called to Kitty as Guy and Claire took their seats.

"Kitty, this is Guy Gardiner and Claire Munro, Saturday regulars of ours, with a preference for this corner window booth. Guy and Claire, this is Kitty Greenwood, a pillar of the place."

She left them to get acquainted.

Kitty greeted them in the thick, husky voice of a chronic smoker. She made no small talk but took their order in business-like fashion, hissing as she spoke through slipping false teeth. Kitty was indeed old, judging from her skin, but her frame was muscular, and she moved with alacrity. She wore a short, brown wig, pink lipstick and heavy foundation make-up over her entire face and neck in a shade darker than her natural skin color.

People, in general, fascinated Claire, unusual characters like Kitty more than most. Claire studied the woman top to bottom and continued staring until Kitty disappeared behind the kitchen doors and Guy interrupted her.

"Come back to earth, Claire. We'll get more on Kitty from Celeste when she gets back. I have a bit of business to transact this morning."

Claire's head jerked to face him.

"An invitation from my mother."

Her eyes narrowed.

"What kind of invitation?"

"Will you join me and my family for Thanksgiving?"

Claire took in a breath. She had already visited Guy's family once and instantly computed the emotional calculus of a second visit. Gardiners two. Munros zero. The imbalance would undisputedly shift the initiative onto her for a reciprocal invitation. It was a normal next step in most relationships, but normalcy didn't apply where the Munros were concerned. Panic mounted in her chest. She self-consciously regarded Guy. His face revealed nothing but patient expectation. Unlike Claire, he wasn't keeping score; he was simply waiting for an answer. She shoved the specter of her own family down deep and smirked.

"Who's cooking?"

With all Claire had found to enjoy during her first visit to the Gardiner's place, the food itself had been dismal. Mrs. Gardiner had piled Claire's plate high with overcooked meat, potatoes, and mushy green beans made palatable only by an excess of ketchup. Claire didn't look forward to disguising the deficiencies of an entire Thanksgiving dinner the same way. Guy, who freely admitted these shortcomings, read the misgivings on her face and laughed gamely.

"I think you'll be safe at Thanksgiving. Some extended family will be there. Mom will roast the turkey, but everybody else will bring the side dishes and desserts. It'll be hit-or-miss to a degree, but where would we be without the adventure of mystery casseroles?"

"Okay, I'm in. What should I bring, aside from a super-sized bottle of ketchup?"

"How about homemade rolls or muffins? Stick to plain food. No one will eat them if they can't identify the ingredients by sight. I'm bringing steamed garden peas and baby onions. What you see is what you get."

"Got it. Thanks for the hint and thank your mom for the invite."

Claire sat back in thought and sipped her coffee. She had just reconnected with her own mother after a six-month break that Claire, in a fit of frustration, had instigated. It had been her only recourse to stop her mother's stomach-churning phone calls about her horrible, live-in boyfriend. Hannah Munro hadn't been pleased but had maintained silence until one week ago, when the calendar turned to November and reignited her annual, you-should-be-home-for-the-holidays pitch. To Hannah, a holiday visit from her daughter was a moral obligation that far outweighed the charitable spirit of the season. Hannah, too, kept score of home visits, less from a sense of fairness or affection than a determination to get her due.

Claire was perfectly content to push her next home visit well out into the new year. She found herself unequal to anything but procrastination just now when it came to introducing Guy to her family. She suspected, once her mother learned of Thanksgiving with the Gardiners, Hannah would redouble her insistence on Christmas. Claire had already argued preoccupation with her new job as an excuse to stay in Mayenne Bay in December but knew Hannah would not accept defeat until all hope was gone.

Claire's and Guy's attention was drawn to stomping feet at the restaurant entrance announcing the arrival of Ben and Louis. They had met Ben through his investigation of an art theft over the summer, and he had since taken Claire into his confidence more than once. They knew Louis from afar for his recent advocacy of Wabanaki interests along the Mayenne Bay shoreline. The two men slung their parkas onto the coat rack and made their way to Guy and Claire.

"Just came from the fire," Ben told them. "Sorry, we both smell like smoke."

"It's no wonder," said Claire. "I heard the sirens. That was an early call. Where was it?"

Ben jerked his head toward the firefighter.

"On the land Louis just bought to the southwest of town."

He made introductions.

"An old shed behind what's left of the house lit up just before dawn," Louis told them. "The whole structure is gone except for the stone foundation and chimney."

Guy's and Claire's faces bore concern, but Louis just shrugged.

"It was in bad shape anyway. I'm just relieved the fire didn't spread to the trees, lucky in all that wind after such a dry spell."

"Do you know what sparked it?" Guy asked.

"Jury's still out on that," answered Louis. "The inspector couldn't see much under the snow cover. We'll reconvene there later today to see if the sun melts enough of it off." He shook his head. "I got off easy. I closed on the place just last week, so nothing of mine was inside. There are items all over the cellar floor, though, that make me wonder if the shed was once somebody's workshop or studio."

Guy's face perked up at the word "studio".

"Don't get too excited, Guy," Ben laughed. "It's too soon to draw conclusions. If Louis had found a pencil and a ruler, they wouldn't make the shed a schoolroom."

The two men left to find a table.

Once alone again with Guy, Claire told him of Ricky Diaz's disclosure at work and the disappearance of his daughter, Valentina, which, aside from the fire, had weighed on her mind from her first waking moments. Her brow furrowed.

"So much can go horribly wrong in a family. I can't imagine being Ricky or Celia right now."

"I'm sure it's hard on them, but Claire, most families manage in spite of the challenges. Don't cast a dark shadow over all family life just because one family is struggling."

She leaned back in her seat and regarded him but didn't dare ask if his words referred to the Diazes or the Munros or both. She reached forward to take both his hands in appreciation. This was not the first time Guy had stepped in, gently, but coolly, to temper her disordered emotions or stop her from chasing fear down a rabbit hole. He had a way of invoking reason, calm and even optimism that kept her from spiraling out of control.

Bayside Squawker, November 15

Readers,

Most of us never locked our doors, but now we have to. Things went missing from stores and yards all last summer. A painting was stolen from the art show. The mayor and town council were duped by a scam artist. Now, there's been a suspicious fire at the Rainwater place. We need answers about what is happening to our town.

Captain Crabbish

To the Mayenne Bay Fire Department:

It's bad enough to have an arsonist in town. We don't have to awaken everybody in fright with that outrageously loud fire siren. It's especially bad for the hospitality business. This is the age of technology. Firefighters can be contacted discreetly by beepers and phone alerts. Bring our fire department up to date and disable that antiquated siren.

Gloria Townsend, Owner
Town's End B&B

3

Times Are Changing

At work on Monday, as Claire took a swig of coffee and opened the first client file of the day, Ricky's face poked around the door.

"Everything working okay this morning?"

He nodded toward Claire's computer as he approached her desk.

"So far, but it's early yet."

She threw him a teasing grin. Ricky waved it off.

"Don't forget our new manager starts today."

His unembellished words spoke volumes.

"Erin O'Farrell," was all Claire said in reply. The expression on her face was more eloquent.

Claire had accepted a lateral position at Mid Coast Accountancy as a means of relocating to Mayenne Bay but had not abandoned her hopes of advancement. Despite her solid performance record and previous experience at New Jersey firms, Mid Coast Accountancy had barred her from applying for the manager position. The reason given, spurious in her mind, was less about competence than the fact that Claire had not yet completed the one-year-of-employment prerequisite for an internal transfer. She had allowed her vexation to ruffle her feathers for only a day or two, then had moved on. There would be other opportunities. Her situation in Mayenne Bay was, in every other respect, exactly what she wanted.

During the hiring process, Claire had been given the dubious privilege of participating in the manager candidate interviews. Erin O'Farrell, a shapely woman of medium height with shoulder-length hair, dyed metallic red, freckles and green eyes, had certainly turned heads as she had been paraded through the office. Claire, too, had thought Erin was attractive until she had detected a disingenuousness of manner that had tarnished the woman's luster. At several points during the interview, Claire had felt compelled to drop her gaze to the floor to hide her unfavorable impression of the candidate, a reaction she sensed Erin mistook for weakness. Erin had been offered the job despite Claire's reservations.

"Any news on Valentina?" Claire quickly asked Ricky in a bid to take her mind off Erin.

"No."

With one heavy syllable, Ricky had quashed all optimism.

"Have you reported her disappearance to the police?"

"No. I've been hoping to find her myself. I don't want her mental illness and past street life to become public knowledge. Dignity is just about all she has now."

"I'm out of bounds here, speaking out, Ricky, but you may not be able to safeguard both Valentina and her dignity. The best hope of finding her lies in outside support even if it's too public for comfort."

She winced at her own frankness. Ricky clicked his tongue and turned away. Claire couldn't mistake his displeasure but didn't regret her words.

"Sounds like you've been talking to Celia," he said

tightly with his back to her.

Claire let the seconds tick by in silence and hope. Finally, Ricky turned back to face her, hands up to prevent further entreaty.

"I guess I just needed to hear that from an objective person I respect. You're right. I'll go to the station today. Celia will declare you a saint."

He left without another word.

Two days later, the newly anointed saint arrived at Guy's loft, just off Union Street west of town, bearing a blessing of Celia's homemade enchiladas in mole sauce. She was greeted by Guy from the floor, where he sat cross-legged on the carpet and swayed to Frank Sinatra's voice sounding from the turntable. He sniffed loudly as Claire made her way to his kitchenette.

"That smells good."

"Enchiladas. Celia Diaz made them, like she has nothing better to do with a daughter missing, to thank me for convincing Ricky to seek help to find Valentina. Honestly, he didn't need much of a push." She pulled plates and utensils from the cupboard as she spoke. "Things with Ricky have been awkward since I nudged him, though."

"You told me once before that people sometimes resent you after sharing intimate stuff."

"Yeah. After the fact, people can feel exposed or afraid I won't be discreet or just angry at something I said. This one hurts, though. I really like Ricky. Celia, at least, is happy, hence the food. And she and Ricky agreed to let me put up posters. I'll be working on that this coming weekend."

She swooped down to peck Guy's cheek and set his enchilada and drink beside him on the floor.

"What's all this?"

In response, she was treated to a boyish, almost giddy, side of Guy she had never before seen, so full was he of Louis's burned-out shack and its possible secrets. Spread before him on an old blanket were the workings of Guy's dismantled metal detector, dragged from the garage where his widowed landlady, 78-year-old Annabelle Clark, allowed him storage room. The Great Detectorist of Guy's youth had re-emerged and was aching for a comeback. Claire ate at Guy's wobbly café table while she watched in amusement as he cleaned and calibrated the machine between mouthfuls of enchilada and song lyrics.

The metal detector was ready to go by Saturday. That evening, the Mayenne Bay Art Club held its November meeting at Claire's place, where Guy approached Meilin Li, club president, about putting it to use at the burn site.

Meilin, a forty-year-old woman of Asian descent, just five feet, two inches tall, radiated energy and enthusiasm for art that far outsized her tiny stature. After years as a Connecticut gallery owner, she had sold out and established the Creative Agenda art supply store on Main Street. She was also the chair of the Mayenne Bay Art Show committee.

"Meilin, did you hear about the shed that burned last week on Louis Rainwater's property?"

"I heard it burned to the ground, but the trees were spared, to his relief." She popped the cork from a bottle of red. "Was there something else?"

"Louis thought the shed might have been an old workshop or studio," Claire interjected. "Guy wants to explore the spot to see if it once belonged to an artist."

"Oh?"

In that single word, Meilin conveyed her shared intrigue, but the words that followed smacked of skepticism.

"And you think you can determine that shed was an old studio from charred remains? Isn't that more of a forensics thing?"

Claire threw Guy an I-told-you-so look.

"We might be able to learn something. I've got a metal detector."

"You make it sound like a superhero cape."

They all laughed.

"Make all the fun you want. If there's a chance it was an abandoned art studio, don't you think that's worth a little delving? With last week's snow melted, we have an opportune window before the next cover. The thing is, I don't have access to the grounds. Ben can't give me permission. Now that the police tape is down, I need it directly from Louis, but we've only just met. I don't feel comfortable asking him for a favor so soon."

Meilin took the bait.

"I'll speak to him and make the request in the name of art and town history. Be prepared. He'll probably want to be part of the exploration. Count me in as well."

"And me, too," said Roxie, who had arrived in time for this exchange and was making room on the table for cans of ginger beer and Moxie soda.

It was Guy's turn to throw an I-told-you-so look at Claire.

"I see I'm outnumbered," she said. "So be it. If you can get the okay, I'll go, too. I wouldn't want to miss four adults bumping heads over a mucky copper penny."

Club members began to trickle in. The apartment crowded quickly in anticipation of the night's guest speaker. They chatted, filled their plates and glasses, then squeezed in—it turned out to be standing room only tonight—quickly enough for Meilin to call the meeting to order on time.

"We have a full agenda tonight, folks, so let's try to stay on task. Once again, we must extend our gratitude to Claire Munro for opening her home to us."

"Hear, hear," the members called and lifted their drinks in salute.

Claire dropped into a dramatic bow.

"And please say 'hello' to Quince Greene, our newest member. Quince is the new intern at the historical society and a budding artist."

Heads turned toward Quince, a beautiful, pudgy, 24-four-year-old in pink overalls over a floral shirt. Her dark brown hair was cut short with a playful tuft of curls at the top, dyed blue. Feather earrings dangled from her ears. Quince pushed her rainbow-colored glasses back on the bridge of her nose, grinned broadly at the others and gave a wave.

Meilin waited for the murmurs to settle.

"Next, I want to announce the result of the votes we took by email on honorary membership for non-artists. As you know, this club was formed primarily for artists, but the by-laws allow up to 20% of the membership to consist of art-related business owners, like myself and Roxie. This latest initiative was intended to expand the definition of that 20% to include non-artists who promote or support the arts, on a case-by-case basis. The vote carried."

There were nods of approval.

"The second vote involved the first nominees for this membership privilege. It also passed. Peggy Cyr, our illustrious town librarian, and Claire Munro, our frequent host, for their volunteer work, are now honorary art club members. Peggy couldn't join us this evening, but we can welcome Claire to our ranks tonight."

Claire turned a shade of pink and looked at her feet as she always did when trying to hide her feelings. Guy squeezed her hand.

The other members smiled and called out their approval—all but one, that is. That one was Gloria Townsend, owner of the Town's End B&B, who stood with her arms folded across her chest, censure on her face. Though a founding club member, Gloria had become a thorn in their side since last summer's art show. A painting she had purchased had, in quick succession, been stolen, found and determined to be doctored, before it was restored to rights and put back into her hands. Gloria seemed intent to keep these injuries fresh in the club's mind and openly exhibited her bitterness at every gathering she attended. Tonight was no exception.

"Now, onto next year's art show," Meilin said, ignoring Gloria's open hostility. "Roxie, Peggy and I will continue to serve as the oversight committee for another year. Peggy will again be managing sale proceeds, which will be donated to the fire department truck fund drive."

Meilin paused to take in the group's reaction. Most gave nods of approval. Gloria displayed continuing displeasure but voiced no particular argument. Meilin simply pressed on.

"We'll be approaching the same exhibit venues as last year: the Main Street Coffee Bar, Mainsail Wine and Cheese and the Unitarian Church, with the awards presentation at the high school cafeteria. We'd like ideas for others, just in case we need to replace one or expand. If you have suggestions, bring them forward tonight or by email."

"I could use more volunteers setting up and moving exhibits," Roxie said. "Please consider helping or recruit some non-member assistance. This summer, we barely had enough hands with the large volume of art."

"And our second show could bring even more," Meilin told them. "As the show is young, the committee is still reluctant to limit entries by jurying. If you think otherwise, please speak up."

"Also, if you have suggestions to improve the registration process," Claire said, "let me know. I'll be handling that again this year."

A general discussion of all these topics followed.

"Thank you," Meilin concluded. "We're off to a good start. I'll make the proposal to the town council at their January session, so try to be there. Now, let's take two minutes for refills and calls of nature, then resettle quickly for our guest speaker."

A few minutes later, Meilin addressed them again.

"Georgia Wilson will be speaking tonight. She's a native Mainer, recently returned from living away, and an ardent art supporter. Georgia has some interesting plans for next season."

Meilin's brief introduction wisely bypassed Georgia's connection to a somewhat awkward history in Mayenne Bay. Georgia was the grandmother of Nicky Littlefield, who had passed herself off last summer as a diva-like artist named Monique Labelle. As Monique, Nicky had adulterated two floral still lifes by a famous American impressionist, one of which, the "Lupines", was at the root of Gloria's bile. Nicky had long since apologized and made amends, but any allusion to this history tended to flare the sense of victimization that simmered so hotly beneath Gloria's tight-lipped façade.

Georgia stepped to the front of the group. She wore a stylish pant-and-sweater combination that conformed to her petite frame, roughly the same size as Meilin's. Her pixie-style, snow-white hair set off a large pair of tourmaline earrings and a matching pendant. Georgia's dignified carriage and intelligent face radiated a presence that far outsized her person and hushed the room. She opened a PowerPoint slideshow that featured photos of a large, historic house in Port Clyde, Maine and began to click through the images.

"This house was owned and used by my mother for gatherings of painters coming and going from Monhegan Island and all over Maine. She was good enough to will it to me. I've begun renovations and mean to resume its service to the art community. My living quarters will be upstairs. Downstairs, there will be a gallery for rotating exhibitions, a classroom and a salon for artist meetups. I've set up a website called 'PortClydeHouseReboot', where I'll post the progress."

A few chuckles circled the room. Georgia joined them.

"Catchy name, don't you think? Guy coined it and is helping me with graphics for the 'Reboot' website and other materials. At the same time, he has agreed to be the first featured artist in our exhibition room, tentatively scheduled for May of the upcoming year."

The room stirred with excitement. Gloria sneered. Guy had been instrumental in exposing the "Lupines" painting as fraudulent last summer. Though, in its restored state, it was worth much more than the purchase price, Gloria resented rather than thanked him.

"Please spread the word about the 'Reboot' among your fellow artists and enthusiasts," Georgia resumed. "If you have any ideas or interest, I can be reached at the number or email address on this card." She passed around a stack of business cards depicting the Port Clyde House in its earlier heyday. "I hope to see all of you in Port Clyde sometime in the near future."

"Thank you, Georgia," said Meilin, moving forward. "What an undertaking." She turned to the group at large. "That ends our formal agenda for tonight. Let's use the rest of the time to network and get to know Georgia."

Animated by the Port Clyde project, the club chattered among themselves and peppered Georgia with questions for almost an hour. Gradually, they began to gather their belongings and head for the door.

"Georgia, you're welcome to stay in my guest room tonight," Claire invited once the crowd thinned, "if you'd rather not drive home this late in the dark."

"Thank you, Claire, but you mustn't worry about me. I'm a native, don't forget."

Guy assisted Georgia to pack up her car and waved her off. The few lingering members left soon after, leaving Meilin, Roxie, Claire and Guy to finish cleanup, and Gloria hanging ominously in the corner. She approached Meilin with a dark expression.

"Obviously, you have something to say," Meilin said sharply, preempting the B&B owner. "Out with it."

"Only artists who bring work for exhibition and art-business owners should be in this club."

"So, what makes you qualify?" Meilin didn't even try to hide her contempt. "When is the last time this group saw anything painted by you? When is the last time, in fact, you contributed anything to this club but tense silence or caustic remarks?"

Gloria snarled.

"At least I'm capable of producing art work."

Meilin sighed heavily.

"Gloria, a vote was taken by the club to change the by-laws. Accept it with grace. You can't expect to agree with all the motions that pass."

Her voice carried a note of finality. Gloria took the cue and made her way to the door. With a final, scathing look at them all, she let herself out and shut the door loudly behind her.

"Any ideas how we volunteers earned her censure?" Claire asked. "You'd think she'd be grateful for the extra hands."

"Not sure," answered Roxie. "She's become unbearable. Meilin?"

"It's partly due to the 'Lupines' fiasco last summer, but not all. Gloria had begun to sour well before the art show. From what I can tell, the B&B is doing fine, but its owner has become an altered creature, contrary about everything, for reasons yet unknown to me." Her face turned wistful for a moment. "She was once a friend. I miss her."

Meilin and Roxie left together, leaving only Guy.

"Don't I get an invitation to stay the night?" he teased Claire. "It's late and really dark out there."

Claire tossed the dish towel onto the counter, smiled invitingly over her shoulder and headed down the hall toward the bedroom.

Bayside Squawker, November 22

Readers and, especially, Louis Rainwater,

America has kept the Thanksgiving tradition since the Mayflower. There's nothing wrong with eating a traditional family meal and giving thanks for our food without dragging up past sins. End of story.

Captain Crabbish

Reply to Gloria Townsend:

Communication devices, like pagers and cell phones, are not infallible. Mobile and internet connections can be delayed or unstable. Batteries die. The fire siren ensures first responders are all informed of an emergency at the same time, wherever they are. It also puts our citizens on alert for fast-moving vehicles, spreading fire, and neighbors in need.

Roxanne Nadeau, Fire Chief

Reply to Ms. Townsend:

No evidence has been found that there is an arsonist in our midst.

Police Chief Manning

4

The Great Detectorist

Guy hurriedly peeled off a paint-coated, nitrile glove to take a call from Meilin.

"I only just heard back from Louis. We have the thumbs-up to explore the shed. Can you make it at one o'clock on Sunday? I know it's just days before Thanksgiving, but we couldn't find another date."

"It's perfect. Claire and I will meet you there."

Claire spent Saturday morning hanging missing-person posters of Valentina Diaz. She did the same on Sunday, then headed to Guy's place for brunch. His boyish exuberance over metal detecting was so fired up, he barely ate. Claire slowed her eating in an effort to restrain his haste to get to Louis's property, but her efforts failed; they arrived well before the agreed time.

The weather was sunny and virtually windless. The snow had held off through the week, and the ground was cold but not yet frozen, perfect conditions for the Great Detectorist. While they waited for Louis, Meilin and Roxie to arrive, Guy unloaded the gear from the car and hauled it over to the shed site. Claire donned work boots and work gloves, then spread a blanket on a bed of pine needles near the shed for the display of discoveries by the unflaggingly optimistic detectorist.

Guy circled the shed remains and grounds and took photos from every possible angle. The structure had been framed in two stories. The lower level had been a cellar set six feet below ground with a floor and walls made solid by the rocks so abundant in Maine. The walls extended two feet above ground to create the upper-story foundation. These and a charred chimney that stood resolutely in one corner, as though conscious it had defied the odds, were all that had survived the inferno.

Guy snapped the last image and pocketed his phone.

"Where are the others? They're late."

"They are not late," Claire corrected him. "We're just very early."

He sighed his impatience.

"Guy, you're as excited as a little kid. Why don't you just let the Great Detectorist loose?"

He didn't need to be prodded twice. He turned on the detector and, with Claire in tow, started at the northwest corner of the foundation and headed east. His face was lit like a child's on Christmas morning, but his eyes focused intently on the ground as he swung the search coil from side to side in an even rhythm. His movements were slow and careful, the better, Claire understood, to demonstrate the technique to a neophyte.

A tone sounded from the detector. Guy stopped the motion to read the digital display and showed the readout to Claire.

"Loud tone, uncertain reading. Let's take a closer look. Ground minerals and rocks can affect detection, so a ping can be misleading."

Claire had to suppress a giggle when he yanked a pin-point detector wand from his belt holster with the speed of the Lone Ranger grabbing his gun, then swept the nose over the swatch of ground that had produced the first signal. To hone in on his target, Guy hovered the wand minutely over the area until it sounded a steady, high-pitched tone. He parked the wand back in the holster, slid his backpack off his shoulders and opened the flap to reveal a tool collection worthy of Inspector Gadget. He extracted some metal stakes, each marked with a tiny, colored flag, and laid them at his side. Then, he pulled out two notched detecting trowels, one narrow, one wider, each with ruler markings. Using the narrower trowel, he began gently cracking the earth in a circle around the spot that had produced the tone.

"Good thing the ground's not solid yet."

Once he completed the circle, Guy dug gingerly with his fingers to remove the dirt. He uncovered a few rocks, then extracted a clump of old nails.

"Not bad for a first go."

He held them up to Claire with a triumphant smile. She rolled her eyes and summed up his anticlimactic find with a wave of her hand.

"All this equipment and effort for a handful of rusty nails."

"Look again. These are hand-forged nails, no two alike. They're historical."

"And you're hysterical. They're rusty, bent and useless."

"Claire, the fun is in the exploration. Any find is just icing on the cake."

"If you say so."

"You'll see. We've only just got started."

Guy pulled a red marker from the pile to mark the extraction location. He clipped a corresponding red tag to the clump of nails and walked over to set it on the blanket. Finally, he returned and waved the pin-point detector above the loose patch once more to make sure he hadn't missed anything. The machine remained silent.

"Guess we're done here."

He restored the wand to its pocket and resumed sweeping the ground with the large detector.

Claire left Guy to the joy of detecting and returned to the car to grab the garden rake and sack they had packed. She swung the sack over her shoulder and lowered the rake carefully down into the shed cellar. Then, she eased herself over the blackened and gritty rock wall and dropped down hard onto the slick and cluttered floor.

Once she found a secure place to plant both feet, she pulled out her phone to make a thorough photographic record, just as Guy had done for the outside of the structure. There were charred chair legs, fractured crocks, metal pieces, paper remnants and other yet unidentifiable pieces not fully consumed by the fire. In the corner by the fireplace, the debris piled especially high where building material had collapsed over a small potbelly stove. After pocketing her phone, Claire slid on safety glasses, tied a bandana over her nose and mouth and drew on her work gloves. With tiny strokes, she began to shift the sooty rubble with the rake tines, working in a gradually expanding circle around her feet, heedful of glass shards and exposed nails as well as possible valuables.

"Oho!" Guy called from above at a second ping from the detector. The hum of the machine stopped while he inspected further.

"What now? Tin cans?"

"Not sure yet, oh ye of little faith."

He pulled out his pocket wand once again. After a few minutes, he leaned over the stone wall and held out an antique, blue-tinted Mason jar filled with old coins and capped with a tin lid.

Claire pulled down her goggles to get a better look.

"Old pennies. No green patina, so they haven't oxidized, maybe due to being in the airtight jar all this time." He looked at Claire brightly. "I'll bet the former owners had no idea this was here or they wouldn't have left it behind. Better hold off for Louis before I do any more. He'll want to explore this himself."

He slid the jar into the ground where he had found it and sat back.

"Oh!" Guy said again.

"Guy?"

"I think the jar is in an underground compartment extending off the foundation. It's about one foot by two feet in size and a foot deep. Looks like it's lined with small rocks, both floor and sides. I'll bet this was once someone's stash."

As he uttered these words, Louis, Meilin and Roxie pulled up in Louis's pickup truck.

"They're finally here," Guy told Claire and stood up to greet them.

The three were at Guy's side in an instant and greeted Claire from above. He walked them through his photos and over to the blanket to indicate his modest find of hand-crafted nails. They returned to the shed, where he indicated the jar of pennies. These were extracted by Louis, tagged green and placed on the blanket.

"After the penny jar, I stopped, not wanting to steal your thunder, Louis," Guy said. He traced the surface dirt with his trowel to indicate the suspected rectangular storage area beneath. "This appears to be a small compartment. There might be more stuff in there."

Louis dropped to his knees, worked the trowel and tugged at the soil. He pulled out a second and third jar in succession.

"Old military buttons," Guy said and passed the jar to Roxie, who in turn gave it to Meilin. "And more old coins. Wow."

"Yeah," Louis said, sitting back onto his heels, his

expression surprised. "Honestly, I thought this expedition was just a lark, and here we are just minutes in."

"Hey up there!" called Claire. "Help me out so I can see what you've found."

Guy's face wore a knowing smile as he reached his hands down. Claire grabbed them, then wedged the toe of her boot in a convenient gap in the cellar wall, about a foot above the floor, to boost herself. When she heaved herself up, one of the rocks slipped out. She fell back hard onto her other foot.

"Ouch," she said, shaking out her leg. "Let's try that again."

"You okay?" Guy asked.

The others looked over the wall in concern.

"Fine. I just came down a bit hard."

Guy reached his hands down again, but this time, Claire's arms remained at her side.

"Claire?"

"Um." She pointed to the cellar floor. "When that rock fell, sand poured out. Why would loose sand be behind a cellar wall? Is that some kind of groundwater drainage thing?"

Louis swung his long legs over the side of the wall and dropped himself neatly onto the small area of floor Claire had just cleared, almost bumping against her. It was a squeeze for just the two of them, so the others had to settle for hanging over the wall to watch. Claire crouched down and dislodged more sand from the wall with her fingers, then made way for Louis. There was a joint intake of breath as they both spied a wide space about six inches further back. Claire looked up at the others.

"It looks like there could be a larger cavity behind the entry hole I uncovered. I hope there's nothing creepy in there."

She made a face and stepped aside. Louis reached up to

grab the flashlight Guy was offering from above, then shone it into the hole and peered in. The angle was awkward, owing to Louis's height, even in a squat or kneeling position, and he had no desire to sprawl onto his belly on the slimy floor. To make matters worse, his hand proved too large for the aperture. He stood up to shake out his legs, then bent awkwardly from the waist to snap a few photos.

"Guess you're missing your Cubby Rat," called Roxie from above.

Louis chuckled.

"I have another one right here." He looked at Claire. "Wanna try? It's going to take a smaller hand than mine and someone who can get closer to the ground."

Already covered in grime from sliding over the cellar wall, she shrugged and dropped to her knees on the slimy floor. Then, with a grimace, she slid her gloved hand up to the elbow into the hole. She withdrew bits of rock and more sand, then leaned back to shine the light inside again. The round rim of a crock gaped at her from about eight inches back. Louis handed his cell phone to Claire, who snapped a few photos.

"Go ahead, see what's in there," he urged.

Eyes shut tight, nose scrunched, Claire felt her way through the narrow hole to the crock. Her eyes popped open, and her hand slid out clasping a squishy object. She and Louis stared.

"Oh, I'm so relieved it's not a rat corpse. Waxed cloth, do you think?" She brushed away grains of sand from the folds. "It's a bit stiff and sticky. Reminds me of the beeswax covers for storage jars."

Guy, Meilin and Roxie hung as far as possible over the wall, rapt with interest. Louis drew out his phone again.

"Go ahead and unwrap it while I video."

Claire squatted down, balanced the object on her thighs and gingerly removed the sticky outer wrapping. Beneath it was a thick layer of plain linen. Inside the linen was a glazed porcelain figurine of a peasant child holding a duck.

"Oh, my." She cupped the treasure in two hands. "Much like a Hummel." She turned it over. "Look here on the bottom. It says 'ES'. Are those initials anybody recognizes?" Claire asked and looked up.

"No," said Louis.

"No," echoed the others.

She rewrapped the figurine, and Louis handed it up to Guy, whose arm was longest. Claire reached again into the crock and withdrew a second bundle, a porcelain of a child eating an apple with a basketful at her feet. After inspection and rewrapping, Louis handed it up to the first outstretched hand. Claire extracted bundle after bundle, pressing her shoulder painfully against the rock wall to retrieve the last one. She shone the flashlight inside to make certain the cavity was finally empty. There were six porcelains in all, each exquisitely wrought provincial children. Louis handed up the last then stuck his foot in the hole and hoisted himself out of the cellar.

"Coming, Claire?" Guy asked, reaching down for her hands.

"No, I'm going to poke around down here, if that's okay, Louis."

He nodded his consent.

"Ha! I knew you'd catch the exploration bug," Guy teased.

Claire sifted carefully through more cellar contents while Guy, Louis, Meilin and Roxie admired the porcelains and took turns with the metal detector. When the sky threw its first hint of fall's early dusk, Claire called out to Guy. It took a few tries, but the detector finally fell silent. His face appeared overhead, and he reached down to assist her out. Claire motioned for everyone to follow her to the blanket, where she spilled the contents of her sack. There were crock fragments, paint brush ferrules and a small brass mortar and pestle, among other items.

"Just some things I thought looked interesting that might be art-related. And I found these as well."

Claire drew some metal pieces from her pocket and laid them onto the blanket, one intact, but tarnished, earring and its half-melted partner.

"They were partially beneath a rock, which must have helped them escape the worst of the fire."

"These aren't old," Guy said.

He passed them to Louis.

"The police team missed these?"

Claire shrugged.

"I accidentally knocked the chair seat with the rake. There's so much slime, it slid across the floor and bumped a rock, making these come into view. They would have been hard to spot otherwise." She looked meaningfully from one face to another. "This jewelry means someone used the shed recently."

Four heads jerked toward the stone cellar and back again.

"You mean like kids goofing off?" asked Meilin.

"Plausible, considering all the trails on this property," said Louis with a wave toward the woods. "Kids use them all the time…or used to."

"Or a squatter," Claire said.

"Oh, God." Guy stood up with an intake of breath. "The fire."

"Oh, God," Roxie echoed.

"You don't think…" Meilin began, uncertain how to finish the sentence.

"I really don't know what to think," Claire replied, "especially after finding this under that thick pile of sodden paper down there."

She pulled out her phone and opened to a photo of the

one remain she hadn't removed from the cellar: a human skull.

5

Big Pants

Thanksgiving Day arrived. Claire obsessed over her clothing, torn between comfort and underdressing. The Gardiners were a bit of a mystery as yet, and Guy had offered no guidance about his family's holiday style. He planned, she knew, to show up in jeans, but as a newcomer, she felt a higher standard applied to herself. Eyeing the outfits strewn across her bed, she decided on sage green corduroy slacks with a festive sweater. At least she would look like she had made an effort.

The kitchen door squeaked open. Guy's voice carried to the bedroom.

"You ready?"

"Coming!"

Claire appeared, bag on her shoulder, coat in hand.

"You look great."

"Thanks."

"How many outfits did you try this time?"

Guy was onto Claire's neurotic wardrobe syndrome.

"None of your business."

She, in turn, took in Guy's appearance. He wore a blue-plaid, wool-blend shirt tucked into a pair of tightly belted blue jeans. The jeans fitted oddly over his slender hips, Claire realized, due to an excess of waistline that bunched under the belt in several places.

"The blue shirt really brings out your eyes, but what is going on with those jeans? They look a bit big."

"These are my holiday jeans. My mother doesn't appreciate sweatpants at dinner, so I got jeans several inches too large. I remove the belt when I need more, um…capacity."

At this, all of Claire's nerves over the visit broke loose. She sank into a chair and doubled over in a fit of silent laughter. Tears streamed from the corners of her eyes.

"Several inches?" she asked finally and wiped her cheeks.

"Yes, to be comfortable. When it comes to Thanksgiving gluttony, it's either big pants or, far worse, in my opinion, opened pants."

"Oh, yes, big pants are preferable to hairy-belly overhang. I take it you mean to dig into those mystery casseroles."

"Plus, the mashed potatoes, corn and peas. I do love the main event, but it's equally about the pie and ice cream afterward. It's a once-a-year indulgence."

"Thank God for that."

Claire gestured to a large cardboard box holding a roasted turkey wrapped in tinfoil, still warm from the oven.

"We need to drop that off at the soup kitchen on our way out."

Guy lifted the box. Claire tucked a container of corn muffins under her arm, grabbed a bottle of merlot from the table and followed him to the car. They swung by the soup kitchen, then easily made their way Down East, thanks to clear roads. The moment they pulled into the Gardiner's driveway, the living room curtain rose and fell, the front door swung open, and two young women spilled onto the porch.

"Looks like your fan club awaits," Guy said. "Believe me, I don't feature in all that excitement whatsoever."

Guy's sisters, Joy and Anna, slender, blonde-haired and blue-eyed like their brother, shivered in the cold air and hopped up and down at the sight of Claire. Giggling and chattering, they emptied her arms, pulled off her coat and, finally, hugged her. Mr. and Mrs. Gardiner, he greying at the temples, she with salt-and-pepper hair, followed behind their daughters with a genuine, but far more sedate, welcome.

Claire stepped from the chill into the warm and toasty house, an indication that the oven was already doing its duty. Rockwell's iconic "Freedom from Want", with its darkly browned turkey at the center, came to mind. Her own imagination supplied a gravy bowl, apple-walnut stuffing and pumpkin and apple pies alongside. The mental picture was so clear, in fact, it triggered her olfactory memory of past holidays. She inhaled deeply through her nose, ready to refresh it with the real thing, but ended by choking. She turned tearing eyes at Guy. *Do you smell it?* she telegraphed to him. It appeared he did. The tantalizing image in Claire's head dissolved into a noxious chemical plant.

"Mom, what's that smell?" Guy asked. "It's like burning plastic."

At Guy's pronouncement, everyone headed to the kitchen, suddenly awake to the odor. It had come on so gradually that only when their attention was drawn to it did it become apparent. In the larger of two ovens, a huge turkey in a black, enamel-coated roasting pan properly spit and sizzled. Nothing amiss there. Above this radiated a smaller oven where a baking dish of homemade cranberry sauce was just visible through the window.

"Oh, Joy," exclaimed Mrs. Gardiner, "you forgot to

remove the lid."

Mr. Gardiner stuffed oven mitts onto his hands, retrieved the offending dish and peeled off the melted plastic top.

"I'm sorry, Hon, but we can't eat this," he told Joy, whose eyes welled.

"It's Grandma's recipe," she said, as if this would change the outcome. "I wanted Claire to taste it."

"I know, Sweetie," sympathized her mother.

"Next year," Mr. Gardiner added simply.

Embarrassed, Joy left the room while the others opened windows, turned on fans and tossed the tainted sauce outside.

The ring of the doorbell drew them all from the cranberry sauce fiasco and back to the foyer, where the first of Guy's extended family entered the house. Claire bit her lower lip for self-control when she spied an overweight woman with several missing teeth and a mustache on her upper lip. Frizzy, gray hair stuck out from under her faded camper's hat. Over plaid stretch pants, she wore a floral blouse that gaped between buttons and safety pins over her large, unsupported breasts. The woman pulled a few cans of cranberry sauce from a large canvas bag, a prescient contribution under the circumstances, shoved them at Guy's chest, then shouted at Claire.

"I'm Guy's Aunt Helen." She sniffed the air. "Something stinks in here. Hope that ain't the turkey."

Without another word, Aunt Helen made her ponderous way into the living room, settled herself with a beer near the hors d'oeuvres and drew a ball of yarn and a crochet needle from her bag.

The doorbell rang again. A seemingly endless stream of Gardiner relatives followed Helen through the foyer. In the end, Claire counted thirty-five. She smiled, shook hands, returned hugs and repeated answers to the same questions for the next hour. In the next room, whole bottles of wine were emptied and plates of hors d'oeuvres devoured before the onslaught subsided and Claire was free to approach the appetizer table. By this time, there was nothing left but a few carrots, one with child-sized teeth marks, and several sad-looking, pimiento-less olives.

Seeing this, Guy took Claire's elbow to escort her directly to the dinner buffet table now laden with innumerable side dishes and a grand platter of sliced turkey. As the family's special guest, she was positioned first in the food line…where everyone could observe her food choices. Acutely self-conscious and thankful in hindsight she had been spared the hors d'oeuvres, she took at least one spoonful from every dish so as not to offend anyone, skipping only her own corn muffins and Guy's peas and baby onions. She made her way to her seat with a plate so full it dropped pieces off the edge as she walked. She winced at the spoiled living room carpet.

"Seems I'm destined to overeat whenever I come here," she sighed to Guy as he lowered himself next to her.

"Makes you part of the family."

He loosened his belt.

Guy's plate was a study. Everything took a back seat to his love of mashed potatoes and corn. Around the spud-and-maize pile, second favorites like peas, meat and casserole were positioned precariously. He dug in. Claire ate slowly with one eye on his progress, biding her time until he cleared some space. When everyone's head turned to listen to Joy's repetition of the cranberry sauce disaster, Claire brushed a huge portion of her plate's contents onto Guy's. He shot her a disapproving look.

"You know I only took all this because everyone was watching. Anyway, I didn't wear big pants."

By this time, Aunt Helen, among others, was pretty foxed from drink. Add to the alcohol the numbing effects of tryptophan and gluttony, and the entire Gardiner contingent looked ready to rest in peace for the remainder of the afternoon. Ignoring the collective stupor, Mrs. Gardiner began to draft guests to clean up, with the exception of Aunt Helen, whose bottom, Claire suspected, would never be coaxed from that chair. Mrs. Gardiner apparently recognized a lost cause when she saw one and skipped past Helen without blinking.

"Let's go," she ordered her recruits, then proclaimed loudly to the whole room, "All hands on deck. No pie or ice cream until dinner is fully cleared away. If you brought a dish, please wrap it up and put it in your car so we can make space on the table for pies."

There were groans of protestation as the day's gourmands struggled to rouse their food-encumbered bodies. Two uncles rose clumsily to their feet, overstuffed bellies protruding from unzipped pants. Claire cringed as they stumbled by her seat, exposed guts at eye level. Guy chuckled, then joined the lumbering parade of gluttons to the kitchen, no longer in need of a belt. On his way, he enlisted two young cousins attempting to hide in a corner behind their cell phones.

Claire remained on the bench next to Guy's discarded belt. She was soon joined by Anna, who shyly took Guy's seat and held her phone screen up for Claire to see. On it was a photo of a black-skinned boy with a pleasant face and intelligent eyes.

"This is the boy I like. Asad. His family came to Bangor as refugees from Somalia. They almost died trying to get here. Asad is top of our class at U-Maine."

"Why are you whispering?"

"I haven't told anyone yet. Mom might be okay with it, but I'm not sure about Dad."

Claire drew a slow breath. "It", she knew all too well, meant Asad's skin color. She understood Anna's circumspection. Claire's own father would not approve of Asad, though Gerald Munro had lived his entire life among a diverse population. Mere exposure to differences, Claire had learned firsthand, did not guarantee acceptance. And this was Maine, the whitest state in the nation, where huge pockets of racial judgment persisted. Of course, light skin didn't necessarily guarantee a free pass. When the Acadian French came to Maine to work, they were oppressed and threatened by the Ku Klux Klan for being foreign and Catholic. Even now, simply arriving in Maine "from away" could raise eyebrows in some areas, though admittedly, a cool reception was a far cry from outright racism. She turned back to the worried teen.

"Asad looks like a fine person, but let's be careful about keeping secrets from your family. If you really want to pursue this relationship, you have to talk to your parents."

"But…"

"Anna, you have to give them a chance. There's a risk they may not rise to the occasion, but what if your expectations are wrong?"

"What if they don't accept him?"

"It's very possible they won't. You're of legal age. If you really like Asad, and he likes you, then you'll have to choose either to please yourself or your parents. It's unfair and a tough choice, I know, and especially hard while you're living in your parents' home."

"I shouldn't have to choose," Anna pouted.

Claire saw no value in sugar-coating the situation.

"No, you shouldn't, but that's the reality of it. But, Anna, before you speak to your parents, you must be absolutely sure of your feelings for Assad and ready to stand your ground come what may. Many will embrace you, but the opposition could be fierce, and not just from family and friends. Your choice will be judged by strangers without the slightest connection to you. Though you'll feel this, the worst of it will be borne by Asad, his family and his community. A faint heart will fail them."

Anna folded her arms to her chest.

"It's just wrong."

"It is. It's not a reason to walk away from Asad if you truly like him, but you and he must be prepared. Truly, I wish the world were different."

Anna's face fell toward her lap. Saddened, Claire placed her palm on the small of the young woman's back to comfort her and scrambled for something else to say.

"Why don't you try talking to Guy about this to get a second opinion?"

Anna nodded.

This was only Claire's second visit to the Gardiners and, already, she was witness to a crack in the family's veneer. Even so, she thought, as she looked across the room at the Gardiner gathering, one crack was nothing when compared to her own family, which was in complete splinters.

"Claire," called Mrs. Gardiner. "As you and Helen are the only coffee drinkers, perhaps you'd like to do the honors?"

"Of course. Excuse me, Anna."

She hugged her and smiled reassurance into her eyes before rising to follow Mrs. Gardiner to the kitchen. As Claire passed by, Aunt Helen emerged from a snore and set her idle crochet needle to work again.

"I take mine strong and black," she commanded gruffly.

After such a meal, and especially with pie, Claire seconded Helen's preference for an unadorned cup of rich, black coffee.

"The tea pots are already brewing out on the dessert table," said Mrs. Gardiner, "so this next kettleful is for the coffee. It should be ready in a minute."

She slid two large mugs and a plastic box in front of Claire. Instant French vanilla cappuccino. Claire felt almost sick but quickly hid her distaste.

"Mr. Gardiner picked this out just for you."

"How thoughtful."

It was far too soon for blunt honesty with Guy's parents. Anyway, the kindness was there even if the flavor entirely missed the mark.

On her last visit, Mr. Gardiner had dug an old jar of instant coffee from the back of the pantry, a generic brand that had tasted like tin. At least, Claire thought, when the vacuum-sealed lid in front of her popped, the contents would be, if not fresh, then less aged. She prepared herself for the sugary beverage knowing full well Mr. Gardiner would be looking on to see how she enjoyed it. Aunt Helen, she suspected, would be less forbearing.

The Gardiners-at-large dove into dessert as though it was the first meal of the day. Guy, Claire observed, did not spare any effort to justify his big pants. Though full to the gills, she politely accepted a fat slice of pumpkin pie with ice cream urged upon her by Mrs. Gardiner. She lifted her mug to signal her thanks to Mr. Gardiner, pretended to sip the sugary cappuccino and bided her time for a safe moment to slide her pie onto Guy's pile. Under the guise of delivering her empty plate to the kitchen, she dumped her coffee down the sink drain unseen. At the same time, Aunt Helen's voice carried overtop the other talk, saying what Claire would not.

"When the hell am I ever gonna get a decent cup of coffee in this house?"

After dessert, Guy and Claire bid everyone good-bye and climbed into the car. Guy shifted awkwardly in his seat in search of a comfortable position. Claire felt no pity. He had gone into the meal with his eyes, mouth and belt wide open.

"And now you pay the price," she said. "Hope it was worth it."

"It was, but tomorrow I fast."

"Only tomorrow?"

"Very funny."

He pulled away from his parent's house with a final wave to Anna and Joy, who had followed them out to the car.

"So, what are the takeaways from this visit?" Guy asked.

"First, a wish that, next time, I'll not be the center of attention. Between Joy's tears over the spoiled sauce, the spectating of my food choices, the monitoring of my coffee consumption…"

"Enough said."

"Second, there was Anna's confession."

"What?"

Claire repeated her conversation with Anna and warned Guy he was destined to be the next confidante.

"You really are a magnet for this stuff. I'm glad she opened up to you, though. Poor Anna. Such a simple thing, to be attracted to a nice boy and have it complicated by her own parents."

"Not only her parents."

"No, it goes far beyond them but it starts there. I'll make sure to talk to her soon."

He shook his head, fell into thought for a few minutes, brow furrowed, then perked up. "Anymore takeaways?"

"Other than I'm supplying my own coffee next time?"

"Yeah, other than that."

"I'm all for memories that last a lifetime, but…"

"But?"

"Crammed guts over gaping zippers. Exposed whitey-tighties. Sadly, some images are indelible."

She shot a meaningful look at Guy's big pants.

Bayside Squawker, November 29

Readers,

Bones were found at the Rainwater place after an unexplained fire. Our children use those trails. Chief Manning, what's going on out there?

Captain Crabbish

Fellow Citizens,

Meeting at the public boat house, Sunday, December 1, 2:00 p.m., to organize a petition for the old canning factory site redevelopment.

Jay Brown

6

Brush with Fire

On Black Friday, Claire and Guy headed out early to the Fish House, hoping to relax over coffee and tea before frenzied holiday shoppers overran the place for the day's featured brunch. When they reached the restaurant, they spotted Celeste through the window. Claire gripped Guy's coat sleeve and pulled him away from the steps.

"I forgot to tell you something," she said and hurriedly recounted her conversation with Celeste in the aisle at Grace Grocery.

"Welcome back," Claire had said. "How was your vacation?"

Instead of the expected tan, Celeste's normally rosy face was pale and tired.

"It wasn't a vacation," Celeste had answered. "I actually went to look for my sister, Denise. She's missing."

Claire had sucked in her breath in shock and stifled the flood of questions in her throat.

"Denise has always been a bit…unconventional. She didn't fit well in school and stood out at work, but we were always close. The last couple of years, we've been sharing a trailer together. About a month ago, she disappeared. I have no idea why she left or where she went. No call, no text, no note. Mom is beside herself with worry. I searched everywhere. As a last resort, I tried our favorite uncle in Florida. Uncle Kenny is very old and doesn't do well by phone. I didn't want to upset him from a distance or spook Denise if she was there. So, I hopped on a plane. Turned out, he hadn't seen her. No one has."

"Have you told the police?"

"Yeah, they're on it, sort of. There's not much to go on, really. No stormy relationships, no drugs that I know of, no clues of any sort."

Claire ended her account here and looked meaningfully at Guy, who let out a long whistle.

"Poor Celeste."

"Poor Denise," she corrected him. "And Valentina Diaz. The skull. I'm so afraid…"

"God, that would be awful. Let's keep a lid on that fear until we hear from Ben."

The Fish House was almost empty, Thanksgiving indulgences having taken their toll on most early morning appetites. Meilin was the sole customer in the dining room where she sat with a pot of tea and the latest issue of the *Bayside Squawker*. Guy and Claire slid into the empty chairs at her table.

"Good morning. May we join you?"

"I'd love it."

Celeste popped out of the kitchen to take their orders. Coffee and toast for Claire. A pot of tea for Guy, whose post-Thanksgiving fast was underway.

"Any word on the skull?" Guy asked Meilin.

She eyed him devilishly.

"You mean like how it got detached from the rest of the skeleton?"

"Yeah, for starters."

She turned the *Squawker* to page two and stabbed the letters-to-the-editor section with her finger.

"Nothing official, but Captain Crabbish got hold of the story."

Guy read the Captain's letter, waved dismissively with one hand and pushed the paper away with the other.

"He's guessing. 'Bones', not 'skull', he says. Anyway, I don't give weight to ramblings in the *Squawker*. Nothing but gossip, trivia and old recipes."

"Don't say that in front of Patty," implored Celeste, who delivered their orders and joined their table with her own mug of white coffee. "She takes pride in owning that paper."

"At least half the town relies on the *Squawker* for local news," Meilin said. "And we all follow the Captain."

"I'm a subscriber," Claire said. "The Captain is part of the experience, a bit of local color and a barometer of public sentiment."

"He's a muckraker and provocateur," said Guy.

"He's an institution," countered Meilin.

"And has been for almost a hundred years," added Patty, who squeezed in another chair. "Crabbish may irk you, Guy, but he speaks the mind of a lot of people here. In doing so, he keeps important issues in front of the town and adds value to the *Squawker*. I'm not sure I'd sell half the copies I do if he wasn't stirring the pot."

"Who is he?" asked Claire.

"The actual writer has never been identified," Patty told them. "It's a long-standing mystery debated even more than Kitty's age. I have a book going on his real name, but, so far, the guesses have bordered on the absurd."

"Is there anything unworthy of a gamble, Patty?" teased Guy.

"Nope. All the bets I take raise money for good causes. Besides, they're fun. As for the Captain, I've never seen the name 'Crabbish' anywhere else. He has written under that pseudonym since the paper's inception in 1900. His mystique is part of the attraction."

"But whoever the Captain originally was, someone else is filling his shoes now after over a hundred years," observed Claire.

"That has to be the case, though the current Captain delivers his letters the same way as he has for decades: typed, in hard copy, by regular mail, postmarked in Mayenne Bay, no return address. He could be someone we meet every day, but no real person has ever been connected to him."

Guy returned to Meilin and the mystery of the skull.

"Do you know if they found more bones at Louis's place?"

"Nobody knows. It's only been a week, a holiday week at that, since Claire found the skull. Anyway, don't you watch detective shows? Ben can't reveal the details of an ongoing investigation. The police have to finish the site examination, then get everything out to Augusta for testing. Who knows how long that queue is? This is going to take time."

On the day of the burn site exploration, after Claire had shown the grisly photo of the skull, Louis had called Ben. The officer had rushed over and cordoned off the shed and surrounding area for a second time. He had also confiscated the detectorists' finds and quashed further amateur exploration indefinitely.

"I'll take good care of these and return them to you as soon as possible," Ben had promised Louis as his gloved hands gently placed each of their discoveries in a separate evidence bag. "Now, Claire, show me where the skull is."

Claire led him to the shed, followed by the others, and pointed to a mound of partially burned, water-soaked paper. There was a tremor in her voice, and her hands gestured expressively as she spoke.

"I was pulling apart that dense pile of paper with the rake thinking there might be a clue in there about whoever used to live or work in here. I guess the fire was extinguished before it could work its way all the way through the paper because the pile had fallen over and then got drenched. It's wet through, heavy and soggy, and hard to separate. I found the skull beneath it, but only after I shifted a good portion of it."

Ben snapped a photo, then slipped down onto the cellar floor to take more. He kicked over the remaining paper pile with his foot, then bent over to take photos of the skull before bagging it.

"At least that explains how our team missed it." He looked up at Claire. "No other bones?"

"Not that I found, but I climbed out right after finding the skull." She shivered and wrapped her arms around herself. "Didn't want to be down there after that."

"Now, show me where you found the jewelry."

Claire walked around to the other side of the stone foundation and showed him the spot.

"I bumped the rake against that wooden chair seat when it was nearer the stove. The floor was so slippery, the seat shot across and dislodged that rock. Underneath were blackened metal fragments, all junk as far as I could tell, except the earrings."

"The earrings are intriguing. Contemporary, not aged like the rest of the stuff," Ben said.

He continued to snap photos.

"That's something that worried us, especially in conjunction with the skull," Guy said.

"Ben," Claire resumed, "I have pictures of everything as it was down there before I disturbed anything. Guy has the same of the exterior. And Louis shot a video of the wall cavity as I extracted each of the figurines. Should we forward these to you?"

"Yes, please," Ben answered and looked up at each of the explorers in turn. "Also, I'm going to need all of you to come down to the station to give a formal statement and be fingerprinted. We'll want to eliminate your prints from any others we find."

They all agreed.

"Our innocent detecting adventure turned out to be more than we bargained for," Guy had said.

"But let's acknowledge that the return of the Great Detectorist has been overshadowed by a curious woman with a rake and a clumsy foot," Claire had teased.

As the group headed for their vehicles, Ben had called out, "Please don't come back until I give you the all-clear. I'll be taping off a broader perimeter and posting 'no entry' at the trailheads as well. It's going to take a while to re-examine the shed, and then we have to cover a lot of ground. Mayenne Bay doesn't have a forensics team, just our regular officers. And all testing will be done at the state level. You can imagine the wait."

"I wonder when I'll be at liberty on my own place," Louis had grumbled within Ben's hearing.

"Patience," Ben had counseled.

Meilin counseled that same patience to Guy today before she rose and headed out to open Creative Agenda to the holiday rush.

Patty also rose and headed for the kitchen to check on the status of the Black Friday brunch buffet preparations.

Guy and Claire took the opportunity to commiserate with Celeste over her missing sister. Afterward, Celeste lingered at the table, looking awkward, as if wrestling with indecision.

"Claire," she spoke carefully, "I hear things. You know how the Fish House is with gossip. There are people saying you're not to be trusted."

Claire colored, non-plussed.

"People? Who?"

"Kitty, for one."

"Does she say why?"

Celeste squirmed in her seat.

"She says she heard you tell a secret out loud. She didn't say what it was."

She reached out and squeezed Claire's hand.

"How would Kitty know something was a secret?" Guy asked.

"No idea. I'm sure there's been a misunderstanding, Claire, but I thought you should know it's being batted about."

Having delivered her message, Celeste cast Claire a consoling look, then headed to the kitchen. Claire sat perfectly still, her back stiff and her color high.

"Claire, you've preached since I first met you about the danger of listening to gossipmongers," Guy cautioned.

"Yes, but this accusation hits a nerve. I've never sought out people's confidences, but once given, I do guard them carefully."

"I know you do."

"Confidentiality is an important part of my job as well. If I'm distrusted at work…"

"Don't get ahead of yourself. Let's take this a day at a time. The rumor is from Kitty, of all people. Patty commended her table service but didn't suggest Kitty was a paragon of integrity. And you have Celeste, the woman who can change town opinion over breakfast, on your side."

Claire laughed. Having Celeste as her ally definitely worked in her favor.

They left the Fish House a few minutes later and walked silently toward Harborview Street until Claire again raised the specter of the skull.

"The idea that there's a headless skeleton out there somewhere is like a movie thriller. Who was it? It's hard to imagine a death gone unnoticed in this little town where everyone knows each other's business, unless it was a transient person or someone who died long ago. I keep imagining some poor soul dying in that fire by accident, or worse."

"Are you suggesting foul play?"

"No natural death separates a person's head from his body, Guy."

Her face was grim.

They ruminated on this as they let themselves into Claire's place, readied hot drinks, and settled onto the living room couch to read and sketch. But Claire couldn't sit still. She set aside her book and went to the kitchen cupboard to grab the broom. Guy continued sketching with a watchful eye on her. He had gotten used to the fact that Claire vented feelings through activity. That she did so today revealed her deep disquiet over the aspersion on her character, not to mention the unidentified skull and two missing women. Claire was a worrier of the first order.

When she shoved the broom back into the cupboard and returned to the living room, her face radiated with determination.

"I have to do something. I can't change the rumor Kitty has put about, not until I learn more about it. I can't imagine where Valentina or Denise is. I wouldn't know where to begin. But I might be able to help with the skull mystery." She pulled her tablet from her work bag and plopped onto the couch. "I'm going to search online this weekend. Monday after work, I'll start going through back issues of the *Bayside Squawker* at the library."

"What do you hope to find?"

"Anything that might suggest an unidentified person or untoward activity on Louis's property or…well, I'm not entirely sure what else. Something apparently benign at the time might have bearing on today. And while I'm combing through back issues, just for fun, I'm going to read the Captain's old letters to get a better feel for him over the years."

On Monday after work, Claire entered the library and headed directly for Peggy, a slightly overweight, middle-aged woman in half-moon glasses and the town's librarian for many years. Peggy dropped off a stool after straightening a painting of beach roses over the checkout counter to welcome Claire as a friend. Claire detailed her mission.

"Can you get me started on the microfiche cache of the *Bayside Squawker* issues? My internet searches of Mayenne Bay news are coming up empty."

"Well, they would. Maine papers, even if they deigned to cover this generally unheralded little town, have been slow to digitize old issues. The *Squawker* has always been the primary source of local news, though that news has never been what I'd call well-investigated. And Crabbish's letters, well, they speak for themselves."

"Thanks for the caution. Reading the Captain's letters is just a lark. I'm mostly looking for hints about unknown or missing persons or events on Louis's property. Even gossip often begins with a kernel of truth." Claire hesitated for a moment, struck by her own words in light of Kitty's recent accusation. She tucked the thought away for now. "Either way, the history will give me a better feel for the town."

"It'll do that all right." Peggy chuckled, then guided Claire through the first few silver-gray pages of old editions. "Sorry for the slow pace, but as the library hasn't had the funds to convert to digital either, your search will be limited to a manual scroll."

Claire bent herself to the task. After only a few hours reading the fuzzy microfiche, her bleary, watering eyes forced her to pack up for the night. She made a mental note to get a pair of those reading glasses at the drugstore to offset the strain.

Outside on the library steps, she paused to calibrate to the early onset of darkness, then slipped into her car and exited the library parking lot onto Main Street. When she reached the intersection of Main and Crest, she stopped and squinted her tired eyes at the scene before her. Gone were the town's ubiquitous turkey placards, pumpkins and fall cornucopia. In their place glowed a riot of light and color. Strings of Christmas lights shone around shop windows and entryways, reflecting off metallic garlands and casting a glow onto evening shoppers. Trees twinkled from inside. Wreaths and evergreens adorned poles and doors. Christmas had burst from eleven months of dormancy into a blazing downtown holiday spectacle.

She rolled forward slowly to take in the transformation, wondering at its suddenness. She passed a fire hydrant wrapped in red and white—was that a knitted scarf?—to resemble a candy cane, another topped with an elf's hat and a bench with leg warmers. Her aunt's crocheted toilet paper covers, the ones made with glittery red and green yarn and topped with a plastic holly sprig, came to mind. Every year, Claire crossed her fingers that none would arrive in her mailbox. Holiday toilet décor was one step too far for her taste, and she judged the town's fiber craze much the same.

As she neared Harborview Street, the dock came into view. A Christmas tree—no, not a tree, she realized, but lobster crates stacked in the shape of a tree—stood tall on the wharf covered in a web of fish netting and strung with bulbs. A large star shone at the very top. Several boats attached to the dock, those housing year-round occupants, the so called "live-aboarders", were strung with lights. One houseboat had a Christmas tree strapped to its bow.

Claire hadn't anticipated how serious a business Christmas would be in Mayenne Bay. As she turned onto Harborview for home, she gawked at the explosion of inflated Santas, deer and snowmen swaying on lawns and the profusion of winking lights on houses, bushes and trees. Mailboxes bore holly and ribbons. Picture windows framed brightly ornamented trees. Front doors were covered in gift wrap. The street she had left behind at first light this morning was now almost unrecognizable, as though a great holiday conspiracy had burst its cover all at once. That the town had made this concerted transition in a single day told Claire she had missed an important notice somewhere or else she was simply out of sync.

For the first time, it occurred to her that her own decorative restraint, more accurately, her complete lack of any attention to holiday décor, especially as a newly minted townie, might be impolitic in Mayenne Bay. As a girl, Claire had happily dragged box after box of lights and ornaments from the attic and spent hours decorating, munching cookies and singing carols. Her Christmas spirit had worked like a talisman against her family's dysfunction and carried her through the holidays. Its magical effect lasted only until New Year's Day, when all the mojo got stuffed back into boxes, and her world returned to normal. By the time Claire had left for her own place, she had seen the Munro holiday ritual for the short-lived charade it truly was. She departed her childhood home without making claim to a single memento, not even to her own baby shoes that hung on her mother's tree.

She pulled into the driveway, conscious of how dismal her place appeared against the backdrop of her neighbors' extravaganzas. She sat for a while in the car as the blackness of her own place engulfed her. It awakened the downheartedness she had struggled to suppress since hearing the rumor spread by Kitty. She climbed out of the car, opened the kitchen door and groped frantically for the kitchen wall light switch. The overhead fluorescent did nothing to dispel her melancholy; it merely illuminated her sense of dejection.

She went to the front window and gazed up and down the street, wishing now for some of that by-gone holiday magic, however fleeting it might be. Perhaps a light or two, she thought, against the darkness.

Fiber art was definitely out of the question.

Bayside Squawker, December 6

Brats,

If I catch whoever is throwing dirt bombs and seaweed onto our boats, you'll wish I hadn't.

Blue Bickford, Harbormaster

Fiber Artists,

We don't have a shortage of Christmas decorations downtown, yet now you are devoting your needles to decorating benches and fire hydrants. I hear this is called "urban knitting". We aren't "urban". We're a small town with more pressing needs: children who need blankets, sweaters and hats. Get your priorities straight and your needles pointed in the right direction.

Captain Crabbish

7

Gloria's Affliction

Through a large, curtainless window overlooking the bay, thirty-five-year-old Gloria Esposito Townsend stared trance-like at the dance of reflective light on the black water. The Town's End Bed and Breakfast was empty of guests just now, a rare but welcome respite between holidays. She nestled comfortably in the tufted easy chair, feet extended onto the ottoman, completely at home in the solitude. Sitting alone in the dark, begun as a necessary break from close quarters with her B&B guests, had become a welcome nighttime ritual to maintain her equilibrium amidst the incessant demands of hospitality. In this, Maine's abbreviated, December daylight suited Gloria just fine. Tonight, she had skipped dinner, feeding instead on the quietude during these sunless hours. Even the glass of wine she had set on the side table was untouched.

Intelligent and attractive, Gloria could radiate charm itself, when she had a mind to. These days, she found herself short on inspiration. It had been over five years since Steven, the love of her life, had traded marital bliss for the enticements of a beautiful, young lodger and abandoned ship. Gloria had been shattered but had stayed the course. In the divorce that ensued, she had fought fiercely to keep the B&B and had succeeded, but the win had been hollow. It had left her to operate a fledgling business on her own, sink or swim, under the weight of an injured heart.

For the sake of the business, Gloria had retained the Townsend surname after her marriage split, not anticipating the psychological drain of this constant reminder of Steven's adultery. She had since purged what items she could from the place, but mementos of his former influence and painful betrayal taunted her like malevolent ghosts from every room of the B&B. Even her remarkable success didn't diminish this history or adequately compensate for its injuries.

In spite of the obstacles, through sheer will and business acumen, she had managed to transform the 1819 Victorian house into the thriving bed-and-breakfast it was today. Proud as she was of her achievement, it was also a deep source of resentment, tethering her as it did to a constrained, small-town existence.

The unending demands of the B&B left its owner no time for life outside of work. Had she relaxed her exacting standards, Gloria might have retained help and found time to enjoy friends, eat at restaurants or drag her easel out to the waterside to paint. Instead, micromanager in the name of perfection, she saw personally to every detail of the place, thereby condemning herself to overwork and almost constant confinement. Off and on, she toyed with the idea of jumping ship but had no place to land except her parents' home in New Jersey, her very Catholic parents, who hadn't yet forgiven their daughter's divorce regardless of its cause.

God knew that, despite the steady swarm of B&B guests, Gloria was lonely enough. In her embarrassment over Steven's perfidy, she had isolated herself from former friends in town and disconnected from family and college chums. For a time, she had flirted with the idea of finding another live-in partner or even just a close associate to share the business, someone from outside town who wouldn't judge her past. She had blocked her guest schedule to attend meet-ups and frequented eateries up and down the coast. She had joined clubs and professional associations. She had even poked around on dating sites. No one she met had measured up, so she abandoned what had been, anyway, a lukewarm pursuit. Alone in Mayenne Bay, she beheld pairings like Guy and Claire, Meilin and Roxie, and Ben and artist Rhonda Grace with a begrudging eye, unable to forgive their happiness.

To add insult to injury, Gloria had fallen victim to an art fraud perpetrated by Nicky Littlefield, operating under the pseudonym Monique LaBelle, at last summer's art show. Gloria had widely broadcast her purchase of the "Lupines" painting, so proud was she to adorn her B&B with original art acquired and not her own. She had come so far, overcome so much, despite the odds, and had chosen this celebratory marker only to learn soon after that Monique had overpainted another artist's work. Gloria had felt mortified by the discovery, heartbroken—again—and furious at Monique's duplicity. The painting was later restored, at Nicky's expense, into something far more valuable, but Gloria still wore this scar of deceit like a badge. The self-righteous resentment it generated afforded her the illusion of actually living.

In these solitary hours, with her window reflection as her only companion, Gloria stirred her wounds into a stew of anger and paranoia that made misery a self-fulfilling prophesy. Her aura of burgeoning self-pity and discontent had made her a social pariah amongst the people in town, but these days, she bore them only contempt. She had disassociated from them all, including those who had once been dear, like Meilin. It was no surprise, then, that, on Thanksgiving, Gloria had found herself eating with only her guests for company. Later that evening, she had sat at the checkout desk in the parlor beneath the refurbished and lighted "Lupines" painting, the symbol of all she had worked so hard to earn and the only reliable company she had.

She reached out now to draw a single sip from her wine glass, then rose from her chair to return to the demands of the B&B. She walked to the lobby desk, opened her laptop and flipped through the reservations for the rest of December and early January. The B&B had full bookings ahead, including a full house for Christmas and New Year's.

People who spent the holidays in Maine were looking for atmosphere. They expected the scent of evergreens, the glow of the fireplace, hot chowder and warm spirit. This morning, Gloria had hung the front door wreath, placed a single LED candle in each window and strung lights along the deck and the dock. Inside, the place as yet showed no indication of the upcoming holiday. In truth, Gloria preferred the simplicity of unadorned darkness to artificially lighted gaiety, but her own sentiments ever bowed to the wishes of her guests.

She steeled herself to what must be done and pulled out her checklist of holiday preparations. The live tree would arrive tomorrow. The wine supply and hors d'oeuvres platters from Mainsail Wine and Cheese were scheduled weekly throughout the month, as were decorative Christmas cookie trays from the Main Street Coffee Bar. The liquor cabinet was stocked with wines, locally crafted beers, soft drinks and Maine's specialties: wild blueberry wine, Allen's coffee brandy, potato vodka, cider, and Moxie soda, classic Maine beverages that seemed to amplify her guests' experience of the place. Whatever. She was happy to take their money.

Gloria pulled back her thick, dark curls into a ponytail using the elastic band she wore perpetually around her wrist for that purpose. She lit the lamps in the parlor, popped open a box and drew out the garland for the banister. After affixing this, she began to unwrap the delicate tree ornaments she had accumulated over the years. Each had been chosen with care and in keeping with the quality and history of the old Victorian. The Town's End B&B stood out as one of the gems of Mayenne Bay, thanks to her commitment to excellence and her eye for quality. The place had been singled out several times by area publications for its tasteful décor and comfort. Her resentful heart beat faster, and her breathing accelerated, as she calculated the town's indebtedness to her singular efforts to raise its prospects by drawing monied people to her inn.

She worked in silent perturbation, hands busy, mind focused on matters outside the B&B's four walls. It settled first on the art club. She seethed over the recent changes in the art club by-laws. Once a club leader herself, her influence had waned as a consequence of her withdrawal from society, leaving governance to Meilin and her cronies. This time, Gloria had been too late in her opposition to their maneuvering but she wouldn't tarry again when it came to governing affairs of the club.

Nor would she lose time when it came to influencing the town's economic development and, specifically, the disposition of the old canning factory site. Leroy Hood, the developer who had shown so much promise this summer, had disappeared with the investment funds for the promised condominiums. The gaping hole left by his departure was being filled, in the mayor's and town council's desperation to save face, by Christy Chase's "A Better Idea for Mayenne Bay" concept. Christy, a local artist and architect, had proposed an "intentional community", in Gloria's estimation, a euphemism for a low-class commune that would undermine upmarket endeavors and devalue property overall, including the B&B. She suspected town leaders were poised, in their lingering embarrassment, to demonstrate rapid progress, possibly even to rubber stamp this alternative solution. She judged the town had better return to last summer's idea of an upscale condo rather than pursue Christy's socialist scheme, or the guests who paid the B&B's extravagant rates would find another seaside destination.

Gloria gulped more wine and continued fuming at the stupidity and shortsightedness of the town leadership. After the fine example she had set, all she had done and invested to raise standards, Mayenne Bay was still a backwater and would remain so without a rudder aimed in the right direction. She pledged herself to instigate a change of tack.

As she pulled tissue-paper wrapping from a set of colorful, hand-thrown Christmas pottery, Gloria's mood could not have been further from the merriment it was meant to kindle. She was solemn as she turned her mind to the methods employed last summer by Leroy Hood to build support for his condominium scheme. The man was a crook, but there was no denying the genius of his personal networking and fund-raising to promote a cause. While she arranged the display on the dining room sideboard, she mentally crafted letters to the *Bayside Squawker* editor contesting Christy's proposal and she outlined a strategy for one-on-one politicking in the style Leroy had so well applied.

Mayenne Bay would soon see who had the better idea.

Bayside Squawker, December 13

Protesters,

Demonstrations are part of the American way, but do you have to crowd sidewalks, shout at passers-by and block busy corners? Our local stores have enough to overcome in this economy. They don't need shoppers skipping town because of you.

Captain Crabbish

Neighbors and Friends,

Two young women, Denise Baptiste and Valentina Diaz, disappeared from our midst this fall and still have not been found. If you sight either woman or know anything about their whereabouts, please contact the Mayenne Bay police department immediately. Photos are posted on the department website.

Thank you,
Chief Manning

8

Holiday Pressures

Claire poured a glass of wine and sank onto the couch to catch up on several issues of the *Bayside Squawker*. When finished, she tossed the papers onto her coffee table, quite in harmony with Captain Crabbish. Fiber artists should find something more constructive to do with their talents than urban knitting, and disruptive sidewalk protesters were getting out of hand. She felt something like kinship with the crusty Captain after all the old *Squawker* issues she had been reading of late at the library. Did this new synchronicity mean that both she and the Captain had their fingers on the town's pulse or that Claire was moving to the far side? Her New Ageist mother would say that Claire was channeling his spirit. Maybe she was.

Right now, the Captain was an abstraction, and reading his letters a mere recreation, while Claire searched out more pressing clues about the skull. Yet, she had read enough of his comments to instill fear that the current Captain could become a hard reality quickly enough if he ever got wind of the rumor of her infidelity. Nothing appeared too sacred to draw his public commentary. Though she didn't intend to publicize any discoveries she made about the Captain, Claire couldn't rely on his restraint in turn. A shiver ran down her spine. She hadn't yet traced the origin of the scuttlebutt broadcast by Kitty, so there was no way to resolve it just now. This left her in limbo, a state she did not tolerate well. She had to get to the bottom of that rumor, and soon. If only she knew where to begin.

Hannah Munro's face appeared on Claire's phone to the sound of the Addams family ringtone as if Claire's unspoken allusion to channeling had conjured her. Hannah would be quick to claim it had. She had long evinced a sixth sense that seemed tuned to Claire's quiet moments regardless of the distance between them and didn't hesitate to pounce when the spirit nudged her. Claire put the phone on speaker, propped it on the coffee table and stretched her legs out next to it. In that short interval, tension rose like great claws to grip her shoulders.

"Hi, Mom."

"Claire, honey, I haven't heard from you. How was your Thanksgiving with the Gardiners?"

"It was nice. We…"

Hannah dropped the saccharine tone and cut Claire off in words both direct and competitive, as though holiday visits were a contest and Hannah was keeping score, which she was.

"They got you at Thanksgiving. We should get you at Christmas. And we should all meet Guy."

Claire pursed her lips, resentful of the way her mother slung "should" at her, as if owed, in lieu of polite invitations for her company.

Hearing no immediate response from her daughter, Hannah shifted from the fairness campaign to food, always part and parcel of the holiday seduction ritual.

"I'll be baking a ham and a turkey with all the usual sides. And I've made loads of cookies, including butter cookies just for you."

Claire sat back and closed her eyes while her mother ran on. She had given up long ago suggesting that Hannah tailor quantities to her shrinking household. With all the family estrangement, and so many moved away, the extended "clan", as her mother called it, had shrunk to a mere few. Hannah simply couldn't adjust. She persisted in cooking massive quantities like in the old days.

Among the few pleasant memories Claire had of Christmas as a girl, baking alongside her mother was one, though she had never revealed the truth about those butter cookies. She hated them. To economize, Hannah always substituted margarine for butter, leaving the sugary sprinkles to carry the day. A mild nausea rose in Claire's throat. She swallowed hard and waited until her mother drew breath before answering.

"Mom, it's not that I don't appreciate all this, but time off at year-end is nigh impossible at any accounting firm. And I'm new on the job and have a new boss. I can't take time off this Christmas, not enough to travel down to New Jersey, anyway."

Hannah disconnected quickly after that but not before conveying, in a painfully high-pitched voice, her extreme dissatisfaction. Claire remained on the couch under the soft light of a single lamp and sipped wine for some time. She was flustered by her mother's refusal to accept her very real job circumstances as a sufficient excuse to stay put. She didn't dare request lengthy time off during the December crunch, especially not this year. But Claire hadn't told her mother the whole truth. Difficult as things were at work, they afforded a convenient excuse to kick a more troubling can down the road: fear of losing Guy by exposure to the Munro family's insanity.

She stuffed her discomfort down deep, picked up her phone again and called Guy.

"You don't sound like yourself," he said, concern in his

voice.

Claire released a long sigh, closed her eyes and massaged the back of her neck.

"Do you celebrate Christmas?"

"Not the religious part, no. I like the gift giving, though. I keep it small and simple. Christmas music is the real highlight. I play the old stuff—Bing Crosby, Dean Martin, Ella Fitzgerald and Nat King Cole. And then there's the food."

"Another opportunity for big pants?"

"No. They make an appearance only once a year at Thanksgiving."

"Thank God for that. Will you visit your family?"

"If I can, but I have end-of-year projects for clients trying to spend what's left in their budgets. My family understands this. Some years, all I've managed is tea with Annabelle. Claire, what's all this about?"

"My mother just called and is planning the usual holiday overdose with an extra pound of guilt because I won't be there. She knows I can't come down with my work obligations but she insists anyway, like a broken record." She stopped herself just short of spilling further into her family's pathology. "Sorry. I sound peevish."

"Peevish? Who uses words like that besides Jane Austen? Maybe you're subconsciously wishing for a quiet hour with Darcy and Elizabeth."

Claire laughed. Guy usually found a way to bring humor into any drama and he was right. An easy read of *Pride and Prejudice* did sound calming.

"Do you decorate?" Claire asked. "I've been second guessing my own austerity after rolling through town. It's like a carnival out there."

"I've always thought the extravagance was a reaction to the short, dark days."

"Maybe I should put candles in the windows for my

neighbors suffering with seasonal affective disorder."

"Leave it to you to make Christmas decorating a psychological therapy. I don't bother in the loft, but I do help Annabelle with her tree. And each year, she crochets a new ornament for me. I make sure to hang them in the windows where she can see them. Could be worse. Aunt Helen crochets toilet roll covers in red yarn with a silver bell garnish. My mother has at least a dozen of them."

This drew a laugh from Claire.

"I have one of those aunts, too. I'm hoping she doesn't have my new address. It seems there are a number like our aunts in town. Have you seen the urban knitting?"

"Yeah. I'm withholding comment in case Annabelle is a participant. Look, Claire, I've got a heavy load, too. We can celebrate quietly right here this year. I'll handle Christmas dinner at my place. You can host New Year's after all the numbers have been crunched."

"Perfect."

When the call ended, Claire's outlook was brighter. Quiet holidays with Guy would be just the thing, and she doubted Hannah would call again until the New Year now that the message had got through. She grabbed her well-worn copy of *Pride and Prejudice* from the bookshelf and curled up on the couch to immerse herself in the comforts of Pemberly.

Despite the demands of their jobs, Guy and Claire found time to attend the Whispering Seabreeze fundraising party the Friday before Christmas. Annabelle, uncomfortable driving in the dark, arranged to ride with them. As the time came to leave, there was a knock at the loft door. Annabelle had climbed the steps to deliver her annual Christmas card and ornament plus a box of homemade ginger snaps.

Claire answered the door and found a chubby old woman with white hair wearing a gaudy Christmas sweater, black knit pants and white tennis shoes. There were large, candy-cane earrings clipped to her lobes.

"You must be Annabelle, the expert rose gardener. I've never seen such beauties before. The scent is heavenly. I'm Claire."

Annabelle was a bit nonplussed by the unexpected flattery but stepped in and coolly eyed Claire from head to toe.

"I seen you comin' and goin' here. You better treat him good. He's a nice boy."

"Hi, Annabelle," said Guy from behind Claire.

The old woman thrust a box, a crocheted star and an envelope toward Guy.

"Hee-ah. Merry Christmas."

"Thank you." He passed the gifts and card to Claire to hold. "I have something for you, too."

He retrieved from his desk a framed painting tied with a red ribbon.

"This year, I painted a yellow one. Merry Christmas."

Annabelle took the painting of her prize rose in both hands. She was lost for words, but her face told Guy all he needed to know.

"Will you come for tea on Christmas Eve?" she asked.

"Would love to. Around seven o'clock? Claire will be here, too."

"Good," was all the old woman said, enough to convey her pleasure at having secured a visit. "I'll put this painting inside, then meet you at the car."

Guy nodded and closed the door. Behind him, Claire had opened Annabelle's box and popped a ginger snap into her mouth. She chewed slowly, taking in the flavor, then popped another.

"These could be addictive. Think we can weasel the recipe from Annabelle?"

"It might not be worth much to you if she copies it by hand." Guy handed Annabelle's Christmas card to Claire. The scrawl below the printed greeting was almost indecipherable.

"I wonder how much the writing is like the person." Guy rolled his eyes and shook his head.

"First you analyze artists' signatures on paintings, now you're onto Christmas cards?"

Claire grinned, shrugged and closed the cookie box. They grabbed coats and headed down to the car, where Annabelle had already planted herself on the back seat holding a wrapped Christmas package and two more crocheted ornaments on her lap.

"I see you're one of our urban fiber artists, Annabelle," Claire observed as she slid into the front seat.

"Not me," Annabelle growled, her expression repugnant. "What a waste of yarn, all wet and muddy in the street."

"Don't sugarcoat your opinion on our account, Annabelle," quipped Guy.

She grunted.

They entered the Whispering Seabreeze home carrying "angel" gifts, a longstanding holiday tradition in Mayenne Bay. Schools, churches and neighbors identified children in need of clothing and other necessities and hung donor requests on wing-shaped tags on Christmas trees at local businesses. Patrons chose tags and acted the part of gift angels. Claire had selected "Female, age nine, child size ten, winter coat" for herself and "Gender neutral, age 14, backpack" for Guy. Annabelle's tag read "Boy, age five, child size 11, winter boots." The gifts would be delivered to the children by volunteers tomorrow morning.

They were greeted in the foyer by their friend, Morrie

Appleton, a short, middle-aged man in a bright red cardigan. Morrie was a local math teacher and a resident of Whispering Seabreeze. This year, he had taken charge of the angel gifts, quite an undertaking judging from the pile under the large tree that dominated the residence dining hall. He directed Guy, Claire and Annabelle to deposit their gifts beneath it and then to help themselves to refreshments.

After hanging their coats, they stacked their gifts atop the mound. Annabelle found bare branches to hang her crocheted ornaments in between lights and stringed popcorn, then headed for a corner of the room where Kitty Greenwood, the Fish House waitress, and Ellie Brown, wife of activist Jay Brown, stood apart from the crowd. When Annabelle reached the pair, the women promptly closed ranks and bent heads in close conversation. Claire took note of this threesome. She couldn't remember seeing Annabelle, Ellie and Kitty together before. They were, in her estimation, an unlikely combination, aside from their proximity of age. Kitty, muscular and angular in her habitual brown wig and too much makeup. Ellie, pallid and immensely overweight, with grey curly hair. Annabelle, rosy-cheeked and somewhat round with white hair in a knot behind her head. A waitress, a retired English teacher and a landlady. Claire giggled. It sounded like the opening line of a bar joke.

Guy and Claire identified many familiar faces in the room. Louis, Meilin and Roxie chatted with the mayor and police chief, the latter of whom wore a full Santa suit. Jay hovered nearby to eavesdrop. Ben and Rhonda stood with Ben's father, town attorney Bobby Tripp, and the Grace family, Thomas, Beatrice, Leon and Sam. Ricky and Celia walked, arm in arm. Christy and her partner, Ken Cross, likewise. Celeste and Patty worked the refreshment table. The eccentric artist, John Mills, privately dubbed Pierre Cliché by Guy and Claire, in a Santa hat instead of his usual beret, watched the gala from a far corner. Quince and Peggy, wearing reindeer antlers, stood with arms across one another's shoulders and swayed to the music. The spirited youth soccer club danced in a conga line to Hall and Oates' "Jingle Bell Rock". Even Gloria showed up momentarily to toss an angel gift on the pile and bestow an Ebenezer Scrooge-like scowl at the bouncing adolescents.

A commotion at the refreshment tables parted the crowd from two different directions. Louis, having the advantage of towering height, could be seen making his way toward the disturbance. Another person of equal influence, but smaller stature, forged a path and became visible only as she emerged from the throng: Roxie. One of the exuberant soccer players had danced and jingled so riotously, he had bumped into the table and tipped a lighted candle, which ignited the paper tablecloth. Roxie and Louis expertly extinguished the tiny blaze, then, casting looks of apology across the room at Mary Bouchard, the residence manager, snuffed out all remaining live candles. She nodded her understanding and pressed her palms together in a silent signal of thanks. There was a smattering of applause for the quick-witted firefighters.

As the smoke alarms and sprinkler system hadn't been triggered, the crowd quickly regrouped to Mariah Carey's "All I Want for Christmas is You". Only Claire remained where she stood staring in wonder at the mettle required to run toward a fire instead of away from it. Guy took her hands and looked up at the mistletoe overhead before waking her from her musings with a kiss.

Guy and Claire drove Annabelle home before settling at Claire's place for the night. There, they sank onto the couch and talked well into the late hours. The next day, Guy would receive a visit from Anna to strategize how best to approach his parents about Asad. It would be Guy's first experience dealing with the threat of family division and alienation, and the prospect sapped him of holiday cheer. Claire helped him push through, being an old hand at family feuds.

Bayside Squawker, December 20

Readers,

In all this rushing to shop, are you paying attention to our town? We have homeless people right here who need food, clothing and beds. I heard tell of a teenager living in a tent and a veteran sleeping in the park bandshell. What are you doing about it?

Captain Crabbish

Bayside Squawker, December 27

Mayenne Bay,

The Town Council plans to increase harbor fees for live-aboarders. With the wharf toilet and shower needing repair, the shortage of electric hook-ups, unreliable internet service and limited potable water, higher fees are hardly justified. And they might price live-aboarders out of their boat homes when we already have a housing shortage on land. Watch for this topic to appear on upcoming council agendas. Be there.

Blue Bickford, Harbor Master and Live-Aboarder Spokesperson

9

New Year's

Christmas Eve tea at Annabelle's earned Claire another friend. Happy to have an attentive audience, Annabelle walked Claire and Guy through the history of the antique ornaments on her tree while they feasted on butter and ginger cookies, tea and vin chaud. Afterward, Annabelle regaled them with stories from the days when she worked in the canning factory and pulled out black-and-white photographs of the time.

"We'd listen for the whistle from the incoming boat full with catch, then rush to the factory in our hairnets and rubber aprons. The floor was always cold and slippery. We taped our fingers so they wouldn't get cut. We'd snip off the sardine heads and tails, then hand-pack them into the tins. It was hard work, not always steady, but we loved it. We were like family. It would be nice to see that place doing something productive again for the community."

Guy had a hard time pulling Claire away, absorbed as she was in his landlady's life story. When they finally retreated, she had, safely tucked in her pocket, the recipe for Annabelle's delightful ginger cookies scratched out in the old woman's contorted longhand. She stayed late at the loft but refused to sleep over. Guy couldn't blame her for shunning his lumpy twin bed; it was uncomfortable enough under his own weight. But it was getting increasingly more difficult to part from her at day's end. The solution, in his mind, wasn't the purchase of a new bed that would merely perpetuate the current back and forth between their respective places. The solution was co-habitation.

Guy had made the proposal to live together several months ago. Claire's hesitancy at the time had told him not to broach the topic again until she was ready. It had hovered over them like a specter ever since. His only recourse was to rely on Claire's increasing discomfort when the time came to part, coupled with her dislike for leaving things unresolved. Until these combined to force a reckoning, the only weapon he had was passive psychological warfare arising from increasing affection, reluctant good-byes and a very old mattress.

On Christmas Day, Claire returned to the loft for an intimate dinner and gift exchange.

When New Year's Eve rolled around, it was her turn to host. With the holidays finally over and their respective deadlines met, some of the tightness had drained from their shoulders.

But not all.

"You know, I felt so sure of my move to Mayenne Bay at first. Then, within just a few months, the town was riddled with theft, deception, betrayal and swindling. Looking back, it seems like a bad movie. The status quo may have needed a shake-up, but not in the way it came about."

Guy listened to this preamble from the kitchen sink where he stood peeling shrimp. He had no idea where this was going, so he held his tongue. Claire went on. Her voice trembled.

"The same is true for my own status quo. My original

plans for life in Mayenne Bay have been completely overturned, first by you—I'm not complaining about that part—and now, by work. I think I'm on shaky ground with Erin O'Farrell."

Guy's head jerked toward her.

"What? Your new boss? Claire, how can that be? Management knows your work is top-notch. Are you sure you're not being paranoid?"

"I don't think so. Being the hypersensitive I am, I often feel off-balance around people without being able to explain it. Something's not right with Erin. And Ricky and Renée have both warned me to watch out for her."

Renée Pincer was Mid Coast Accountancy's administrative manager, and Ricky its IT lead. Both were friends of Claire and well placed to have their fingers on the firm's pulse. They had her interests at heart.

Claire looked earnestly at Guy.

"Do you think she got wind of the rumor of my untrustworthiness? I could see her latching onto that. Breaches of confidentiality don't fit well in an accounting firm."

"But it's a rumor, Claire. You're giving it far too much weight."

"I'm not sure I am. You know how these things take on a life of their own in this town." She sank into a chair. "Putting my integrity into question cuts me to the core. No one has approached me with a problem for some time. The rumor might be the reason for that. I should feel liberated, but if it's because I'm not deemed reliable…"

Guy walked over and gently pulled her to a standing position. Not for the first time, Claire felt as though she could drown in the ocean blue of his steady gaze.

"It is possible to live life contentedly, Claire, without the endless burdens of strangers and their problems."

"And so, we circle back to the disruption of my status

quo. Trust is a big deal for me, and hearing people out has been a part of my life for as long as I can remember." She forced a weak smile. "Well, at least the holidays are over, and we're relieved from the pressure to conform to that commotion for another year."

"Yes, but we have to wait a full year before Chief Manning appears again in a Santa costume."

Claire laughed.

"On a boat with a fishing net full of goodies. That was a first for me."

She reached on tiptoe for a Main Street Coffee Bar box sitting atop the refrigerator and opened it.

"And these butter cookies, Maine-inspired red lobsters, green crabs, candy-cane-striped starfish, will soon disappear from the shelves. I haven't been able to walk past the Coffee Bar without buying a cookie since they first crammed the bakery case after Thanksgiving. The whole place smells like gingerbread and warm butter. We'll have to survive without them until next season."

Guy regarded the box contents.

"Are you sure they gave you your money's worth? Seems a few are missing."

"Someone had to sample them."

"And this after you scarfed up Annabelle's ginger snaps. I thought I had a cookie addiction, but mine involves only Oreos and milk and is triggered by crisis. With you, it's any cookie, anytime."

"That's not precisely true. I don't like Oreos. No butter."

She set down the cookie box, retrieved Annabelle's ginger snap recipe and waved it in the air.

"It's some consolation I'll be able to make Annabelle's ginger snaps myself. But look at her writing. It's like another language altogether. It was a trial to decipher the recipe, but it spurred me to look into handwriting analysis using her as my guinea pig. Her writing is so distinctive with long, narrow 'y' loops and stray 'i' dots. I was sure it would suggest fascinating insights."

Guy rolled his eyes.

"Claire, is there anything you don't turn into a behavioral lab? You're always postulating about people. This summer, you psychoanalyzed artists' styles and signatures. You put Christmas candles in your windows against your neighbors' seasonal affective disorder. And now this."

"You're the one who suggested the mania for Christmas lights is to compensate for the darkness of winter."

"You have a psychology obsession, not to mention a cookie addiction. Maybe somebody should study you."

She laughed.

"Maybe they should. But aren't you curious about subliminal compulsions?"

"My God, I'm dating Freud reincarnate."

Guy's face bore an expression mingled of feigned censure, amusement and affection. Say what he would, he loved this side of Claire.

She laid the recipe before him.

"Look here. Annabelle slants her cursive in both directions. Slants are supposed to involve emotions, so what does it mean if the letters flop haphazardly left and right? She's a fascinating study. Ooh, just wait until I get around to all the artists' signatures."

"I don't think handwriting analysis is an exact science."

"That doesn't mean it's completely without merit."

"Next thing I know, you'll be studying tea dregs."

"Whatever works. I have you right at hand as a test case."

When they sat down to cold shrimp, Claire relayed her conversation with Annabelle from that morning. She had dropped by with some homemade ravioli and Coffee House butter cookies for the old woman's New Year's Eve. While Annabelle went to the kitchen to prepare tea and coffee,

Claire had begun poking through the photos spread across the dining room table.

"Reminiscing again?" asked Claire when Annabelle re-emerged. They both leaned into a class photo. "Which one is you?"

Annabelle indicated a young woman with shoulder-length dark hair.

"Annabelle Boisvert," Claire read aloud. "Did you speak French in your childhood home?"

"Oh, yes. We spoke at home. If we hadn't, the language would have been lost to us. Until 1960, speaking French was forbidden in Maine except at home or in a foreign language class. Outside of that, we could be punished for it. When I left to get married, I started speaking English at home—my husband was an anglophone—but I had French-speaking family and eventually joined the French Club to keep up my skills."

Annabelle had then lapsed into a recital of her youth that left no doubt of the pains she and her fellow francophones had endured. Claire had been very affected.

"It's one thing to read about history. It's another to meet someone who has lived it. It's hard to imagine such oppression, though there are countless instances of it throughout history."

Guy didn't disguise his resentment.

"You can say the same and worse about the Wabanaki people. Just spend five minutes with Louis on the subject. What disturbs me is that they never taught us about this stuff in school, not more than a mention, anyway. History is full of mistakes, but they shouldn't be buried under a rug." He could see from Claire's face this discussion had put her in a stew. "I sense more research projects coming on."

Her mouth curved at one corner.

"I'm not a history buff, but when it teaches you something about the people you know, it's worth delving a bit. Did you know Annabelle Clark was once Annabelle Boisvert? 'Boisvert' translates to 'green woods', as in Kitty 'Greenwood'. I wonder if the origin of their names was the same and then, at some point way back, 'Boisvert' was anglicized to avoid mistreatment. It wouldn't be the first time immigrants have changed their name to fit in."

Her brow furrowed, a sign, Guy had learned, that she had sunk into her own thoughts. He left her to it while they feasted on shrimp, finger food. and a dozen butter cookies, minus two or three.

The rest of New Year's Eve passed just as quietly as Christmas, with mellow music playing from the turntable Guy had brought. He planted a Nat King Cole album, one of several vintage, 33-RPM LPs Claire had gifted him for Christmas for his collection, on the platter, positioned the arm and started the record. They sipped drinks and ate during the first side of the album. Then Guy rose, flipped the disk over and pulled Claire up from the sofa for a slow dance. She snuggled against his shoulder—she loved the way her head landed just right, like they had been molded for each other—while their bodies swayed in synchronous rhythm to Nat's "Unforgettable". Guy stroked her hair.

"I hope you don't mind an early night," Claire whispered into his ear. "I figure the new year will be here in the morning whether we watch its arrival or not."

Guy gently drew her closer, making his answer quite clear. After a few more dances, Claire's place fell completely dark except for a solitary LED candle in each window, sentinels for her neighbors against the winter blues.

On January 2, Claire stepped quickly across the office parking lot, head down against the cold wind while, at the same time, her body burned with the heat of anxiety. The holidays had temporarily distracted her from her worries. Now, as life returned to normal, they swarmed her like hungry children. Her job insecurity. Kitty's nasty rumor. And worst of all, her uncertain future with Guy. Nothing short of a Munro family face-to-face would decide it. Claire didn't miss the irony that, just six months ago, she hadn't wanted Guy or any man in her life. Now, she lived in terror her family would scare him away.

In recent weeks, she had taken to force-filling every spare waking minute to keep her mind from all this. Anything served—books, cooking, Captain Crabbish, visits to Annabelle, even cleaning her already immaculate apartment. The Munro-visit-avoidance campaign, in particular, was beginning to sap her energy. The prolonged indecision was, in itself, unnatural for her and exhausting. She had no idea how practiced procrastinators maintained their sanity. Soon, very soon, before she completely wore out, she would have to come to grips with herself.

She closed her office door, hung her coat on the hook and roved about the room to clear her head, stretching, bending and deep breathing. It had always been thus: Her troubles rose to the surface in the tranquil moments of the morning. She found, when she applied her mind to other things, she could block them out for a time. Spreadsheets and calculations would do the trick. She went to the break room to grab a coffee and returned to find Erin hovering in the doorway.

"Good morning, Erin."

She gazed steadily into the woman's green eyes and raised her eyebrows in question.

"You promised me those calculations first thing when you returned. I need them now."

"I said they would be done by the end of today," Claire corrected her.

Erin started to speak, but Claire cut her off.

"But I finished them before I left for the New Year's holiday. They've been in the client file for over a week."

She turned away from her boss, lowered herself into her desk chair and tapped her keyboard, taking no further heed of Erin, who spun on her heels and left, the wind gone from her sails. Claire sighed. She had learned long ago the art of "under-promise and over-deliver" but felt no triumph having been a step ahead of her boss. One victory in battle did not win a war, and Erin did not seem the type to tire of these irksome workplace power demonstrations. Claire would have to stay on her toes.

Bayside Squawker, January 3

Readers,

After that crook last summer, not a word from our mayor about housing development. Here we are, starting a new year, and still, nobody can find an affordable place to rent, while our mayor sits in her big house on The Point. The factory site is back on the town council agenda for January 16. Come and be heard.

Captain Crabbish

Fellow Business and Property Owners,

Our mayor and town council are again considering development of the old canning factory site into housing. Last summer, they were duped by a scammer, but the upscale condo concept itself had real value. Beware of the populist "A Better Idea" plan. Let's not replace a rusty eyesore with a downscale commune that will further degrade property values in
Mayenne Bay.

Gloria Townsend, Owner, Town's End B&B

10

A Better Idea

With the new year rung in, the town settled back to wait out the remains of winter, which progressed at its slow-as-chilled-molasses pace through the frigid temperatures and intermittent snowfalls. Christmas decorations disappeared, though a few trees lingered in living room windows and some dirty, soggy urban knitting drooped obscenely from town fixtures, bringing to mind soiled diapers. Retail stores posted shorter winter hours or closed entirely for the needed breather before the next tourist season began. The streets resumed their usual off-season dearth of pedestrians and traffic.

But all was not quiet.

Like bees in hibernation, the denizens of Mayenne Bay clustered where it was warmest and buzzed unflaggingly amongst themselves in anticipation of the upcoming January town council meeting. Last summer, the council and mayor had entertained an upmarket condo scheme for the town's abandoned canning factory site and, to the consternation of the general public, had negotiated the deal behind closed doors. Before ground had been broken, the developer, Leroy Hood, had left with the investment proceeds, leaving the town flat and the mayor and council eating humble pie. The townspeople wanted action. They planned to make themselves heard.

Mayor Sandra Edgecomb folded her copy of the *Bayside Squawker* and leaned back as she ruminated on the latest commentary from the Captain. It was a wonder she bothered to read his provoking posts, but had she not, she would have missed Gloria's shot across the bow. In the past several years, the B&B owner had turned from congenial colleague to reclusive adversary, prone to criticize and slow to lend a hand. Sandra kept tabs on all business owners and their standings on town issues, however opposed to her own views, but the contrary B&B owner had become so negative and tiresome, Sandra was almost numb to her. Anyway, as mayor, she had far bigger fish to fry. It didn't take a letter in the *Bayside Squawker* to inform her she was in deep water with her constituents.

Sandra had been stunned by Leroy Hood's betrayal, but more so by the collusion of her then-trusted assistant, Sally Eaton, in his scheme. Shortly after Leroy scarpered, Sally had covertly bolted to escape reprisal. Where she had flown, Sandra did not know, but Sandra doubted Sally had found solace with Leroy. Hurt and a bit at sea, Sandra had pressed on unassisted these past months, too paranoid to trust another helper.

Residents of Mayenne Bay had grudgingly endured those months of apparent inaction from the town leadership, but though Sandra had been silent, she hadn't been idle. She had spent the time evaluating the only other development option on the table: Christy Chase's "A Better Idea for Mayenne Bay". She met at length with Christy and sounded out the town council, the town attorney, the area chamber of commerce and business and property owners. She spoke to Jay Brown, self-appointed defender of citizens, and to Celeste Baptiste, town news broadcaster at the Fish House. She even stopped people at random on the streets and kept a watchful eye on the *Squawker*'s Letters to the Editor. All this, she had done with an ironic and reluctant nod to the vanished scammer, Leroy, who had used this style of up-close politicking and data gathering to collect supporters and substantial investments.

When the town council posted the January 16 agenda, the popular reaction was swift and palpable. Residents who had smoldered with impatience to learn how their mayor planned to fulfill her promise of economic development found their voices. Sandra didn't resent those who complained about her missteps with the Hood debacle but she was flummoxed by insinuations she was a privileged silver spoon. She didn't disguise her pride in her family's ancestral home on The Point, the stretch of Mayenne Bay's shoreline that jutted farthest out into the bay, but the derision directed at her, as though the place had been a windfall, was galling. In truth, she had inherited a money pit and spent ten years working an out-of-state job to afford all the renovations required to make it fit for habitation. Finally, she had come home to Mayenne Bay to devote her energies to the town's improvement only to be confronted by baseless spite.

On January 16, Mayenne Bay citizens packed into the council meeting room, filling it to the gills, as expected. Jay, who usually arrived early and positioned himself front-and-center before the podium to voice popular demands, was conspicuously absent tonight. Sandra had hoped he would prove an ally with respect to the building plan—she knew he had called a citizens' meeting about it last month—and delayed as long as she could. At 6:15, she tucked a few loose strands back into her classic French twist, tapped the mic and rapped her gavel on the podium. Conversation dropped to a low hum.

"Good evening. Our first order of business is to introduce our new Town Manager, Jerome Allen."

Mayenne Bay had terminated its last manager for his duplicitous involvement in the Hood scam. His ruggedly attractive replacement, a young man with dark brown hair with blonde highlights, intelligent, brown eyes and caramel-colored skin, stood and waved to acknowledge the crowd while Sandra read a brief bio, then took his seat. The room audibly rustled. Sandra suspected the rush of female pheromones, were she able to smell them, would be overwhelming.

"Jerome's first project will be to investigate the live-aboarder harbor fee schedule. He'll begin by conferring with Blue Bickford. Next, we'll hear from Louis Rainwater on his proposal for a Mud Season Bash this spring. Details of Louis's plans were published in the *Squawker* and on the town website last week. The proceeds will benefit our fire fighters."

A flutter of applause sounded for these vital volunteers.

After a brief statement from Louis, Sandra sought a motion and a second, then proceeded with the council vote. It was unanimous.

"We're looking forward to the Bash, Louis," she said before turning back to the general audience. "Now, we'll hear a brief word from Meilin Li on behalf of the Mayenne Bay Art Show committee regarding this year's proposed sequel. Again, details were published last week."

Meilin took the podium. She underscored last year's achievements, briefly outlined this year's plans and requested approval for the second annual show to go forward. Again, a motion, a second and a unanimous vote in favor.

Sandra took the mic again, grateful to have breezed through the first few items.

"Let's be sure to support these events with our time, talents and money, folks. They're large undertakings that benefit all of us and can't be managed by just a few hands."

The next agenda item, the mayor knew, was the one that had the greatest potential to test temperaments.

"We now move to tonight's primary topic. As you already know, the abandoned canning factory is not only an eyesore but unproductive to the town in every possible way. This is the first of several open council discussions regarding the disposition of that site."

The crowd stirred. From the corner of her eye, Sandra saw Gloria, whose dark expression was easy to spot amidst the undisguised optimism of the other business owners, rise and begin to make her way toward the podium. Sandra felt a momentary foreboding but pressed on.

"Last year's development attempt was a complete failure from start to finish, for which I sincerely apologize to you all." She paused for effect, certain from the crowd's reaction it hadn't expected a public apology. "The silver lining of that fiasco is that we already have clearance from Environmental Protection and Maine Historic Preservation to go ahead with demolition under a new plan. Christy Chase, a fine artist but an architect by trade, will speak tonight about her original idea for the factory site, 'A Better Idea for Mayenne Bay'."

The eruption of calls, the applause and the sudden flash of yellow-and-blue "A Better Idea" signs were raucous enough to stop Gloria in her tracks. She quickly ducked back to her seat.

Sandra stepped aside for Christy, sat down and dropped her gaze to her shoes. That Sandra had allowed herself to be blinded by Leroy's personal charms mortified her to this day. She had expected and felt she deserved a demonstration of some kind from her constituents for her past sins. Even now, she wasn't sure she would escape a public flogging, but her blunt confession and prompt apology had, at least temporarily, stayed a spontaneous combustion. It had been a risk worth taking regardless of the outcome, the first step toward healing wounds for which Sandra held herself largely responsible. She looked up at the audience. Most had upturned their hopeful faces to Christy. For the first time in many months, Sandra felt the town could move forward.

Christy was a picture of ease in a soft lavender sweater and grey slacks, though her brown eyes radiated an intensity of mind. Her fit body and head of blonde curls gave her a youthful look that belied her forty years. Ken Cross, her partner of the same age, stood nearby, one thumb poised over the remote, ready to open the slide presentation at her signal. He, too, looked relaxed in worn jeans and a navy sweater stretched over his slight girth, his wavy, salt-and-pepper hair loose and a bit disheveled.

"Thank you, Mayor Edgecomb, and good evening, everyone," Christy began. "Many of you are familiar with the 'Better Idea' plan. It grew out of the belief that profitable development can be achieved without sacrifice of Mayenne Bay's charm or the public's interest in the waterside."

There was more applause. Christy held up her hands.

"Please. Let's set aside the demonstrations so everyone can hear."

The crowd calmed.

Sandra leaned back against her chair.

Ken brought up the first image onto the screen, side-by-side drawings of the present site and the proposed housing complex. He zoomed into the latter while Christy detailed its features. Low-rise, cedar-shingled duplexes with metal roofing started at the water's edge and continued up the rising ground to the highest edge of the property, just below Harborview Street. Each unit had a small porch overlooking the water. Aesthetically, the design fitted the factory's sloping ground so well that the structures might be imagined to have sprung from the earth.

"We submitted this plan to an environmental consultant for advice on sea-level-rise risks," Christy continued as Ken clicked to the next slide, a close-up of a single unit. "Each duplex will be built—those nearest the water on pilings—for year-round occupation, not seasonal. The houses are single-storied to preserve the water view from behind, to maintain the natural look of the shoreline and to protect from wind off the bay. All units will use heat pumps with a supplemental source and will capitalize on passive solar heat and natural light. Native greenery, maintained by the complex, will fill the spaces between structures to preserve the soil."

She paused to scan reactions from the audience and to give Ken time to shift through a few more illustrative slides.

"This isn't a true co-housing complex in the sense that there are no common facilities or shared spaces. The location so near the town center and park makes those features unnecessary, so we devoted all the land to much needed housing. The public walkway along the water's edge in front of the complex will not only remain but will be enhanced as you see here."

Ken used the cursor to trace a re-routed pathway that extended over the water, then returned to the slide depicting the entire complex. Christy was again met with applause and hoots of approval.

"The plan will generate several local jobs," she resumed, "and the units will be geared to a sliding scale of incomes."

The crowd shifted and murmured. Gloria, Sandra noted with a sideways glance, glowered.

"You're probably wondering about how we will pay for all this, as you should," said Christy. "I apologize for getting technical here, but bear me out. I propose we create an LLC, a limited liability company, with a tripartite general partnership of the then-current mayor, one rotating major investor and an elected citizen, coupled with limited partnerships for private investors. We're looking into a scheme for smaller investments to allow more Mayenne Bay citizens to participate financially."

She paused to give everyone a moment to digest this concept.

"The tripartite partners will oversee governance. Returns on the property will go first into maintenance, improvements and property taxes. After all expenses are paid, investors will receive dividends when available. Our town attorney, Bobby Tripp, has reviewed and approved the idea from the legal side. He'll continue on a pro bono basis for now. I'll provide architectural support at no charge until project completion."

She stopped and looked meaningfully around the room.

"Tonight, I've presented a simplified overview, the outcome of many conversations with Mayor Edgecomb and Attorney Tripp, to name just two of those involved. This development is critical to the town's future, but I must emphasize it isn't a handout or a slam dunk. We need to attract enough investment and general support to make it work. And we need patience and understanding from you. This won't happen overnight, and the devil is always in the details. Thank you for your attention."

The applause was appreciative but more moderate. Christy's cautions had sobered the room, and their most vociferous representative, Jay, was still absent. Sandra took advantage of the lull.

"Thank you, Christy. You've given us much to think about. Everyone, please take a printed copy of Christy's proposal from the table in the back or view it on the town website. February's session will be devoted to questions and comments about the proposal. We adjourn here. Good night."

As soon as Sandra rapped the gavel, the crowd began to rise and talk amongst themselves. Sandra fully expected to be accosted by Gloria but, instead, caught sight of someone else elbowing her way through the packed room toward the mic: Celeste. She looked pained, almost frantic.

When she reached the podium, Celeste tapped the mic. It was still live.

"Can I have your attention?" she called out, panting from exertion.

Everyone stopped talking instantly at the sound of her familiar voice.

"It's Ellie Brown. She died. A heart attack. This afternoon."

Celeste sank onto the nearest chair and buried her face in her hands. Sandra reached over to turn off the mic and stood among those gathering around the aggrieved waitress. Jay had missed this critical council meeting to be at Ellie's bedside. It was the first time Sandra could honestly say she was completely on his side.

Bayside Squawker January 10

Readers,

Another winter, and mailboxes are again being taken down by plow trucks. The township should be held accountable for this damage. Mailboxes don't come cheap. I say we deduct the cost from our property taxes.

Captain Crabbish

11

Yin and Yang

Among those who flocked to Celeste's side were Patty, Claire and Guy. With tear-streaked cheeks, Celeste smiled gratefully into their faces. The rest of the crowd poured out onto the sidewalk, their enthusiasm for "A Better Idea" dampened by the news of Ellie's death. A select few walked somberly toward Grace Grocery for a prearranged gathering to toast tonight's milestone in the "A Better Idea" campaign. Guy, Claire, Patty and Celeste trailed behind them at an uneasy pace.

Thomas and Beatrice Grace were on hand to greet guests at the door of the second-floor meeting room over the grocery. It occurred to Claire in this moment how well their surname suited them. They were frequent and generous hosts with friendly manners. Thomas radiated kindness, and Beatrice moved with elegance and an open, unaffected air. Both exuded an ease among people that belied the grit and drive that had won them success at various business enterprises around town.

"Please, make yourselves comfortable," Beatrice called invitingly with a sweep of her arm toward the array of seating and stand-up cocktail tables.

When Celeste appeared in the doorway, Beatrice intercepted her, gently grasped her elbow and, with the other hand on the small of Celeste's back, guided her to a sofa positioned in a corner of the room. Guy, Claire and Patty followed. Beatrice pressed Celeste down on a cushion and maintained a grip on her shoulder to prevent her from rising. Claire sat down on Celeste's left, Patty on her right.

"But Beatrice," protested Celeste, "I promised to help serve."

"Not tonight. We'll find other willing hands."

"I'll do it," Guy said, relieved to find something to do besides sit alongside the grieving Celeste and grapple for the right words. "Just show me where to go." He extended his hand to Beatrice, then Thomas. "Guy Gardiner, Rhonda's friend from the art club." He nodded toward Claire. "And this is Claire Munro, also a friend."

"Rhonda has mentioned you two fondly," said Thomas. "Come on, Guy. You and I can handle this."

The two men disappeared into the kitchen and, within minutes, emerged with trays of drinks and hors d'oeuvres.

Guests continued to arrive. Beatrice stayed close to Celeste like a mother bird and waved to Christy, who had just come through the door.

"Christy, well done tonight. But where is our mayor? She showed a lot of courage in that meeting."

"She's gone to find Jay to see if he needs anything." She took in the surprise on several faces and added in a slightly indignant tone, "These last few months, working through the factory project, Sandra has earned my respect. It doesn't surprise me that, despite their past antagonism, she's ready to extend a hand to Jay."

"Wasn't he planning to support your proposal tonight?" Beatrice asked.

"Yes. I was looking forward to having him on my side. I've never seen him in action when he hasn't been adversarial."

She ended with a shrug and half grin. Her listeners tittered. Jay was generally at swords with someone.

"It's unfortunate that Ellie so often bore the brunt of his antagonism," Claire said soberly, "but he had his priorities straight today and was exactly where he should have been."

"Poor Mrs. Brown," Celeste said wistfully. "She was my eighth-grade English teacher. My all-time favorite."

"Mine, too," added Ben, who had approached to condole with his schoolmate. "She inspired me to read for pleasure. It changed my life. By the time I returned from the police academy, she was retired and an altered creature. Jay has been hard on her these past years. His energy went into a lot of causes. Mrs. Brown wasn't one of them."

"You're right," said Celeste, "but I never heard Mrs. Brown complain. Not once."

Ben alone knew that, though Ellie may not have spoken her marital discontent aloud, she had found at least one outlet for its expression. Last summer, she had clandestinely damaged or disposed of all of her husband's beloved garden gnomes. Ben had discovered Ellie in the act but never reported her. He had allowed the frustrated, wounded woman her own form of justice then and wasn't about to go public now.

Guy leaned into the group with a platter of food.

"I can't imagine Jay without Ellie, in spite of their difficulties," he said, as many hands reached for hors d'oeuvres. "Something held the Browns together for over forty years. Maybe their opposing personalities drew them together, you know, the magnetism of the yin and the yang."

"Jay had a little too much yang, I think," Claire said. "I didn't know Ellie personally, but whenever I saw her, she looked exhausted. Jay can't have been entirely insensible to it. My guess is he'll feel her loss all the more because, underneath, he's decent and knows he contributed to her unhappiness."

Everyone stopped speaking, nonplussed by their sudden sympathy for a man whom they had long dismissed as cantankerous and annoying.

When the guests began to thin, Claire rose and approached Ben.

"Any news about the missing women?"

"We've determined that the earrings you found in the burned shed belonged to Denise, at least originally. She makes and sells homemade jewelry. Celeste was easily able to identify Denise's creation."

"So, Denise may have been at the shed?"

"Or one of her customers. Her jewelry is pretty popular, and just about anybody could have been in that shed. The trails running through Louis's property are familiar ground to people who grew up here." A sheepish grin overtook his face. "When I was a kid, word was that the huge house was haunted. You had to brave the ghosts or risk being branded a loser." Claire rolled her eyes, and Ben shrugged. "Even back then, I wanted to be a cop, so I couldn't be seen as yellow." He chuckled, then sobered. "Anyway, with all the traffic, there's no telling, without more clues, if anyone was in the shed when the fire started."

"So, we're still at square one."

"Yeah. Still searching for both women. Denise should be the easier of the two to spot. She's a bit conspicuous. To start, she's built like Celeste… you know…" He gestured vaguely to suggest large breasts, then stuffed his hands into his pockets and rocked on his feet, eyes on his shoes for a few seconds, before regaining his cool. "And she has lots of piercings. It almost hurts to look at her. Roughly chopped hair, dyed in bright colors. Billowy clothes with bizarre patterns. She was always a standout, even when we were in school. Here, I'll shoot you a photo."

He pulled out his phone.

Claire drew out hers and opened the image she had just received.

"Wow. The small black-and-white in the *Squawker* didn't do justice to her flamboyance. I'll keep my eye out." She leaned in. "What about the skull? Could it be…could it be recent?"

"Honestly, I have no idea. It's in Augusta at the lab. They called in a forensic anthropologist from the University of Maine, but there have been delays due to the holidays and her other commitments."

"Just the skull? No other bones?"

"Just the skull. Nothing else was found even after an extensive search of the property."

Guy, passing by with an empty food tray, caught the word "skull" and hesitated.

"I'll catch you up later," Claire told him.

Before he left, he threw a teasing look over his shoulder.

"Claire, don't forget to tell Ben about your *Squawker* research at the library."

Ben looked expectantly at Claire. Patty was next to approach, having heard the word "squawker".

"My original purpose was to look into past issues of the *Squawker* for hints of missing persons or weird events that might relate to any of the things we found in the shed. I decided, at the same time, to read the Captain's past letters to get a feel for the guy. I'm sure that's the part Guy wanted you to know so you could have a good laugh."

"What did you find out?" Patty asked.

"Just interesting tidbits about the town and the daily life of the time. Nothing yet that could possibly help Ben. I began at the paper's inception in 1900 and have got as far as the 1930's. The microfiche is blurry, blinding actually, and the words are unsearchable, so it's a tedious study, page by page."

When Ben returned to Celeste's side, Patty guided Claire to a private corner and pressed her about the Captain.

"There's not a hint about his real identity, Patty, or even where he might have resided. His writing style was more formal at first, perhaps a sign of the times. It changed in the late 1930's, when I guess the original must have passed the baton to a successor. Both the original and first successor—I haven't gotten far enough to flesh out a second—enjoyed finding fault, a lot like the current Captain. Their commentaries track the town's history, so they're illuminating. The first successor's writing seems to bear some French influence, judging from the occasional odd syntax and spelling. That would be possible, wouldn't it? The influx of francophones began in the late 1800's, so the language would have been pervasive by the 1930's."

"But not permitted in public since 1919," Peggy reminded Claire. "That could explain it—a francophone forced to use English." She lowered her voice. "Please, Claire, keep your findings to yourself. If the Captain's identity is discovered, he'll lose all his appeal. And if the French club ever gets wind of the remote possibility that he was one of them…well, you can imagine the ruckus."

"Mum's the word. I promise to come to you first with any discoveries about the Captain, Patty."

The gathering was beginning to break up. Thomas and Guy finished cleanup and hung up their aprons. Claire rejoined Celeste and, with Guy alongside, walked her to her car. From there, Claire and Guy made their way to Claire's place. As they walked, Claire repeated her conversation with Ben about the missing women and skull.

"So, in all three matters, we're still on hold," she concluded.

After an affectionate good night, Guy made his way home from town in a mental fog, full of Claire's last words.

"We're still on hold," he repeated to himself.

What had begun as a casual observation about the police cases had struck a subconscious chord and devolved into a tuneless earworm. Still on hold. Still on hold. Still on hold. It wasn't the first time words had taken on a life of their own. As they looped in his head, he awoke to the cause: "Still on hold" was a distillate of his stalled relationship with Claire.

He had lost count by now of the nights they had spent together since meeting last April. They had grown increasingly close, shared one another's secrets and even occasionally completed one another's sentences like an old, married couple. Together, they were easy and compatible. They conversed openly about all things. On only one topic, the idea of sharing a place, was Claire mute.

The heat of frustration flared inside Guy's chest and rose to warm his face. Almost four months had passed since he had first suggested moving in together. For him, the desire was overwhelming, and the uncertainty excruciating. He and Claire saw one another almost daily, yet nothing broke her silence on the subject. He had promised himself not to press her and to give her a wide berth, hoping the space would ease her worries. It hadn't, at least not enough, not yet.

Normally clear-headed and decisive, Claire's reasoning on this one crucial matter was tangled in a net of uncertainty woven by her past. Her paralysis left them drifting as a couple, rudderless, a course Guy sensed she was in no rush to correct. What did it mean? They had talked at length about moving in together on that memorable October morning when he had nervously floated the idea. She had expressed only one reservation, more of a prerequisite, really: He would first have to meet her family. Guy would have gone to see them that day if Claire had been ready. She wasn't and hadn't been since.

In all other ways, Guy felt confident about the future.

Through his thriving graphics arts business, investments and frugal lifestyle, he had already built a substantial capital reserve. His fine art career was taking off. On the near horizon were the Port Clyde solo exhibit and a second Mayenne Bay Art Show. He derived a sense of fulfillment from these achievements, but they counted as next to nothing if he couldn't have Claire at his side. She had come to give all he did meaning. It was that simple.

Guy was not unmindful of the distractions—the shed fire, the holidays, job demands, and now tax season—that gave Claire excuses to ignore the proverbial elephant in the room. By his reckoning, that elephant was going to sit undisturbed until at least Tax Day, when Claire's work pressure would lift. The topic of living together was, until then, taboo, unless Claire raised it. Yet, it hung in the air around him, bumping his head like a half-deflated helium balloon after a party.

Guy entered his loft, flicked on the lights and tossed his keys onto his desk. Feeling lost and powerless to change it, he wandered the place, half-consciously straightening piles and picking up clutter. Then, he stopped, stared at the dirty clothes in his hands and laughed out loud. This was Claire's influence, cleaning to channel feelings and clear confusion. A wave of sadness followed the laughter. He would give anything to break this impasse.

He plopped onto the tired loveseat and dropped his head into his palms. He needed a way forward, a fresh perspective, a different tack. Then, it hit him, and his head came up. Daniel, Claire's cousin and best friend. He would know what to do. Guy grabbed his phone.

Bayside Squawker, January 17

Fellow Business Owners,

If the town council elects to move forward with "A Better Idea", the specifics should be approved by the general membership of the Chamber of Commerce. We are the ones creating employment and contributing most heavily to the town treasure chest.

Gloria Townsend, Owner, Town's End B&B

12

On Hold

Daniel Munro was, fortuitously, coming north on the third weekend in January for some cross-country skiing with friends. At midday on Saturday, while Claire plowed through microfiche at the library, he arrived at Guy's loft with a steamy, mushroom-topped pizza and a six-pack of ginger beer. While Daniel removed his coat and restored his mop of red hair from the tight fit of a ski hat, Guy cleared space on the tiny kitchenette counter for the box and gestured to the place settings on the small café table.

Daniel pulled out two slices, plopped them on a plate and popped open a can of beer before swinging a leg over to straddle a stool.

Guy joined him opposite and wasted no time. Looking hard into Daniel's eyes—they were hazel, like Claire's— and ignoring the sizzling pizza, he got right to the reason for this tête-à-tête.

"Thanks for agreeing to see me. I need your help."

"So you said," Daniel mumbled through a mouthful. "What's going on? Is Claire all right?"

"That's the very question I want to ask you."

131

"I'm not aware of any issues, aside from her new boss."

"Did she ever tell you I asked her to live with me last October?"

Daniel nodded and continued chewing.

"Well, she didn't say 'no' but she didn't say 'yes', either. All she said was that I'd have to meet her family first. Since then, she's been silent on the subject. Not a word about a visit to her family. I'd bring it up myself but I don't want to scare her off."

Daniel took a long draw from his beer can, set it down and eyed Guy appraisingly.

"Does Claire know you invited me here?"

"No."

"I have no secrets from her." Daniel spoke the words like a solemn oath.

"Me, either. I promise to tell her we've spoken as soon as I can. Just give me some time, will you? I have no right to ask but, at the same time, I don't want to broach the topic without being better prepared."

Daniel laughed.

"Now you sound like Claire. She's always preparing. Got it down to a science."

"So, she's not delaying out of procrastination? I didn't think she had that in her."

"Not one cell in her body, not in its usual sense, anyway. She's dragging her feet, but with a purpose. Claire does nothing without a purpose."

"What could that possibly be, unless she's waiting to resolve doubts about me?"

"Guy, open your eyes. It's not about you. Well, it is, but not the way you're thinking. She's struggling to think how to prepare you for her family."

"Is that really necessary?"

"It is in her mind. Claire told me about your family. Polite, civilized, sensible."

"Or repressed, eccentric and dull, sometimes racist and drunk on holidays," returned Guy. "She met my Aunt Helen, after all, and knows of my dad's close-mindedness. I love my family, but in no way are they perfect."

Guy's knee started bouncing with nerves under the table.

Daniel stared at him for a long minute before speaking again.

"Maybe that's the tack you should take. Claire sees your family through rose-colored glasses right now…except for the cooking and instant coffee. She told me about those." He laughed. "Look, Claire's parents, my Aunt Hannah and Uncle Jerry, are decent at heart but they're loud, crude and uncontrolled. No boundaries. Conflict reigns and always has at their house. It's the same even after the divorce. Mind you, I can be this blunt because I'm a relation."

"Why would Claire think I can't handle that?" Guy's tone was desperate now.

"Again," repeated Daniel, a bit impatiently, "it's not about you. Claire is like oil to their water. Trying to stay close got her all screwed up. She's finally achieved a sort of balance for herself, but that's much more difficult for an outsider. She cares for you and doesn't want to subject you to that nuthouse. At the same time, not to do so would feel dishonest. How can she open her life to you and protect you at the same time?" Daniel leaned in for the punchline. "And will you walk out in the end, regardless? Her history with men hasn't been great. The family hasn't helped."

Guy's jaw dropped at Daniel's insightful and succinct summation of Claire's quandary, and his chest tightened. He stared out the window across the room, his own face twisting as he turned her emotional contortions round and round in his head. All the time he had spent with her had not taught him this. Claire wasn't underestimating him. She was fighting for him, fighting a moral dilemma because she cared.

"I wonder if she'll ever stop surprising me," Guy said finally and took his first bite of pizza.

Daniel chuckled, swigged more beer, then grabbed a third slice.

"Don't count on it. But understand that she likes you and has already entrusted you with more than anyone but me. Her fear that you might be repulsed by her family and abandon her is monumental. It has some basis in reality and, whatever you do, it may never disappear completely."

Guy's head spun wildly, and he ran his hands through his blond hair, making it stick up. Daniel frowned, concern on his face.

"I've crossed a line here. If the subject comes up, I'm going to confess this conversation to Claire without hesitation. Even if it doesn't, I'll only wait so long. The only reason I'm not calling her right now is because I want the two of you to have a chance."

Guy nodded his appreciation.

Daniel clammed up about Claire after that in apparent self-condemnation that he had overshared. For Guy's purposes, he had shared just enough. The remainder of the visit involved chat about Captain Crabbish and the prospect of good snow at the resort. When the pizza box was empty, they rose and shook hands. Daniel grabbed the remaining cans of beer and headed out to his car to join his friends waiting at the Main Street Coffee Bar.

Guy sat for a full thirty minutes trying to work out what to do. Broaching the topic directly was out of the question. Claire was making that clear. He had to act in a way that reassured her, but how? He grabbed his phone and thumbed through his calendar. He couldn't rely on words—a circumstance that, before Claire, would have filled him with relief—but he could use time to advantage. He would carve out hours from his schedule, be more present in her life, show her he could be trusted. He would work through the night if that's what it took.

Later that day, while Claire listened, Guy talked of walks in the falling snow, snowshoeing trails and crossing the lake to visit ice fishing huts. Hot chocolate by the fire. Stargazing. The toboggan chute and snowtubing at the Camden Snow Bowl.

"Tomorrow," he invited, "let's do some snowshoeing, then visit a maple syrup shack."

Not one word escaped Guy's lips about living together. Not every rough tide is best met head on.

Cheeks rosy from several hours outdoors, Claire listened intently to the maple syrup producer while Guy milled around the shop trying to keep a straight face. The owner was wearing a colorful, Alpaca wool chullo hat whose flaps fluttered and strings flung every which way each time he turned his head. The only way Guy could listen seriously was to avoid looking at him.

"The weather can be frustrating because we rely on the freeze-thaw cycle. When temperatures rise above freezing, positive pressure in the tree causes the sap to flow out through the tap hole. Below freezing, suction develops, drawing water into the tree through the roots and replenishing the sap. Not every year is a winner, but this year looks very promising. I hope you'll come back for Maple Syrup Sunday at the end of March."

"Thank you. That was fascinating," Claire told the man.

She selected one each of the Grade A syrups, Amber, Medium Amber and Dark Amber, and set them on the counter. To Guy's questioning face, she said, "To see if I can taste the difference."

He answered with an incredulous roll of the eyes.

Claire handed her credit card to a young, round-faced woman behind the counter whose shirt strained to cover her large chest and pregnant belly and, at the same time, reach the waistband of her yoga pants. A ponytail of dark blonde hair, tied roughly with a black scrunchie, swung to and fro with her movements. Claire, who had always preferred a natural look, admired the clerk's make-up-free face and unadorned appearance. It fitted her expectant state, even enhanced it. She thanked the clerk, grabbed her bag of syrup and exited with Guy.

Within seconds of pulling onto Route 1, Claire sat up straight and slapped her hand over her forehead.

"What is it?" asked Guy. "Are you okay?"

"Guy, we have to go back. Please turn around."

She pulled out her phone and began flipping through screens at a fast pace.

Guy did as he was bid, though his face bore nothing but confusion. He had barely brought the car to a stop when Claire jumped out and ran into the syrup shop. There, she found the producer gone and the clerk alone stocking shelves.

"Hi, again," said Claire.

The woman jumped.

"Um, I saw your nametag. Is 'D' short for Denise?"

The woman shrank back.

"Are you Denise Baptiste, Celeste's sister?" Without waiting for an answer, Claire clapped her hands together. "Oh! Thank goodness we found you. Celeste will be so relieved."

"I didn't say my name is Denise."

"But it is, isn't it?"

Claire herself could barely believe the understated woman before her was the long-lost, exotic Denise in the photo on her phone. Guy, who had just re-entered the shop, stared.

"If it is, why would I tell you?"

Claire's tone shifted from excited to soothing.

"Because Celeste is so worried."

"She won't be if she sees me. Mom, either."

Claire observed her for a moment.

"Are you worried about the pregnancy?"

Denise gave a single, almost imperceptible nod, and pressed her lips together. Tears emerged from the corners of her eyes.

"Who are you, anyway?" demanded Denise, wiping them away.

"I'm Claire Munro, and this is Guy Gardiner. We live in Mayenne Bay and know Celeste from the Fish House."

"Like I said, I don't want to see her. I can't go home like this."

Denise broke into sobs. Claire approached her very slowly, then slid her arms around Denise's enlarged body and held her against one shoulder until Denise stopped shaking.

"Denise," Claire whispered and held on, "if you don't want to go home permanently, we understand that and will drive you right back here ourselves. But there are people out looking for you, possibly putting themselves at risk but certainly using valuable time and energy at the expense of other things. And Celeste is so overwrought with worry, she flew all the way to Florida to look for you."

"To Uncle Kenny's?" Denise gasped as she separated from Claire's embrace.

"Yes. Won't you at least consent to show her you're alright? I think that's all she needs. Why don't you see for yourself?"

Denise pulled away, sniffed and drew her sleeve across her eyes.

"Okay." The word shook with emotion.

"When do you get off work?"

"Fifteen minutes."

Claire threw a glance at the clock.

"Guy and I would like to drive you back, if that's alright. We'll wait."

Denise nodded her agreement and blew her nose.

"Celeste will be working when we get back to Mayenne Bay," Guy said, finally recovered from the surprise. "We'll take you directly to the Fish House."

About an hour later, Claire and Guy delivered Denise into Celeste's arms at the restaurant, then sat and watched the reunion from their favorite booth by the window. The sisters clung to one another, then broke apart, several times. Celeste's eyes sought permission, then she reached out to touch her sister's belly. They both laughed and hugged again.

Suddenly, the restaurant door burst open, and Jerome Allen, the new town manager, rushed in with Ben Tripp in his wake.

"Denise!" Jerome called. "God, I've been so worried." He stopped and stared at her mid-section. "Mine?"

Denise nodded.

Jerome ever-so-gently surrounded her with his arms and held her close.

"Why didn't you tell me?"

Celeste stood aside, mouth agape. The handsome newcomer ogled by every woman in town was already taken by her own sister. Judging from the size of her belly, Denise must have known Jerome well before the mayor had introduced him to the town. For once, Celeste, Gossip Queen of Mayenne Bay, had been out-scooped.

Ben headed for Guy and Claire.

"Thanks for the text," he told Claire.

"How did Jerome find out?" Claire asked. "Denise arrived only five minutes ago."

"I texted him. Anyway, Claire, you're sitting in the town newsroom. By now, all of Mayenne Bay knows." He looked from Claire to Guy. "How did you find her?"

Guy tilted his head toward Claire and waited, anxious as Ben to hear her answer. Everything had happened so fast, he hadn't had time to put the pieces together. Ben slid onto the bench next to Guy while Claire explained the stop at the maple syrup store that morning. She opened her phone to the photo of Denise that Ben had shared, complete with crazy-colored hair, tattoos, piercings and wild clothes, and handed it to Guy.

"What struck me first was her odd name tag. 'D'—just an initial. Then, there was her stature, so much like Celeste's, discounting the pregnant belly, of course, and her facial resemblance still evident despite the added plumpness. The tattoos were covered up, but she has remnants of several bright hair colors in the ends of her ponytail and a multitude of piercings, minus the jewelry."

"Well done," said Guy, giving her hand a squeeze.

"You'll have the chief thinking of asking you to join the force," teased Ben.

"All in a day's work," she joked.

"Denise is found, but am I right that Valentina's whereabouts are still a mystery?" Guy asked.

"Yes. I received a bit of news that'll give you some relief, at least. Forensics determined the skull Claire found is very old. They're working to be more precise about age, but it can't be Valentina or any other recent victim. I'm going through cold cases, but I don't expect much. I've informed the Diazes."

They all sat quietly for a few moments adjusting to this information.

"I'm sticking to the theory that the shed was once an atelier," Guy said.

"It might have been," agreed Claire, "but there may be more to the history. Did you know flotsam used to wash up on the shore of La Palourde Island just off The Point? I read about it in the old *Squawker* issues. In 1903, an entire steamship from Boston went down out there, burned at sea." She shuddered. "Everyone was lost except a few crew members and passengers. They were a well-to-do crowd on their way to new homes in Canada, so there had to be valuables on board. Much of the ship's surviving contents supposedly landed at La Palourde. I had the figurines and older coins in mind. Those aren't artist paraphernalia."

"The flotsam is common knowledge," Ben said. "Word is that a lot has reached the shores of La Palourde and The Point just below Sandra's place over the years. With the sandbar that leads to the island, her forbears had ready access and are thought to have captured many hidden treasures. Rumor has it these were hidden somewhere in the Edgecomb house."

"Several old Captain Crabbish letters insinuated that," said Claire.

"The Captain's letters aren't reliable sources. The steamship incident is pretty well known, though. Anyone could have grabbed that flotsam."

"And hidden it in the cellar wall of a shed," Claire persisted. "Anyone who discovers flotsam is allowed to claim it unless ownership is otherwise proven. If no one made a claim…" She gave Ben a meaningful look. "I asked the historical society for the steamship's passenger and cargo manifests. They're looking into it."

"All this you got from microfiche?" Guy asked.

"Plus, a visit to the historical society."

"Claire, you're either working or with me or eating and sleeping ninety percent of the time. When do you find the time to do all this stuff?" asked Guy.

"Somewhere in the remaining ten per cent," she said, cheeks flushed, and looked away.

He regarded her closely. He was familiar with this emotional tell of hers. Claire wore her feelings right on her face. If she wanted to hide something, she was forced to avert her eyes and change the subject.

"Have either of you been out on La Palourde?" she asked.

"Lots of times," Ben answered. "I doubt you can find a local who hasn't been there."

"La Palourde," Claire repeated. "The Clam. The island is supposedly shaped like one. I checked the map and think it's a stretch. The sand bar access is a challenge, isn't it, getting over and back before the twelve-foot tide rolls back in?"

"People have gotten stuck out there, but it's hard to do if you're paying attention. You can start out as much as two hours before low tide and return up to two hours after its lowest stage," Ben said.

"Let's plan a trip as soon as the weather warms," suggested Guy.

"You'll have to keep that on hold until at least April," said Ben. "It's frigid out there."

Guy was unfazed. He was inured to putting things on hold.

Bayside Squawker, January 24

Readers,

Gloria Townsend wants the rich and privileged to drive the factory site rebuild. We don't need to feed more to the already fat and happy. Regular citizens should be part of the decision and building process and share in the benefits. Make yourselves known. Sign the petition in support of a citizens committee for the factory project. And don't forget to show up on February 20, 6 p.m.

Captain Crabbish

13

Burials

Having seen Annabelle with Ellie Brown and Kitty Greenwood at the Christmas party, Claire knew they were friends and suspected, from the intimate way they conferred that evening, the three had been close. In the weeks leading up to Ellie's funeral, Claire made several attempts to visit Annabelle to condole with her. She was met each time by a dark house and no answer. Finally, it occurred to her that Annabelle might be with Jay, and that is exactly where she found her, in his little bungalow on Castle Street. Annabelle, not Jay, answered the door to accept Claire's homemade New England clam chowder and cheddar cheese biscuits. She didn't invite Claire in, and they didn't talk much. Gifts of food had an eloquence of their own.

Late January underwent a brief warmup, a typical mid-winter teaser, just in time for the funeral on the last Saturday of the month. Claire and Guy, along with much of the town, attended the service at the local Catholic church for this beloved English teacher. The upbeat weather, incongruous with the event, seemed to lift the crowd a bit, though it did nothing for Jay. Annabelle and Kitty flanked the crestfallen man and guided him mechanically through the proceedings.

No one had ever seen Jay so pliant or lost for words. The public outpouring of admiration for a partner he had so blatantly neglected overwhelmed him, and his grief, Claire suspected, now commingled with a good deal of shame. Jay, it seemed, now felt the pain of belated understanding, though it was far too little and far too late. Head drooping, eyes downcast, he seemed to manage an upright stance in the receiving line only by means of support from Annabelle and Kitty.

Predictably, the weather aberration didn't hold. Winter reasserted itself with snow and ice like Claire had never before experienced, forcing her to upgrade her winter boots and gloves to arctic thermal and to invest in ice cleats. Walking became a hazardous sport, even the short distance from her car to the door.

On the Monday morning following the funeral, in the office parking lot, she stepped from her car, misjudged the ice beneath the snow cover and completely lost her footing. Her backside took the brunt. She grabbed her car door handle to try to heave herself to her feet but hung there, feet scrambling to gain traction, until forced to give in and collapse again onto her bottom. In spite of the pain, she broke into hysterical laughter. Fortunately, the only other early bird to the office that day was Ricky who, though he laughed until he almost cried, rushed to lift and steady the mortified Claire with a promise to tell no one.

While she worked that morning, Claire repeatedly stood to shake out her smarting limbs and shifted uncomfortably on her bruised rear end. She popped pain relievers to calm the throbs and aches interfering with her concentration. By late morning, when Ben Tripp called to request her presence at the police station over the lunch hour, she was ready to throw in the towel at work. She rose, her sore body stiff and unyielding, packed her belongings and headed with rigid steps back to her vehicle, determined not to land on her duff a second time. Ricky caught sight of her awkward gait. He grabbed her computer bag, hooked his elbow around hers and supported a grateful Claire to her car door. She would drop by the station, then head home to doctor her pains.

It was just past noon when Ben ushered a hobbling Claire into the police station conference room, where Louis Rainwater was already seated. She lowered her throbbing body carefully onto the nearest chair. On the table before them sat an opened laptop bearing two images side by side: the old skull found in the burned shed and a woman's face.

"Thanks, both of you, for coming on the fly over your lunch hours," Ben said. He motioned to the images on the screen. "I just received these images from a friend at the police academy who's studying forensic art and science and, specifically, digital facial reconstruction. She's working under a grant at U-Maine and agreed to give me a hand on the sly." He pointed to the woman's face on the screen. "This is the 3-D likeness my friend developed using the old skull. She styled the hair this way, as the evidence strongly indicates a female."

"How does this work?" asked Claire.

She winced as she shifted her chair closer.

Louis bent forward with interest.

"Facial reconstruction involves twenty-one markers for fatty tissue, muscle size, and skin thickness that help construct the size and shape of individual features. From skeletal remains, you can discern sex, age, and height and make an educated guess about ethnicity."

"This is fascinating, Ben, but why bother with a skull that's so old?"

"Curiosity first. Certainty, if I can get it. The DNA sample was inconclusive, so I turned to facial reconstruction for clues. I felt like we should at least try to find out who this person was, even if the chance is remote. The discovery site was not a grave, nor did we find other bones anywhere on the place. The skull was probably, as Guy originally guessed, used for artistic reference. But I can't let go of the fact that it came, no less, from a person."

He paused to allow the other two to digest this explanation, then resumed.

"Claire, I invited you today because you made the initial discovery of the skull and might want some closure." He turned to Louis. "Louis, I thought you would want to know, as it was found on your place, if the skull might have belonged to an indigenous person."

Louis looked at the young cop with a new appreciation while Ben explained to Claire.

"Anyone can legally possess human bones in Maine unless they're the bones of an indigenous person. Those must be returned for traditional burial."

Claire looked impressed.

"I can't take credit for all of this," Ben said, holding up his hands. "It was Quince Greene who tipped me off. She's fascinated with skulls, even sketches them. She made me see this one, despite its probable use, with more humanity. Quince is trying to take this facial image a step further using facial identification software, hoping she can find an old image or a current-day look-alike that may be a descendant. It's a long shot, I know, but she's pretty keen on trying."

"I'm guessing, based on the evidence at hand, you don't believe this is the skull of an indigenous person," Louis said.

"My friend doesn't think so, no," answered Ben. "She can't be 100% certain, of course, but this is her best assessment."

"Thank you, Ben."

"I have an ulterior motive, of course. I need help with the disposition of the skull. From the standpoint of the police investigation, we're finished with it. It could, of course, continue serving as reference material for art or science. Quince would take it in a heartbeat and she would treat it with reverence. But, Louis, the skull was found on your land. To the extent ownership of human bones is possible by law, it belongs to you. What is your preference?"

"I'll bury it on the property."

Ben rose to retrieve a plain brown box in which the skull was stored and handed it to Louis.

"I thought you'd say that."

Louis accepted the box solemnly, bade the other two good-bye and returned to work. Claire rose slowly using the chair's arms to brace herself and headed for home where she had an appointment with a hot bath and a heating pad. She dialed into work to inform the office.

"Erin, I won't be in for the rest of the day. I hope to be back in the morning." She cut off Erin's testy reply before it gained traction. "Please put me through to Renée. I fell on the ice in the office parking this morning and want to report an onsite injury."

It was standard procedure to report any injury on the job, but Claire relished the moment. Erin's emerging objection to her unplanned departure was bested by the claim. Erin huffed audibly into the phone and transferred the call to a far more sympathetic Renée Pincer. Claire and Renée were close friends, allied in their dislike of their new boss, though even were this not so, Claire knew she would be in good hands. Renée promised to file the claim and arrange a doctor's appointment the following day.

At home, Claire sprinkled the bath water generously with lavender Epsom salts, then slowly lowered herself down against the bath pillow. She soaked for a long time, freshening the hot water again and again by turning the spout with her foot—far less painful than sitting up—until she was limber enough to pull herself out. She gently performed a few yoga stretches, poured some wine and set herself up on the couch with a book, a heating pad and her phone. Just in case, she kept her tablet within arm's reach, too.

After a quick text to Guy telling him where she was and what had happened, she checked the clock on the kitchen wall and, ignoring her book, sat back for a while and watched the minutes tick by. With all that had happened this morning, she had lost track that, today, Guy had met Anna at their parents' house to discuss Asad. Claire imagined they were all sitting around the table right now hashing things out over heavily piled lunch plates. She was wrong.

The sound of stomping feet could be heard on the stoop. Claire sat up a bit straighter. The kitchen door opened.

"Claire?"

"In here," she called.

Guy removed his coat and boots and rushed over to her. "Are you okay?"

"I will be, yes. Just a little stiff and sore right now." She studied him closely. "And you? Are you okay? You're back far earlier than I expected." She had asked the question, though she could already read the answer.

He sank into the nearby armchair, shut his eyes and rubbed his temples.

"I had to get out of there before I said or did something I would regret. Anna was impressive, remarkably strong and clear. Joy was right by her side. Mom is fine with Asad but struggling with the family tension and living in the same house with Dad, who is, for all intents and purposes, a complete stranger to us all right now. He shut the conversation down before it even got started. How can we all have missed this side of him? They say all people are a mixture of good and evil. Well, the good man my father can be was entirely overshadowed by ignorance and obstinacy today." He sighed heavily. "I'll be helping Anna move out this weekend. She's found a place near the university campus. Joy will very likely follow."

It was a long speech for a man who normally struggled for words. Claire watched sadly as Guy trudged to the kitchen to put the kettle on for lemon balm tea, a fitting selection as he needed all the balm he could get just now in the face of such bitter disillusionment. His parents had lived their whole lives in Maine among people who looked just like them while cultivating convictions about those who didn't. Today, Anna had tested their worldview. Mrs. Gardiner had taken the high road, but her husband had fallen short and failed his daughter.

Claire lamented the tenacious foothold old attitudes had on this otherwise kind man and prayed he would find reason before his relationship with his daughters was permanently damaged. Sad for Anna and, at the same time, proud of her, Claire reached for her phone and texted some words of encouragement. Then, she sank back onto the couch and prepared to let Guy unload his troubles in the first counseling session she had given in quite some time.

Bayside Squawker, February 7

Dear Mayenne Bay,

Thank you, Neighbors, for keeping the conversation about the "A Better Idea" proposal alive and meaningful. Please continue to send constructive comments and ideas to my office email or drop off your letter in person. I personally hope this project can become a reality for this town. It's only a first step to alleviate our housing and revenue pressures, but it's an important one.

Mayor Sandra Edgecomb

Dear Business Leaders,

The town is entertaining the creation of a citizen committee—persons with no background in property, business or building—for the populist "A Better Idea" scheme. The factory project is too significant to the town to be in the hands of the uninformed and inexperienced. I will host an informal get-together at the Town's End B&B on Sunday, February 16, 2 p.m. for business and property owners to discuss this potential development.

Gloria Townsend
Owner, Townsend B&B

14

Nor'easter

On Valentine's Day, the first Nor'easter of the season blew through town. Snug at home, Claire pushed the *Bayside Squawker* carelessly aside and sat with her morning coffee, mesmerized by the icy flakes whipping past the windows. She opened her tablet meaning to set to work, but her eyes flicked frequently to the scene outside. She had seen the aftermath of Nor'easters on the news and feared the rapid snow build up would prevent her from opening the door. The idea of being caged in by immovable drifts induced a mild claustrophobia that propelled her outside to clear her dooryards. She repeated the precaution about every hour or so. Each time, she watched impotently from the window as the storm replenished the piled snow almost before she removed her boots.

A childhood on the East Coast's hurricane alley had schooled Claire how to prepare for severe weather. All her devices were charged. There was food in the cupboard, including an ample stash of her three staples: coffee, wine and chocolate. She had stocked oil lamps, candles, bottled water and a kerosene heater. But none of these preparations, including her backup power supply, could ensure a remote connection to the office all day. She disciplined herself to accept this reality by repeating Daniel's strictures on the futility of overplanning in an unpredictable world.

While power remained, Claire forced her attention from the blasting snow to the computer screen and worked with rapid-fire keyboarding while the utilities held out. Everyone else at Mid Coast Accountancy was running the same race, wanting maximum speed and efficiency from an overburdened IT system on a day when connections were under threat. Tax Day waited for no one. Claire envisioned Ricky on a day like today, scrambling to keep the systems running, even as he ached over his daughter's disappearance. As far as Claire knew, Valentina was still missing and now she was missing in a Nor'easter. The outlook, like the weather, was bleak.

In her confinement, Claire busied herself with office work but consoled herself with cooking. Today, her first-ever batch of homemade baked beans was slow-cooking in the gas oven. In anticipation of the much-predicted storm, she had stopped at Grace Grocery for ingredients the night before. After soaking the beans overnight, she had boiled them this morning, then dumped them in the cast iron Dutch oven with dry mustard, black pepper, onions, salt pork and maple syrup instead of molasses. The sweet fragrance and warmth filled her kitchen. The method fell short of Maine's famous bean hole beans, but the recipe itself was authentic, as far as she knew. She planned to verify this with Annabelle at the first opportunity. Annabelle had all the old Maine recipes, like her ginger cookies, and wouldn't hesitate to give Claire an honest thumbs-up or thumbs-down as to flavor. She was frank like that.

Mid-morning, Claire's phone rang. It was Guy.

"Power's still on here. You?"

"Yeah."

"Looks like tomorrow's outing to the Toboggan Championship at the Camden Snow Bowl is a 'no-go'. With this storm continuing through the night, even the main roads won't be passable. I'll keep an eye out for the snow date. But we have the ice carving in Belfast yet to see and the ice carousel—I read it's 1,200 feet wide this year, possibly a world record—up on Long Lake in Sinclair. You haven't been up in Aroostook County yet."

"No, I haven't."

Claire loved winter outings with Guy, but his sudden and ambitious itinerary made her head spin. While he rattled on, she pulled up her calendar. February was already half over. How they would squeeze all his plans into one season with all their other obligations and before the weather gave way, she didn't know. When Guy had first volunteered to introduce her to Maine in winter, she hadn't expected a full-court press. Now, he was so intent upon it, he had shut out all else. It was an absorption untypical for Guy, almost obsessive, and carried out with uncharacteristic intensity, much more like something Claire would initiate. What did he mean by it?

She set aside her misgivings for the duration of the phone call. She would wait to voice her apprehension in person when next she could read Guy's eloquent blue eyes and watch for revealing change of color on his fair face. She kept the chat light for now—snow, baked beans, painting, work. When they disconnected, she leaned back in her chair uneasily. Something lurked beneath Guy's nervous enthusiasm, if she could only put her finger on it.

Seconds after she hung up with Guy, Claire's phone rang again. With a groan, she put an end to the Addam's family ringtone and set the device on speaker. Not for the first time, she marveled at the uncanniness of her mother's timing. Hannah Munro telephoned at the exact moment when Claire, sequestered by the storm and confused by the call from Guy, was feeling discomposed and needed to think.

"Hi, Mom."

"Hi, Honey. I saw the weather report. Are you really having a blizzard on Valentine's Day?"

Hannah often connected unrelated dots in ways that confounded Claire. In this case, Claire inferred the link was meant to condemn nature's impudence for asserting itself on a holiday.

"Pretty much. Complete whiteout right now. But I'm toasty and comfortable here. Listen, I can't talk long. I'm in the middle of baking."

It was a bit of a stretch to claim slow-cooked beans demanded her immediate attention, but it served the purpose. Hannah went right for the soft tissue.

"When are we going to see you?"

"We", of course, meant Hannah. Claire was sure no one else was pining for a visit. Funny how holidays seemed to draw her mother out. Today's, at least, was already half over.

"I know it's been a while. I needed time to settle into my new place and job, plus all the year-end financials and now the tax work. There's no way I can think of coming until after tax season."

Claire closed her eyes and let her mother rant while Claire came to grips with herself. Guy and she had discussed a Munro family visit back in October. It was already mid-February, and she had met the Gardiners twice. She wrestled for the umpteenth time with her fear of giving Guy the lowdown on her family. It seemed simple enough on its face, and she had dropped enough hints that all was not as it could be. But to really know the Munros...to *really* know them... would require facetime. Anything less would fall short of the full story, as Daniel could attest.

She fretted, too, about how much longer she could put her mother and Guy off or endure her self-imposed program of avoidance. She recalled the "fish-or-cut-bait" resolve she had mustered back when she had been vacillating about dating Guy. She reached deep inside now and found something like it, then sucked in a gulp of air and plunged, one arm gripping her stomach crosswise to counter the punch.

"How about the weekend after Tax Day?"

"And you'll bring Guy with you?" came her mother's immediate reply, not missing a beat.

"Yes. And Daniel wants to come, too." Daniel, Claire's pillar. "I'll make sure they're available that weekend and let you know for sure."

Her mother squealed so loudly that Claire had to pull the phone away from her ear, then abruptly ended the call. Date set. Claire and Guy locked in. There was no value in squandering time or words after that. For once, Claire and her mother agreed on something. After they hung up, Claire released a long breath of pent-up steam, quivered and coached herself through the aftermath.

"Maybe you should thank her instead of being annoyed," she said aloud as she rose to pace the room. "At least now, the moment of reckoning is, well, not quite done, but in motion."

She looked at the clock. Eleven forty-five. She reached for a bottle of red Bordeaux and the corkscrew. As she opened it, Claire recalled once laughing at Guy when he told her that lunch was always at noon, regardless of his appetite. At noon, you ate, case closed. And here she was, watching the clock to justify a midday glass of wine.

"Breathe fast," she told the bottle. "You have fifteen minutes."

She pulled on her hat, jacket and boots to clear the dooryards and her whirling emotions yet again.

By early afternoon, the storm had slackened from blinding whiteout to steady snowfall, making it possible to see a reasonable distance beyond the window panes. In that time, Claire had calmed as well, though just a degree or two. She alternately sipped and swirled her wine in a slow, hypnotic rhythm that had more to do with easing tension than the beverage itself. Breathing restored to normal, she dialed Daniel, knowing he would likely be at home, as Portland had been as much under winter's siege as the Mid Coast.

"Hi, Claire. Keeping warm?"

"Yeah, nice and comfy here. You?"

"Power's been out for two hours. I'm starting to feel the cold seep through the walls. What's going on?"

"I did it."

"You did what?"

"This morning, I agreed to visit my mother with Guy. The weekend after Tax Day. Can you make it?"

"I don't see why not. How are you feeling about this…wait, this morning? Let me guess. You've already had a glass of wine."

She laughed.

"A wonderful Bordeaux. I'm about to pour my second glass."

"I'm going for hot chocolate until the heat comes on. For what it's worth, Claire, I think you're doing the right thing. What did Guy say?"

"I haven't told him yet."

"What? Then why are you on the phone with me? Stop torturing the poor man and tell him. He's been on tenterhooks for months."

"What? How do you know that?"

"I'm going to hang up so you can make that call."

"Daniel, wait…"

But Daniel had disconnected.

Claire stared out the window. Tenterhooks…for months? Is that really how it was? And how would Daniel know that? She would find out the "how" later. Today, the mere fact of it was more pressing. She drained the last drops of wine from her glass and straightened her spine for the second time. Daniel was right. The call to Guy was the call that counted. She could always retreat from her mother at this safe distance. Daniel was flexible. Guy was another story. The visit to her family carried weight in their relationship and their future. For the second time that day, Claire heard herself say aloud, "Fish or cut bait," and picked up the phone.

"Hi, again. Can you reserve the weekend after Tax Day?"

"What?"

"Save the date."

"I think so. For what?"

She detected a touch of hesitation in his voice.

"For a trip to New Jersey to meet my family. Daniel is coming, too," she added quickly.

An uncomfortable silence followed while Claire awaited his answer.

"I didn't think you'd ever do it."

His voice was heavy, and his angst no longer masked. It was so apparent, Claire flinched, and tears immediately filled her eyes.

"I'm really sorry it took me so long. Will you come?" she asked again in a husky voice.

"Of course, I'll come."

Guy had accepted her invitation without complaining about the wait, without casting blame on her for the long delay. More copious tears arising from his pain and her own shame now leaked from Claire's eyes. Despite her skills of observation and her emotional sensitivity, she had managed to overlook the person closest to her, the one who meant the most apart from Daniel. She had been blind to the toll her procrastination had been taking on Guy. The revelation explained so much, for starters, why he had been in hyperdrive urging an exhausting winter schedule at her side. He had been striving to demonstrate his commitment while she hadn't found strength enough to endure something as reasonable as a visit to her family. There was no telling what the outcome of the visit would be, but she owed Guy, and Guy was worthy of, this chance.

"I'm really sorry," Claire repeated and meant it.

After they hung up, she remained on the couch for a few minutes engulfed in a cloud mixed of guilt, relief and burgeoning dread. She felt momentarily adrift, unable to concentrate on anything. Now that the impasse was overcome, would the whirlwind of winter entertainments downshift into a slower gear? Would Guy forgive her? Would their relationship survive the Munros? One thing she knew for sure: she no longer wanted that second glass of wine. With all the turmoil roiling inside her, she had to move. She went to the closet in search of a dust rag and attacked the living room furniture as though it hadn't been cleaned in ages. After an hour's frenzy, she stopped at the window to stare out at the winter wonderland, then texted confirmation to her mother and Daniel.

One demon vanquished.

Bayside Squawker, February 14

Neighbors,

Calico lost near Castle and Crest. Expecting. If found, contact the Fish House.

Kitty Greenwood

Dear Bayside Squawker,

We seen no letters from the Captain these last weeks. Word is you shut him down for tearing into the mayor and town council. The Captain has always spoke his mind, which we like. Folks count on him and have done for years. Bring him back.

Unhappy Reader

15

Icy

At the end of Bay Street, in the beautiful Town's End B&B, Gloria Townsend stuffed the latest issue of the *Bayside Squawker* into the waste bin, disgusted. The preoccupations of the townspeople with cats and the rude and elusive Captain Crabbish were inconceivable to her when there was so much more at stake. To say she was angered beyond words was to understate the fiery resentment burning in her belly.

Several weeks ago, she had published a letter to the editor offering to host business and property owners at the B&B for a meeting to formulate a plan to modify the "A Better Idea" proposal and to combat the involvement of ordinary citizens in the design process. Today, she expected those invitees to collect in her dining room to forge a strategic alliance and, after an inevitable exchange of grievances, lay out a scheme of activism. She would invite her peers to step away from the fray, to look ahead with clarity and to unify with purpose for the town's betterment. This forum would establish her as a town visionary and business leader.

She glanced at the clock. The gathering was scheduled to commence at two o'clock, less than an hour from now. She had scheduled it thus, anticipating her Valentine's Day weekend B&B guests would be on their way home by that time. It had been a useless precaution; all her holiday guests had canceled. The storm had seen to that.

Circling the dining room, she scanned her preparations and smiled her satisfaction. As a demonstration of bon ton, she had laid out a huge cheese and charcuterie board, a fruit platter, quality wine from Mainsail Wine and Cheese and French bread baked by her own hands. She stepped to the sideboard to pop open two bottles of red to breathe, then added a few more chairs to the room, just in case. All was in hand. All she needed now were her co-conspirators.

When two o'clock rolled around, Gloria poured herself some wine and stationed herself at the front window, though she doubted her guests would arrive exactly on time. Business people had full plates, even on a Sunday, and might straggle in according to their own timetables.

At a quarter past two, she continued her vigil and walked from one front window to the next, peering out onto the wintry but still empty driveway. Perhaps the storm's aftermath was delaying people or, like her guests, preventing their coming altogether.

At two-thirty, she stepped onto the front porch, swept away some windblown snow from the entryway and paced vigorously in the chilly air.

Finally, at two forty-five, Gloria stormed inside and slammed the door, seething. She briskly collected up all the food, chipping an antique serving dish in the process, and stuffed it into her refrigerator, then restored the dining room to rights. She hastened to clear all the evidence of the intended meeting so that no one could witness her utter and complete failure to draw allies to her side. Her anger and resentment intensified with every moment that passed.

Not a single person had answered her call to arms. The monied people of Mayenne Bay, the town's de facto elite who had tripped over one another to support a con man last summer, hadn't deigned even to hear her out. She fumed at their poor judgment, their lack of confidence in her and their complete lack of foresight. It didn't occur to Gloria that her own vision might be clouded, blind as it had been for some time to the effect of her increasing antagonism on her fellow townspeople.

She refilled her wine glass to the brim and dropped onto a hard chair in the empty dining room, where she sat for some time, stewing in her own juice.

Bayside Squawker, March 6

Dear Captain Crabbish,

Can't remember many *Squawker* issues without your letters. We haven't seen one for over a month. Most times, your letter is the reason I buy the paper. Don't let us down.

A Concerned Fan

Readers,

Gloria Townsend should be voted off the mainland.

Captain Crabbish

16

March

February slid into March. Anybody still breathing was ready for nature to signal a change and hint at an underlying onset of green, but winter wasn't willing to relinquish its chokehold without a fuss. The temperature crept up above freezing enough to bait the gullible, then quickly dropped again. Snowfall threatened perpetually overhead and fell often, alternating between icy dustings to heavy, sodden stuff that challenged even the strongest of backs. Snow plow markers remained fixed in place, a constant reminder that a fierce Nor'easter could again blow through at any time. Claire kept her snow shovel in the dooryard, always prepared. And though some days were warm enough for rain, she braced every morning for the cold and damp, the kind that didn't leave her fingers.

The interplay between the seasons seemed to test Mainers' temperaments even more than the very depth of winter. "March is the coldest month." "The worst." "It lasts forever." And, as if the weather's indecision wasn't enough, March marked the early stages of mud season, the resurgence of deer ticks and the renewed prospect of flooding as the spring melt got underway. It was no wonder so many took temporary refuge in March Madness and St. Patrick's Day celebrations. In the little spare time tax season allowed, Claire distracted herself with early garden plans, books, baking and, of course, the Captain. She was nearing his letters from the more recent decades.

No one lost sight of the actual calendar date despite the weather's caprice. By mid-March, grumbling over the fluctuating damp and cold was displaced by restive impatience for spring to finally work its magic on the waterways. In the office coffee room, at the Fish House, everywhere she went, Claire found people keyed up, chafing for the icy lakes and rivers and the bay to dissolve again into reflective, blue water. Already, ice fishing shelters were being dragged to shore off Loonwater Lake (alternately called Nebilinto Pond, Wabanaki for "water" and "sing") in anticipation of the great melt. But as the ice was still thick and strong—four inches were needed for persons on foot, seven for an ATV to haul a shack—Claire guessed the lake's transformation would grate nerves for many weeks to come.

Claire and Guy listened from their favorite booth at the Fish House as bets were cast on the date the Loonwater-Nebilinto's ice would melt through. Fifty percent of the proceeds, Patty's sign promised, would go to the Mayenne Bay Fire Department toward its new truck.

First thing that morning, before a crowd of spectators, Chief Manning had ceremoniously placed a rock formation, shaped much like a hiking trail cairn, on the frozen lake surface. The genius who guessed the date closest to the day the lake gave way under this stone pile, the day the ice would officially be "out", would be the contest winner. And once the ice was "out", spring would be "in", no matter what the date on the calendar or how much more snow fell. Spring was a season so hard to identify in Maine, one simply had to be decisive about it. Already, there was excited talk of clamming, fishing and boating.

Through the chatter, an argument arose between two tables at the back wall. At issue was whether Loonwater-Nebilinto Lake was technically a lake or a pond, a distinction often blurred in Maine and heatedly contested in Mayenne Bay on an annual basis. A number of diners rose from their tables to add weight to one side or another.

Over the din, Kitty arrived at the booth with coffee and tea. Claire immediately wrapped the fingers of both hands around the steaming mug.

"Hi, Kitty. I'm surprised to see you here again. I heard you retired."

Claire smiled, hoping to engage the eccentric woman before she sped in another direction. Kitty returned an icy look.

"Filling in for Celeste, not that it's your business."

Her deep smoker's voice croaked, her jaw twitched, and her loose dentures clicked as she spoke. A slight whistle accompanied the "s's". Then, without another word, Kitty headed for the next table.

Claire stared after her, stunned.

"Claire, you're staring," Guy told her.

She jerked her gaze back to him.

"Guilty as charged. But did you catch her tone?"

"I did. Ignore it."

It was advice Claire found impossible to follow.

After breakfast, they each placed a bet on the future date of the ice melt and handed their money to Patty. Guy chose March 31. Claire chose April 5.

"Wishful thinking," Claire said as they exited.

"Pessimist," Guy returned.

They made their way up Main Street to the frame shop. Roxie greeted them from behind the counter and was quick to reach for a small frame wrapped in brown paper. She laid it on the counter, unfastened the paper and pulled the wrapper away. The frame held an oil painting of spring bulbs—soft yellow daffodils, paperwhites and blue grape hyacinths—in a clear glass vase. In the lower right corner was the artist's discreetly placed signature: "G. Gardiner".

"I spent a lot of time looking this over, Guy. It's fantastic," breathed Roxie. "I didn't realize you painted still lifes."

"Only for Claire and my landlady, it seems, at least, so far."

"It was his Valentine's Day gift to me. It's perfect, isn't it? I can't wait to hang it," Claire said.

Not twenty minutes later, Guy stood on a stool, ruler and hammer in hand, in the doorway between Claire's kitchen and living room. He shifted the rose painting he had given her last summer a bit to the left and banged a starter hole to the right. The two works would hang side by side.

"You really surprised me with this," Claire said, handing the bulb painting up to him. "You were so busy with your work, not to mention escorting me all over Maine, I can't imagine how you found the time. I love it. You're turning me into a collector."

"That's music to my ears."

"But I really struggle with what to do for you. I don't have your talent. And I can't keep stuffing you with sweets and buying you records."

She gestured to the classic 33LPs on the table, her present to Guy for his 31st birthday, much as it had been for Christmas.

He replied awkwardly due to the nail between his teeth.

"I honestly wouldn't mind. There's no such thing as too much music. And I'd trudge through a blizzard for another slice of this lemon pound cake."

He stepped down from the stool and took another large bite of the cake Claire had baked. Then, the two backed up a few feet to admire the wall.

Claire was especially self-conscious over Guy's gift after so spectacularly underestimating his feelings about the visit to her family. It had been over a month now since they had set the date with Hannah, and he had still not breathed a word of criticism, but his palpable relief at her invitation had spoken volumes. He had been less anxious over the visit itself than the prospect it might not happen at all. Now that the date was set, Claire's steely resolve to see it through had her by the throat. She turned to him, slid her arms around his middle and laid her head on his shoulder. With every stroke of her hair, Guy, master of wordless communication, let her know he understood.

On Sunday morning, Claire took a walk in the park while Guy painted by the water's edge. It was chilly and, by afternoon, turned blustery. The wind was almost deafening. Gusts rushed past her ears, but Claire welcomed the wild wind against her face as she made her usual circuit of the park. On the south side, she fell into step with Jay Brown and turned with him onto Castle Street, searching for a way to open conversation.

"Jay," she began. "I'm Claire Munro. I'm somewhat new in town—been here about a year—and haven't managed until now to introduce myself. I hear your name a lot due to your activism for the town."

"Pot shots, I'm sure," he growled.

"You are a bit controversial, but I think you already know that."

Jay released a combination grunt-snort. Claire, pleased to have elicited something akin to a laugh from this morose man, pressed on.

"Headed home?"

"Kitty's."

The wind tugged at the papers he carried under his arm and flapped the corners. Jay squeezed his elbow tighter to press them against his rib cage. Claire walked with him in silence to the top of Castle Street where, just before the intersection with Crest Street, Jay turned left onto a private, dirt lane marked "Bayberry", whose entrance was obscured by overgrown roadside vegetation. Claire waved him off and bore right onto Crest to make her way back to Guy, whom, she suspected, the wind had probably driven from the shoreside by now.

A strong gust whipped across the intersection with such force, it loosened some papers from under Jay's arm. He scrambled with remarkable agility to retrieve the runaway sheets, stuffed them into his jacket and proceeded down the lane at a quick pace. As he disappeared from view, Claire spotted a sheet stuck in the brush and missed by Jay. She called out to him, but due either to distance or the wind in his ears, he didn't hear. She bent over to pick up the sheet and followed.

The trees and brush along the lane were untamed but provided a welcome break from the wind. As she walked, Claire squinted all around in the dappled light for signs of a house. About two hundred feet in, the path curved slightly, and there, surrounded by a wildness of bushes and brambles and fronted by a tiny yard strewn with nature's debris, stood a small, red-and-white cabin with a crooked number five on the door.

The structure at first appeared upright, helped in this appearance by horizontal siding, but to Claire's inner sense of perpendicularity, it leaned ever so slightly to one side. The exterior was in some disrepair—peeling paint, old windows and a chipped front stoop. A weathered outhouse stood in the back. There was no car, lawnmower or other sign of modernity aside from the electric service pole that extended a lifeline to the house. Several cats prowled the grounds. Claire saw, as she stepped up to the porch door, that there were more inside. She sneezed loudly just as Jay rapped on the door.

He swung around.

"What do you mean by following me?"

She reached out to pass the lost paper to him.

"When you picked up the papers, you missed this one. I called out, but you didn't hear. Don't worry, I didn't read it."

"Who's that?" came a low, gravelly voice from inside.

"Jay and, uh, Carol."

"Claire," Claire whispered into Jay's ear.

Under the wary eye of Kitty Greenwood, Claire entered the cabin with Jay. She had not intended to be part of his visit but felt, now that Kitty had seen her, this was the courteous thing to do. She stood mutely, attempting invisibility, hands at her sides, eyes cast down at the cat litter beneath her shoes.

Jay handed the papers to Kitty.

"Hee-uh."

Kitty's eyes darted to Claire and narrowed.

"Carla didn't read them."

"Claire," Claire corrected him again.

Kitty grabbed the sheets, flipped through them and shoved them under her arm.

"That one's not to be trusted," she snipped and stared icily at Claire. "Heard her telling Ben Tripp she was 'breaking a confidence'."

A very tense silence ensued. Jay stood there, his primary mission accomplished, apparently uncertain what to do next in the wake of this bombshell. Claire wore a momentary expression of absolute surprise. She flashed back to her conversation with Ben about Valentina's bipolar diagnosis and her own concerns about confidentiality and remembered that Kitty was one of two persons who had passed closely by while she spoke. The other had been Erin. Finally, Claire knew. Finally, she understood the rumor. She had grabbed Ben by the arm and pulled him aside, to the extent possible, in the busy Fish House.

"Ben, any word on the two missing women?"

"Nothing yet, but we're looking actively."

"Ricky Diaz is a co-worker of mine and a really fine human being." Claire's voice had been low, her tone confidential. "He's private, though, and may not have told you Valentina is bipolar and has gone missing before. I wanted to be sure you knew because it could complicate the search."

"He did reveal that, and I could tell it was a wrench for him." A corner of Ben's mouth upturned. "You know, I didn't think Mayenne Bay was large enough for the police to have an informant."

Claire had bristled.

"I'm not an informant. I'm sharing information because it's the right thing to do. These women might be in harm's way."

"Whoa." Ben had raised his hands in surrender. "I meant no disrespect. It was a joke."

"I'm not laughing, Ben. I broke a confidence just now. I don't want to read about it in the Captain's next post."

Kitty, bearing a full breakfast tray, and a red-headed woman with a computer bag over her shoulder had brushed past them while Ben stood stock still, studying Claire as if seeing her for the first time.

"And you won't, not because of me, anyway. I'm sorry, Claire. I unburdened myself to you a few times and I see now I chose the right person. I will keep any information you bring me close to the chest. You have my word."

Now able to account for Kitty's attitude, Claire addressed her.

"You're right, Kitty. I did tell Ben. I did break a confidence at that moment in the interest of someone's safety but quickly afterward confessed it to the woman's father. He understands what I did and why and has no objection, so I'm not sure why you would. Really, it just isn't your business."

Claire had the momentary satisfaction of throwing at Kitty the same words Kitty had thrown at her yesterday morning but couldn't dwell on the topic any longer. There were other demands on her attention. The strong smell of cat urine, the abundance of flies over spoiled cat food—these were nothing compared to the feline swarm that had collected around Claire's legs, purring, drooling and rubbing her calves. God, she hated cats, and they knew it. No other animal sensed repugnance and retaliated with slow torture like a cat.

She sneezed several times as she worked to disengage her legs from the cats in a way that wouldn't harm them. They threw her off balance, and she grabbed onto the nearest stable object, a rolltop desk so covered with desk miscellany, it was barely discernible beneath. She identified oak wood and suspected the desk was antique. It held an old black typewriter, boxes of paper and carbon sheets, clean and used, *Life* magazines and a tall stack of *Bayside Squawker* issues. Pencils, ballpoints and fountain pens were strewn everywhere. At the edge of the desk sat several very full ash trays, adding cigarette odor to the cat stench. It was all Claire could do not to retch.

"Excuse me," she choked to Jay and Kitty, "I've got to get going."

She made for the door, tripping over cats as she advanced, and didn't breathe deeply again until she had covered a safe distance from the house. The welcome wind brought fresh air to her lungs and a means to dislodge cat hair from her nostrils and clothing. She sneezed, shook out her hair and brushed her clothes with her hands as she rapidly put distance between herself and Kitty's cat zoo. By the time she found Guy, he was at his car, having folded up his easel in surrender to the elements. Claire recounted her visit to Kitty's place, Kitty's revelation about the rumor and her contest with the feline plague, a story punctuated by more sneezes.

"Well, at least now we know where Kitty got her name," was all Guy said.

Bayside Squawker, March 20

Neighbors,

Support Maine Maple Sunday, March 22 this year. Some sugarhouses are offering events on Saturday, too. Check your local sugarhouses online for their hours and activities.

Your Local Maple Syrup Producers

Bayside Squawker,

Just one letter from Captain Crabbish in 2 months. What's going on?

A Loyal Reader

17

Winter Purge

Late March brought definitive signs of spring. "House-For-Sale" placards, Maine's "state flower", sprung up to mark the advent of prime house-buying season. Not to be outdone, nature sprouted her own early blooms wherever the ground was warmest. In the woodlands, there were skunk cabbage, jack-in-the-pulpit and trout lilies. Yellow coltsfoot appeared on the roadsides. Crocus, pussy willow and forsythia popped open in town yards.

Inside, spring-fevered homeowners began their post-winter purges. They cleared the last of the preserved garden goods from pantries and freezers to make space for new season produce. They dragged furniture marked "FREE" to the foot of their driveways. The bins at the consignment store were piled to overflowing with items judged recyclable after a winter of disuse and dust collection. Those looking to capitalize on discards advertised early spring garage sales in the *Bayside Squawker*. Claire was keen for these, especially if they boasted used books for sale.

"Jay's having a garage sale today," she announced as Guy entered her kitchen rubbing his wet hair with a towel. She pushed a folded *Bayside Squawker* marked with yellow highlighter toward him. "The 'library of an English teacher', it says. I don't want to miss that. It starts in an hour, but I'd like to arrive early, which means leaving now. Want to come or join me later?"

Guy was accustomed by this time to Claire's early-bird nature and knew better than to delay any mission that involved books. Besides, he, too, was a fan of garage sales. They were almost as much an adventure as metal detecting. He quickly transferred his tea to a to-go mug, stuffed a piece of toast in his mouth and exited through the kitchen door behind her. They drove rather than walked to Jay's place on Castle Street, an indication that Claire hoped to score big.

In spite of the early hour, the sale was already well underway. Just outside the garage, Jay sat in a lawn chair, wrapped in a jacket and lap blanket, thermos of coffee and money box at his side. People milled around racks of clothing, tables of kitchenware, knick-knacks and cartons of books. Yard tools leaned against one garage corner, and over a dozen garden gnomes stiffly lined the inside wall, looking to Claire like they were awaiting execution.

Guy began to wander the place with no particular goal in mind.

Claire headed straight for the book boxes, where Peggy was already rummaging.

"I should have known you'd be here already."

Peggy stood up straight to stretch her back.

"Jay gave me a call and told me to take whatever the library needed as a donation. I never turn down free merchandise. Not finding much I need, though. A few replacements for my worn classics, but otherwise…"

"So, I'm free to look without impinging on the library collection?"

"Help yourself."

And Claire did. She was soon met by Roxie and Louis,

both wearing firefighter jackets. Louis held a large sack full of leaflets, and Roxie carried a small fire extinguisher.

"Thought we'd stop to check out the goods on our way to the boathouse," Roxie told her. "Everything will be gone by the time we finish the fire prevention seminar with the live-aboarders. Louis got us grant money for outreach to educate groups like theirs with unique needs."

"Live-aboarder. I've read that term in the *Squawker*. It's a strange label," Claire said. "It's not like anyone would be dead aboard a boat."

The pair laughed.

"It just means people who live aboard their boats all year round," Roxie said. "There are about ten live-aboard slips down at the wharf, all full. Not surprising with the lack of housing on land."

"I saw one of those boats over Christmas. Red with a lighted tree strapped to the bow."

"That would be Blue Bickford's."

"The harbormaster who complained in the *Squawker* that things were being thrown at her boat?"

"The very one," answered Roxie. "And the one who's leading the opposition against increased harbor fees. She's an old sea dog but she's smart and has a good heart. Not one for outside interference, generally, but we're hoping she'll show up today. She has electrical appliances and lights on that boat rigged with very wonky cabling. She's in as much need of safety and exit strategies as the rest of the bunch."

"Exit strategies? With bay water all around, aren't the boaters in a favorable position for a fire?" Claire asked.

"It's counterintuitive," Louis replied, "akin to a house burning in rain or flood waters or even heavy snow, as you saw at my place. Fires burn hot. Imagine standing on a small burning vessel trying to access bay water, especially at night."

"And fire moves fast," Roxie added. "On board, there are only small water tanks. There's a communal water spigot on the dock, but it isn't hooked up permanently to a hose. It's shut off completely during winter because it freezes otherwise."

Roxie and Louis left Claire to contemplate the perils of living on a moored boat and moved along to take in the rest of the sale. Claire stayed put and rummaged through the remaining book boxes until she accumulated quite a pile. She carried the stack over to the table where Jay sat.

"Cash only," Jay barked at a tattooed man wielding a checkbook.

The man dropped his intended purchases at Jay's feet, stowed his checkbook and walked away. Grumbling, Jay tossed aside his lap blanket and rose to shift the goods to a nearby table, then returned directly to his chair. Maintaining some distance, Claire spoke gently to the man.

"Okay if I leave these here by you while I look around some more?"

Jay's eyes flicked to the pile of books then resumed their stare straight ahead. He nodded almost imperceptibly, lips pursed, informing Claire just how much of a wrench it was to let go of Ellie's things. She held back words of comfort, judging the very last thing Jay wanted at the moment was a public display of sympathy. Then, she waved her hand toward the collection of garden gnomes, once Jay's prized possessions, displayed proudly throughout his garden beds.

"Jay, that's some gnome collection. Do you really mean to part with it?"

"Ellie hated them," was all he said, but those three words were enough. Jay was clearly purging on more than one level.

Guy arrived with his own selections and set them to the side on the driveway next to Claire's book pile. Three bird feeders. An Audubon bird guide. Binoculars. A squirrel baffle.

"Since when are you into birds?" asked Claire.

"Always have been. It's just that I have no place to hang the feeders where I can see them. I was hoping you'd let me put them outside your kitchen window."

Claire hoped this was as near as Guy would come to talking about a joint domicile just now. The mere hint jump-started her nerves and set her mind to whirl over the upcoming visit to the Munro family. She was saved from further comment by her discovery of an old Smith Corona manual typewriter in a box under one of the nearby tables. She rushed over to take a look. Guy followed.

"Oh, I've always wanted one of these!"

She lifted the machine to examine it.

"Claire, I thought you were getting into fountain pens," Guy said.

After seeing fountain pens on Kitty's oak desk, she had ordered one to try it out.

"I am, but a manual typewriter…" She looked longingly at the machine and came close to caressing it. "The whole experience is sensory—sight, sound, touch and even smell. You're working right on the paper."

Guy rewarded this reply with one of his customary eye rolls followed by a smile of indulgence and amusement.

Claire approached the old man again.

"Jay, how much are you asking for the typewriter?"

"Ten dollars."

"So little?" Suspecting it had been Ellie's, Claire squatted down next to his chair and asked discreetly, so as not to be overheard, "Are you sure? It's in such good condition."

"Ellie kept it clean," said Jay. He turned his face away. "Can't stand to look at it no more. She used it all the time, clackin' away. Now the house is silent, but that thing just sits there, scoldin' me. Take that box of paper with it," he said and gestured to the stationery box under the same table.

Claire rose.

"Sold," she said, no triumph in her voice. "I promise to take very good care of it, Jay."

He continued to look away, lips tight. She placed the machine and box next to her pile of books, paid him and whisked her purchases away to the car. After seeing the pain on Jay's face, she couldn't leave them any longer right under his nose.

Claire spent the ride home in sullen silence instead of her usual fever over garage sale finds. Every item she had bought was in near perfect condition, a mark of the tender care Ellie had taken of her cherished possessions, but each carried the taint of Jay's grief, so palpable, it hurt. He had, perhaps rashly, unloaded Ellie's belongings in his present inability to cope. Claire decided to brace herself in case he had second thoughts. She would regard the typewriter as a loaner for now.

Guy was also silent on the ride home but, unlike Claire, ecstatic inside. This morning had been yet another proof of Claire's zest for life. She didn't require anything extravagant or sensational. Over a simple, neighborhood garage sale, she came alive—Guy couldn't think of another way to say it— through small joys, like books and an old typewriter. She thrilled over art and history and good food and fountain pens and even handwriting analysis. She made an adventure of the most insignificant things. What other person would consider taste-testing three syrup grades? He eyed the bird feeders on the back seat, sure he would have a fellow bird enthusiast before the season was out. Life with Claire would never be dull. If only he could be sure she would spend that life with him.

Once back at Claire's apartment, Guy got right to work on sinking the bird feeder pole into the ground just outside the kitchen window. Claire set aside the books and typewriter on her kitchen table, filled a bucket with soapy water to scrub out the feeders and set them in the sun to dry. As soon as Guy ran to the hardware store for bird food, she slipped back inside. She popped off the lid of the typewriter case, rolled a clean sheet of paper into the Smith Corona and looked around for something—anything—to test it. She grabbed her grocery list from under the refrigerator magnet, sat down and typed it out, grinning like mad.

That evening, the Mayenne Bay Art Club, joined by the Mayenne Bay French Club and the Mayenne Bay Historical Society, convened a special, Sunday gathering in the library conference room.

"Time to get settled, everyone," Meilin called out.

While she waited for guests to seat themselves, Meilin was approached by Sandra. She suppressed a gape at the version of the mayor standing before her. Sandra's habitual, meticulous upsweep of her brown hair had been replaced by a soft, French braid that trailed down her back. Her lipstick was gone. She wore hoop earrings and a green Mayenne Bay sweatshirt over faded jeans. Well-worn but colorful socks protruded from a pair of Birkenstock clogs. Sandra looked like a throwback from the hippie era. Meilin wondered if anyone recognized her at all tonight.

"Please don't announce me," Sandra begged under her breath. "Let me be a civilian tonight."

Without fully understanding, Meilin agreed to this odd request, and Sandra slipped discreetly to the back of the room. Claire, who had overheard, followed Sandra with her eyes and caught the half-smile on Louis's face as she stationed herself at his side. The mayor had priorities outside her office tonight. Sandra had long been unattached, except for a brief infatuation with last year's duplicitous condo developer. Louis was a widower with a teenaged son. Together, the pair exuded an ease Claire hadn't perceived before.

"Welcome all," Meilin said. "First, thank you, Peggy, for use of the library tonight. Second, please welcome the French club and historical society to our midst. And third, thanks to the French club for refreshments." Cheers and applause followed. "We have a lot to cover, so let's get down to business. You've all heard about the discoveries from the shed fire on the property owned by Louis Rainwater. Louis has allowed us to display some of the findings this evening. First, however, Officer Tripp is here to clear up a few things about that fire. Ben?"

Ben stepped to the front of the room.

"I apologize to all the would-be crime novelists, but the skull found in the shed was determined by forensics to be about a hundred years old. No other bones were found after an extensive search of the area. My research of cold cases came up empty. So, Mayenne Bay can't claim a murder or even a recently deceased person by any means." There was an unseemly moan of disenchantment, at which Ben raised his palms. "Please. The skull, which we believe was once used by an artist for reference when painting the human face, has been respectfully laid to rest in private ground."

"Thanks, Ben. Now that we have the macabre aspect in perspective," resumed Meilin, "let's consider the skull in a different context. Peggy?"

The librarian rounded to the front of the room, this time in her capacity as president of the historical society. From the bright, uplifted faces, it was clear Peggy was a well-known favorite.

"The historical society is fortunate to have Quince Greene, a master's degree candidate in archival studies with undergraduate degrees in both history and art history, as this year's intern. Quince identified the other remains from the burned shed. Taken collectively, these and the skull suggest the shed was very likely once an art studio, as Ben intimated: a wooden table easel, now somewhat charred, a paint box, a mortar and pestle, a palette knife, ceramic crock fragments, tin cans, tin paint tubes and brass ferrules from old paint brushes."

She paused to let the crowd digest this information.

"There have been many painters on the Mid Coast throughout history. One prominent artist, Percy Sanborn, was born in 1849 and died in Belfast in 1929 of a vehicle accident. He worked primarily in Belfast painting marine landscapes, signs, theatrical back drops, murals and pet portraits. He certainly had the talent to paint a human portrait, but we have no proof that he did. Before Percy, Dolly Smith of Searsport, born in 1824 and died in 1891, was renowned. She produced landscapes and was well known for her portrait paintings. But the shed studio could have belonged to anyone, amateur or professional. All of the studio artifacts, except the skull—we've displayed only a photo of that—are laid out on the back table where Quince stands ready to field your questions."

Peggy continued speaking as she signaled to Claire to come forward.

"On the other back table are six small porcelain figurines, fully intact and also found at the burn site. These were unearthed by Claire Munro's fortuitous placement of her right foot." The crowd tittered. "If not for this happy accident, these artworks would have remained hidden and unenjoyed, probably forever. I'd like Claire to tell her own story."

"Thank you, Peggy, for putting a positive spin on my clumsiness. Louis allowed me to be among the party that explored the burned shed remains. While the others worked the metal detector above, I explored what had collapsed onto the cellar floor in the fire and found the artifacts on the back table as well as the skull. When I stuck my foot into a wall crevice to boost myself out, I knocked loose some rocks." Giggles from the audience drew an amused shrug from Claire. "The dislodged rocks revealed a hollowed space behind the wall where a large storage crock had been embedded. The figurines were stashed in that crock, carefully preserved in wrappings of linen and oil cloth, as you'll see on the back table, and cushioned in sand. Celeste Baptiste, president of the French club, has found out more about them."

Celeste rose to speak while Claire returned to Guy's side.

"Hi, everybody. Thanks to a joint effort by the historical society and the French club, we have a working theory about the origin of these figurines. They may be the creations of the French porcelain maker, Edmé Samson, based in Paris until he died in 1890. Each bears the mark 'ES', though Samson's mark varied and, apparently, was often omitted. This is all speculative, of course. We have some outside expertise coming in to take a look. How these pieces got stuffed into a crock full of sand in the cellar wall of a woodland shed, though, remains a complete mystery."

"Flotsam!" someone called out.

Peggy stepped in again, laughing, to speak for the historical society.

"Quince is looking into the idea. Most of you will already have heard of the steamship, the 'Bold Coast', on course from Boston to Halifax, Nova Scotia, that burned and sank off La Palourde in 1903. All but a few were killed in the fire that sunk the vessel. Some cargo may have survived. The ship's passenger list from the Boston shipyard archives indicates elite personages on board relocating to Canada, so it's reasonable to suspect there were valuable possessions among them. As of now, we have no way to confirm the figurines were on board."

She paused to allow a flurry of movement and whispering among the guests to pass.

"Flotsam from the Bold Coast, if any, would have landed at La Palourde or The Point. Sandra Edgecomb's family diaries and records—she allowed us complete and unsupervised access—note the disaster, but no salvage. It's possible this was an intentional omission to hide the acquisition. It's equally possible another enterprising person found and stashed the figurines or even that they came from another source entirely. Quince is looking into the original owner of the house on Louis's place just in case that gives us a lead."

Peggy ceded the floor back to Meilin.

"Thanks, Louis, for allowing us to display these treasures. The art studio artifacts will end up on permanent display at the historical museum. The figurines' destination is undetermined. Now, please help yourself to refreshments and circulate."

"Claire," came Louis's voice from behind her, "Sandra tells me you two haven't formally met. Claire Munro. Sandra Edgecomb."

The women greeted one another.

"I hear you were instrumental in getting the historical society and the French club to work together. If that's true, you're a miracle worker," Sandra declared. "I've been mediating their differences since I came into office."

"The joint research was my idea," Claire admitted, "but it was their willingness that made it happen. You know, the rapprochement might just be the culminating effect of all your previous efforts."

"That's generous of you." Sandra turned to Guy with a hand extended. "And you are the artist, Guy Gardiner, who exhibited the painting of The Point last summer that had my house in it."

"Mayor…"

"Sandra," she interrupted. "I admire your work and the good your art is doing for the town."

Guy didn't hide his surprise.

"I wonder if the painting is still available."

"It is." His face was equally incredulous and hopeful.

"Great! I let it go last summer and have regretted it ever since. May I see it again? Would you be willing to bring it to the house so I can see how it looks on the wall?"

"I'd be honored."

He punched in Sandra's phone number as she spoke it and let the call ring so she would have his.

"Text me when you have an opening, will you?" she asked. "I'm free most weekends. And when you come over with the painting, why don't you bring Claire? I'll lay out some wine and cheese…and iced tea." She nodded toward Guy's glass.

"I never turn down a glass of wine," Claire joked aloud but finished her thought in her head. *And I'd love to get a look inside the mayor's infamous house.*

Bayside Squawker, March 27

Dear Captain Crabbish Fans,

We at the *Bayside Squawker* cherish Captain Crabbish and miss him, too. He has not been banned from the paper. He's taking a needed break. I'll keep you updated.

Patty Libby, Owner, *Bayside Squawker*

18

Plein Air

Nature signaled April's arrival with the usual muck born of ground thaw and melted snow. The landscape turned from white to dirty white to a ubiquitous brown except for slowly receding pyramids of snow plowed into parking lot corners, though the threat of snowstorms was far from over. Drivers kept one eye on surface conditions and the other on low-lying roads prone to overflow from melting snow, ice jams and heavy rains. Mainers slogged through their yards trying to keep the mud from sucking the footwear off their feet and splattering their pant legs. For yet another year, Maine's rubber boot market would be secure. Mud Season, the state's "fifth season", having ramped up in March, was now in full swing.

Sandra sat on a chilly park bench drinking coffee and reading the *Bayside Squawker* front page, filled with resentment at the article entitled "Peeved at Potholes". Like anyone could stop the forces of nature. As it did every year, the cycling freeze-thaw and the spring melts and rains wreaked havoc on town roads—cracks, buckles, ruts and potholes. The article advocated reporting these travesties to the Maine Citizens' Transportation Watch, which offered a prize for the worst road in Maine, according to its particular standards. Strangely, Captain Crabbish was silent on the subject this year, but Sandra wasn't complaining. The article itself instigated enough trouble. When things settled down, the road department would attempt to reverse the damage on a shoestring budget in the few months the weather allowed. Really, sometimes people had no idea.

With an indignant huff, she stuffed the paper inside her jacket and started down the path toward the boathouse. Her face lifted to enjoy the brisk sea breeze and the returning geese that circled overhead and then lowered to watch the lively activity in the park, where volunteers were getting it ready for tonight's first-ever Mud Season Bash.

Over on the boathouse deck, she spotted an artist setting up his easel. The ski hat drawn down over his ears made it difficult, at first, to identify Guy Gardiner. He hung his overstuffed backpack from a hook beneath the easel tripod to secure it against erratic gusts off the bay. As she got closer, Sandra detected the layer of insulation beneath his paint clothes and fully appreciated his insulated boots. Only the tips of Guy's fingers, protruding from fingerless gloves as they did, had cause to take issue with the cold sea air.

A pang of regret passed over Sandra at the sight of this talented artist hard at work memorializing Mayenne Bay. Guy's painting, "The Point", exhibited at last year's art show, highlighted her own historic home overlooking the bay. Generations of her family had lived and died in that house. When she had inherited the wreckage, Sandra hadn't shied from the extensive restoration required, nor spared labor or expense. Yet, she had let Guy's painting celebrating this heritage and investment go not only unpurchased but unacknowledged.

It hadn't been her finest hour, nor her finest summer, in

truth. Her infatuation with Leroy Hood, the cunning and charismatic condo developer, continued to elicit a visceral mortification, but Sandra welcomed it. She wanted to keep that memory alive as a prodding reminder and unshrinking guardian against ever again losing her grip on common sense. She rejoiced now at having met Guy and arranged for him to bring the painting to her house for a viewing.

As Sandra walked across the boathouse deck toward Guy, he waved at Christy, who was heading toward the small beach next to the boathouse with her easel and a large canvas. Christy bobbed her head in return, her hands too full of gear to do otherwise.

"Hi, Guy. Do you expect the whole art club today?" Sandra asked.

"I emailed all members plus a few other artists." He scanned the park as he spoke. "Not all paint en plein air as a rule. Some just not in the cold. Several expressed an interest to experiment today. Christy just arrived, and there's Pi…John Mills, just heading in."

Guy's tongue had tripped on John's name because he privately used a nickname for the man: Pierre Cliché, chosen for John's cartoonish painter-attire and affected behavior. Even in this cold, John-Pierre wore his blue beret poised at an angle over the stringy, white hair on his head, a paint-spattered coat, white painter pants and a red necktie. Guy and Sandra watched this caricature make his way across the park green to the jetty. With a half grin of understanding, Sandra took her leave and headed toward Christy's easel.

Guy continued his watch for incoming artists. Christy and John-Pierre were followed by…he squinted…Geoffrey Bristolwaite! Guy almost dropped his brush. He had invited Geoffrey on a lark, never dreaming this established fine artist would deign to appear, especially after their last, disastrous encounter. They had met over dinner with Claire and Geoffrey's wife, Caroline. Geoffrey and Caroline had openly sparred across the table and had left, mute and humiliated.

Geoffrey spotted Guy, signaled and joined him directly on the deck. He bore no sign of residual embarrassment and offered no explanation for the dinner disaster. He simply dropped his gear at the opposite end of the deck from Guy and bent over to unpack his easel, humming as he did so. Guy preferred it this way; he would never have found the right thing to say. He heartily shook Geoffrey's hand, the only clean thing Geoffrey had to offer, for the moment, anyway. His backpack and easel were caked with paint, his clothes spattered, and the silver hair that poked from his hat generously flecked. With the high price of paint, Guy had to wonder about the cost of so much misdirected medium.

"Glad you could make it."

Geoffrey pumped Guy's arm, eyes bright.

"Been wanting to get up here again for some time. We never did get to talk art last visit."

There was little time for conversation while the two men focused on their respective creations of the morning. Every half hour or so, each broke concentration, stretched and hydrated. And so it went until noon, Guy's habitual mealtime. He laid down his brush, secured his painting and easel further against the wind and dug into his sack for his packed lunch. After a long draw on his water bottle, he sank down and sat cross-legged against the now sunny boathouse wall to eat a tuna salad sandwich. Geoffrey followed suit, spreading out his meal and digging in.

Footsteps sounded on the deck, and Christy rounded the corner with her lunch and gear to join them. John-Pierre remained alone at his easel out on the jetty.

"Doesn't look like John's had much inspiration this morning."

Christy jerked her chin toward the odd man. The others stared. John-Pierre stood as though posing for a tableau with one leg forward, one hand holding his palette and the other suspending a brush over the canvas. His painter pants, stuffed into untied boots, puffed in the wind. He had secured his double-breasted, Navy pea coat up to the neck and donned a Ushanka hat on top of his beret. The fluttering ear flaps brought Goofy to mind. With dramatic gusto, John-Pierre swirled his brush in paint, reached out toward the canvas, then swirled and reached out again. Anyone watching from a distance would think he had a well-progressed painting before him after almost three solid hours on the jetty. Instead, he had achieved nothing more than a large, muddy blotch.

"I've been debating whether or not to paint him in," Guy said, gesturing to his own canvas. "What do you think?"

"I'd add a few seagulls overhead instead," Geoffrey said, chuckling.

"I agree," said Christy. "Adding John would detract from your composition. He'd be the only element that doesn't seem quite real."

Geoffrey and Christy rose to lean their wet paintings du jour next to Guy's against the side wall of the boathouse protected from the wind. They studied one another's work while they ate and called out comments. Each had been looking out at approximately the same scene from one angle or another, yet style and work product couldn't have been more different. Christy painted in broad strokes and abstract shapes. Geoffrey's work was representational but executed loosely with a palette knife in thick texture. Guy's realistic style involved the greatest degree of detail of the three. Not surprisingly, his painting was the least progressed, whereas Geoffrey's was nearly complete, and Christy had begun her second.

A strong gust blew against the far side of the boathouse. It was followed by the sound of raucous laughter emanating from the park. Guy, Geoffrey and Christy stretched their necks to find the source. Mayenne Bay's firefighters, identifiable in their white-lettered, red jackets, and accompanied by Sandra, were shaking their heads at a tepee-shaped woodpile that had toppled over in the wind.

"Looks like they're setting up a bonfire," Geoffrey said.

"It's for the Mud Season Bash tonight," Christy explained.

"The what?"

"The Mud Season Bash. It's the brainchild of one of the firefighters, Louis Rainwater, but friends of the firehouse have all worked on it. They're raising money for a new firetruck." She pointed to what looked like large metal bowls placed at intervals in a circle around the bonfire site. "The bonfire will be the center attraction, but there will be small firepits all around. Fire is the theme in every sense of the word. Hopefully, the wind will die down as predicted."

"There'll be craft beer and locally made sausage to roast over the fires," Guy added, "among a great deal else." He turned to Geoffrey. "I hope you'll stay for the event. That's why I suggested you bring mud boots. You're supposed to wear traditional Maine dress, however people decide to define that, to the Bash." He chuckled. "Claire will be in her glory people-watching tonight."

A seagull swooshed over their heads. The three ducked and spun around to follow its path toward the jetty. Only in this moment did Guy, Geoffrey and Christy realize that the wind that had toppled the bonfire wood had also taken hold of John-Pierre's easel and spilled it into the bay. The artist lay on his belly stretching over the rocks, one fist grasping the easel's leg. From this prone position, he slid backward and pulled the easel back onto the jetty with him. Out of reach flashed the white and brown of his unfinished canvas as it bobbed over and under the choppy waves, soon to be waterlogged and claimed by the sea. To make matters worse, while John-Pierre inched to safety, the seagull dove for the lunch he had left spread on the rocks.

"Not one of John's better days," remarked Christy.

"No, but it'll be interesting to hear what he makes of the saga and his lost masterpiece," joked Guy. "There's a touch of the dramatic in him." He cupped his hands around his mouth and called, "Need help, John?"

John-Pierre turned his head toward his compatriots and shook it dumbly, flapping the ear covers of his trapper's hat against his cheeks. Once on his feet again, he hastily gathered his belongings and headed out. Guy, Geoffrey and Christy also packed up. The four converged briefly on the boardwalk.

"Bad luck today, eh, John?" Guy asked the obvious.

John-Pierre grunted, his face crimson. The front of his pea coat and white pants were smeared with rock slime and bits of seaweed. His Goofy hat was askew. His easel dripped with bay water. He looked at the other three glumly, then walked away without a word.

"I guess I'd pack it in if I were him," Christy said.

"I probably would, too," agreed Guy, "but as I'm warm and dry, I'm heading over to the boatyard to paint some more."

"I'll join you," said Geoffrey.

"Guy!" a high voice called from a distance.

The three artists turned. It was Claire. She waved as she jogged her way toward them in a red, cloche-style hat that becomingly framed her face. In keeping with the Maine-centric theme of the Bash, she sported an oversized, cable-knit fisherman's sweater and navy-blue Wellington-style boots. She looked so crisp and clean, there was no mistaking her for a working fisherman who had hastily grabbed gear off the mudroom hook, but she had clearly grasped the spirit of the thing. Guy made a mental note to ask how long it had taken her to put this outfit together.

"Geoffrey, how nice to see you again," Claire gasped, holding her side. "Christy, I haven't seen you since the night of your presentation to the council. Well done. The prospect is so exciting."

As the foursome walked toward the boatyard, Christy filled Geoffrey in about "A Better Idea for Mayenne Bay" and called his attention to the old factory site at the far end of the wharf. The conversation then turned to the particular challenges of plein air painting, so aptly demonstrated by John-Pierre's mishap.

"This was my first attempt," said Christy, "so I don't have any first-hand war stories yet."

"None of us is immune," Geoffrey said. "Not long ago, I stood on a rocky beach to paint an ocean scene and underestimated the slickness. Down I went, easel and all. My left thumb hasn't been the same since." He held it up and attempted to bend it, unsuccessfully.

"Once," Guy told them, "I was surrounded by a cloud of gnats that kept landing in the wet paint on my canvas. I kept picking them off, then decided one looked like a faraway bird in the sky, so I just painted a few right in."

"I hope you raised the price of that painting," teased Geoffrey. "Organic products cost more."

Christy waved the others off and left for home to clean up for the Bash.

While the two men painted, Claire wandered aimlessly along the boardwalk and in the boatyard among the assortment of crafts. The boats housing live-aboarders were huddled together in their usual winter cluster on moorings close to the boardwalk. Blue Bickford's red houseboat was the most conspicuous among these. Other boats had already been cradle-lifted into the water for the new season. All were rocking madly in the wind. Some—lobster boats, tugs, sailboats, yachts, speed boats—had yet to emerge from winter hibernation and remained nestled in their storage racks in various stages of undress. The unique wear and tear on each gave it a distinct character. If boats could speak, Claire was certain these would have stories to tell.

One small boat, tightly shrink-wrapped, sat snugly between the side of the large warehouse building and the neighboring retaining wall. Claire imagined it must be a pet project tucked away until the owner found time or else a relic too cherished to discard. As she drew nearer, woolgathering, she saw that the elements had torn a hole in the protective plastic cover. Poor thing, Claire sympathized, having had to weather the winter in a torn robe.

Her footsteps halted, and her eyes grew wide. She saw…or thought she saw…a head peer out from the hole. She stood motionless, staring at the spot. Really, she'd had enough of bodiless heads for a lifetime. But again, a head in a blue ski hat emerged from the hole and then shrank back inside. The third time it appeared, a body followed. Claire released a breath, relieved to see the person intact. One leg reached from the boat to the top of the retaining wall, and then the occupant pulled himself across the breach between the boat and wall and scampered up the hill to Harborview Street. It wasn't the long winter, but a squatter, who was to blame for the boat cover puncture. Full of her discovery, she quickly made her way back to Guy and Geoffrey to report the sighting but stalled at the sight of the small group now gathered around the artists' easels.

The people-watcher in Claire threw the throttle wide open as she took in their respective interpretations of the Maine-centric clothing for the Bash. Morrie and Quince were among the group. Morrie wore a brown Irish fisherman's sweater, most likely, Claire guessed from the hole in the elbow, from the consignment shop, and a pair of lowcut Bean boots. Quince had got more holistically into the spirit of the thing. She wore a sailor's beanie on her head and lobster buoy earrings. Her blue sweatshirt featured the skull of an old salt, complete with mustache, beard, pipe and sailor's cap. And she sported bright yellow, waterproof pants and Bean boots.

By this time, the stream of people milling around the park in anticipation of the first-ever Mud Season Bash had grown considerably. The artists packed up, and they all made their way toward the crowd gathering at the entryway.

Bayside Squawker, April 10

Calling All Maine Artists,

The second annual Mayenne Bay Art Show will begin accepting registrations on May 1. Maine resident artists working in all media are welcome to apply. Go to the Creative Agenda store website for more information and to register.

Meilin Li, Art Show Committee Chair

19

Mud Season Bash

The entire town park had been roped off for the Bash. Entry was permitted from one corner only, where a historic, red firetruck stood like a sentry, leaving no doubt of the event's purpose. Well before its siren wailed to signal the opening at five o'clock, a long queue had formed. Guy, Geoffrey and Claire joined it. Sandra and Peggy were on hand in Mayenne Bay hoodies and ankle duck boots to collect the admission fee that allowed visitors to warm themselves by the fires, access the vendor trucks and mix with friends. Louis, Roxie and other firefighters, conspicuous in their red jackets, patrolled the park to monitor the fires and redirect would-be Bash crashers attempting to jump the rope barrier.

A huge teepee of bonfire wood, expertly stacked at the very center of the park and having survived further onslaughts from the wind, awaited ignition at dusk, around seven o'clock. Six lighted firepits encircled it at even intervals, and a large, incinerator barrel for paper trash burned in the corner nearest the vendor trucks. Cocktail-height plywood tables, picnic tables, benches and even logs for seating dotted the grounds. Lined up just inside the waterside park path stood tables featuring the baked bean cookoff, the homemade Needham-potato-candy contest and the New England chowder competition. On either side of these were tents selling Bash T-shirts and sweatshirts and local crafts to benefit the fire department. The garden club sponsored a tent to conduct the town's annual seed sale and swap. Against the rope barrier along Park Street, vendor trucks offered local microbrews, craft ciders, hot chocolate, coffee, baked goods, lobster rolls and blueberry pancakes with maple syrup. Red snapper hot dogs, parboiled potatoes and sausages were available on long skewers to roast over the fires. Ten percent of all Bash food sale proceeds were destined for the fire department.

Claire left Guy and Geoffrey to talk art while she strolled the grounds alone to observe. The crowd was spirited, appreciative of this taste of early spring free of both insects and snowfall, however chilly the air. Mayenne Bay was out in full force and, judging from the swarm of unfamiliar faces, word had spread far and wide about the Bash. The locals weren't the only Mainers itching for a cabin-fever reliever. Fires crackled, sausages sizzled, and hands rubbed together over the flames. The smells of wood, smoke and enticing foods wafted through the air. Warmth, company and food—the Bash offered the perfect combination of ingredients to revive winter-weary souls.

The varied interpretations of Maine-themed dress captivated Claire most. The majority of attendees had simply thrown on worn boots and an old barn coat or cable-knit sweater, but a number had taken their Maine fashion statement very much to heart. A few tribal members milled around in traditional Wabanaki winter dress. The French Club, not to be outdone, paraded in historic, Acadian-style costumes. Blue and a large group of fellow fishermen wore heavy sweaters, bright orange overalls with suspenders and black rubber boots. There were outdoor guides sporting hiking pants and boots, multi-pocketed vests and official "Maine Guide" caps. Jerome came dressed as a lumberjack with Denise in tow, her pregnant belly looking very near term under her fleece moose pajama pants. Claire counted five young pirates, the fiercest among them a girl in a pink fairy costume with wings, a black eye patch and a sword.

She picked up a large, black coffee and two warm crullers and lowered herself onto a bench, a perfect vantage point for spectating. She was surrounded by happy faces…all except one. In the corner next to the incinerator fire sat the widower, Jay, a beer mug in his hand, an absent-minded stare on his face. Claire frowned. Jay had formerly exuded energy, quarrelsome though it had been. Ellie's death had changed him. Without his usual bluster, the man looked small, almost pitiful, like a deflated balloon. Instinctively, she stood up and made her way toward him.

"Jay, may I join you?"

Without waiting for an answer, she sidled up to the welcome heat from the incinerator then sat down next to him. She popped a piece of cruller into her mouth and washed it down with a gulp of coffee.

"Have you tried the crullers? I could eat an entire batch. I used to help my mother bake crullers when I was a girl. These are very similar."

She handed her second cruller to Jay. His hand came up and accepted the gift before his face reflected consciousness of the act.

"I, uh, have beer."

He reached out to return the confection. Claire held up her hand to refuse it.

"Just like my grandfather. He had beer with everything—ham on rye, fish and chips, even homemade crullers, I imagine. I never saw him dunk a cruller in beer, though, like we did with our coffee."

Her eyes sparkled devilishly with the dare.

This produced a snort from Jay and drew out the contrarian in him. He plunged one end of the cruller into his beer mug, drew it out and chomped off the saturated end. His contorted face set Claire to laughing, which caused Jay to laugh in turn, before the cake had fully cleared his gullet. He sputtered and coughed.

"Tell your grandpa I gave it a go, but…"

"He's passed now." Claire's tone was soft as she took advantage of the segue. "I haven't had a chance to speak to you about Ellie. I'm very sorry about her passing. She was beloved in Mayenne Bay, judging from the extraordinary turnout at her funeral. I feel so honored to have a few of her belongings in my possession."

She said no more, wondering if Jay would suddenly demand the return of Ellie's old books and typewriter. Instead, the old man turned his ashen face toward her, his grief so obvious, it made her flinch. Ellie's death had taken the wind from her husband's sails.

"We met in high school," he said shakily, head hanging. "I don't know why she married me. I never deserved her. Everyone saw that but me. I just gave her trouble."

Claire, despite her practice with unexpected disclosures from strangers, was astonished at Jay's openness. She had judged him a man who spouted his political grievances loudly but held his intimate feelings close to his chest. He had revealed some emotion at the garage sale, but she didn't think that was intentional. Now, he was volunteering it. She strained for a way to leave him with something…something useful, hopeful…in return for his confidence and honesty.

"Jay, may I tell you what I think?" Again, she didn't wait for an answer. "I think you loved Ellie, even if you didn't show it as you should. And Ellie saw something in you to love, or you two wouldn't have stayed together all these years."

Jay stared at her with rapt, wet eyes while she continued.

"Perhaps you didn't treat Ellie as you ought while she was here, but there are ways you can make her proud of you now."

He sat up stiffly in the wake of these words. They both understood Claire had suggested a way forward.

"Take care, Jay," Claire said as she gently touched his shoulder and rose to take her leave.

She walked away wondering if Ellie would be surprised to see Jay so bereft. How ironic and how piteous that Ellie's legacy might lay in her death and its belated transformation of her husband into a more amiable man. Claire became so lost in thought, she bumped into Ben and spilled coffee down her leg onto her boots. She dabbed her pants quickly with her crumpled napkin before looking up to see Rhonda standing at Ben's side.

"Hi. I'm so glad I bumped into you." She rolled her eyes. "I can't believe I said that. How are you, Rhonda?"

She listened to Rhonda gush about college, then, judging from Ben's tight face, thought it wise to change the subject.

"Ben, are you familiar with the boatyard?"

He gave a nod. He had just taken a mouthful of lobster roll timed, Claire suspected, to avoid talking about college.

"Do you know that small boat sandwiched between the warehouse and the retaining wall?"

He nodded again.

"On the retainer wall side, there's a hole in the shrink wrap. At first, I thought it was just a casualty of winter weather. Then, I saw a guy climb out of the boat, hop over onto the wall and climb the hill to Harborview."

Ben swallowed.

"They're probably working on the inside of it."

"A man wearing a full face-cover ski hat who peeked out several times before exiting and then scooted up the hill?

On a Saturday off season? Doesn't sound like an employee to me."

"No, it doesn't." He turned to Rhonda. "Claire is now on the force, unofficially of course." Claire started to protest, but Ben didn't give her the chance. "She's always spotting something useful." He turned back to Claire. "I'll look into it."

There was a tussle between two boys by a firepit. Ben made his way over to separate them.

"Rhonda?" Claire asked, looking at the young artist's gloomy face staring after Ben.

"Ben didn't want to come tonight. I came home this weekend to tell him I'm going to France for the fall semester to study art. It's a program through the college. Ben's outwardly supportive, but I can feel him struggling."

"It's never easy to be the one left behind, waiting, not knowing, especially when the other is off for a life-changing adventure. A semester is a long separation at such a distance."

"But we'll connect by videochat the whole time," Rhonda insisted, her voice cracking. "And I promised I'd come back to him. He's so sweet."

"I'm sure you mean it but I suggest you give Ben space. The harsh reality is that your present intentions may not be the ultimate outcome. He knows this but isn't getting in the way despite his own wishes. It's a generous gift to give."

Rhonda nodded glumly, and tears leaked from the corners of her eyes.

The raucous youth soccer club ran by in a rush, waving sparklers and alerting Claire to the oncoming darkness. Though the moon was almost full, all the tents, tables and vendor trucks around the periphery had lit portable lamplights. She searched the grounds for Guy, who had planned to paint a nocturne this evening—his first ever. With fire in it—another first. She spied his easel just outside the rope barrier in the darkest, least traveled corner. If he'd hoped this position would protect him from spectator curiosity, he hadn't counted on the LED lamps clamped to his easel to foil his plan. Bash attendees drew to him like moths to a flame, but Claire was pleased to see he was holding out, determined to make the attempt despite the invasion.

Guy had explained beforehand the challenges of painting fire. Like water, fire was all motion. Dancing flames twist into teardrop and tendril shapes, thin and thick, haphazard and unpredictable. Colors shift fluidly– red, orange, yellow and white hot with blue and black contrasts. Smoke, sparks and ashes rise into the air. He had made painting fire sound so difficult, Claire wondered at him even trying. His brow was furrowed with concentration now as he raced to capture the Bash scene before dusk fully gave way to night, when the brilliant glow of the roaring fires against even a moonlit night would turn the background detail to solid, indistinguishable pitch.

Not until the dark fully engulfed the place did Claire and Guy leave the Bash. He spent the remaining waking hours that night and all day Sunday refining the nocturne.

As part of his invitation to paint en plein air at the park, Guy had invited participants, as well as other interested art club members, to an informal gathering at Claire's place the evening after the Bash. Geoffrey and Christy arrived and leaned their wet works against the living room wall next to Guy's. They stepped back with the other guests to study the paintings and mingled over drinks and food. Guy hung back in the kitchen to watch the reactions to his nocturne, fingers crossed behind his back that the response would be favorable enough to include this canvas in the Port Clyde show. The fires had been, predictably, a wrench to paint but worth the effort for the education alone. But was the end result worthy of a public exhibit? Judging from the body language of his peers, he needn't have tied himself so tightly into knots.

Bayside Squawker, April 17

Neighbors,

Do you know the person in this photo? The Mayenne Bay Historical Society is hoping to identify this woman. She may have lived here as much as a century ago. A larger, color photo can be viewed on the society's website. Contact me at the society office if you have information about this person.

Quince Greene, Intern
Mayenne Bay Historical Society

20

The Munros

The dreaded weekend for the Guy-meets-the-Munros tragic comedy—or was it comic tragedy?—finally arrived. Claire stuffed the last few things into her travel bag, sat down on the edge of the bed and closed her eyes. Tonight, she and Guy would drive to Portland and stop overnight at Daniel's place. By late tomorrow morning, she would be in the impatient arms of her mother.

It was just past six o'clock as Guy and Claire raced down route 295 to a Spotify mix of the Rat Pack. Guy sang along and tapped to the beat on the steering wheel and, from time to time, took Claire's hand in what she knew were grips of reassurance. Once at Daniel's, they didn't tarry long in light of tomorrow's early wake-up. Daniel went to his room. Guy and Claire slipped into the sofa bed.

The threesome hit the road at first light and ate breakfast in the car, nibbling and sipping coffee and tea to a collection of instrumental movie soundtracks. When they crossed the George Washington bridge into New Jersey, Claire reached over and turned off the music. One way or the other, her future with Guy lay fully in his hands now, but she couldn't allow him to meet her family entirely blindfolded.

"Guy." She twisted to face him. "I haven't given you much information about my family. Honestly, I haven't known where to begin. You'll meet them soon enough, but you can't show up entirely unaware."

He kept his eyes on the road, but Claire could tell from his face that her preamble had drawn his attention. She ran through a brief description of the occupants of her mother's house and a condensed history of her years living there. She touched on her parents' divorce and her mother's string of boyfriends. She described her relationships as they stood today.

"The Munros are a loud, unruly clan," she concluded. "I'd give you a rule of thumb, if there was one."

"The rule of thumb is to just roll with it," interjected Daniel, who had poked his head forward from the back seat. "Both of you."

He threw Claire a meaningful look.

Guy said nothing, but reached over to squeeze Claire's hand again. She left him to ponder her history and flipped on the music again, grateful for the distraction during the rest of the drive.

They pulled up to the Munro residence in absolute silence. Guy took in the place. The house was a modest, yellow split-level with black shutters whose paint was sun-bleached and peeling. The front lawn was covered in loose stone and cluttered with lawn chairs, an old surfboard and stray weeds. The shrubbery was overgrown, and a cedar tree leaned at an angle in front of the living room window. A wooden fence stretched across the front of the yard. Two cars were parked alongside the road in front of it. There was just enough room for Guy to squeeze his car behind a third in the driveway.

As Guy turned off the ignition, Claire stared straight ahead, lips sealed, face impassive, body tight. They had reached the moment when further explanation was superfluous, when the reality was directly before them. Even after her lengthy explanation this morning, Guy had no idea what to expect from the Munros, largely because they were wild cards. Even Claire couldn't predict their behavior. That was the problem, the reason she had delayed this visit for so long, He heard her inhale deeply and release her breath. Then, she straightened her shoulders and climbed from the car.

The front door flew open with a bang—the pneumatic closer was broken—and Hannah Munro dropped nimbly down the front porch steps with a piercing squeal, arms flung wide in the direction of her daughter. Claire had warned Guy of her mother's trademark caterwaul, but the real thing was more jarring than he had imagined. He shook his head from side to side to clear the ringing from his ears and pulled himself from the car. Daniel did the same.

Hannah was muscular but scrawny—Guy guessed about a hundred pounds soaking wet—with neck-length hair dyed strawberry blonde. She wore black slacks, a mustard top with a large broach pinned at the collar bone, and matching earrings. She approached Claire with a great, lip-sticked smile, pulled her into a full body hug and squeezed hard, all the while verbally streaming in a single, unpunctuated breath.

"I'm so glad to finally see you it's been too long is that a new haircut I'm so excited Guy came how was the trip oh Danny I see you made it."

Claire uttered "thanks" or "fine" at all the appropriate moments, though Guy doubted Hannah heard a word.

"Mom," Claire said when she broke away, "this is Guy Gardiner. Guy, my mother, Hannah Munro."

Hannah walked right up to Guy and delivered him a powerful, bony hug as if she had known him for years. Daniel was next.

"Guy, you're a Pisces, I understand," said Hannah in a high pitch as she let go of Daniel and rounded again on Guy, clapping her hands together. "A water sign. Sensitive. Artistic. A perfect match for our Virgo, here. I can't wait to do your chart!"

Guy had no response to this summation of his being or his and Claire's astrological compatibility, nor did Hannah wait for one. She hopped back up the front steps and held the door open wide in invitation. He, Claire and Daniel entered the house where they were greeted by Charlie, the family dog, who repeatedly poked his nose in all the most sensitive places. While the three fended him off, Hannah leaned around the wall that hid the central staircase and yelled upward.

"Boys! Your sister is here!" No response. "Markie! Bobby!"

Only three minutes had passed, and Guy already wondered if the woman was capable of speech that didn't end with an exclamation point. A thunder of footsteps sounded overhead, and four twenty-something men descended the stairs en masse. The two in front, Guy guessed from their looks, were Claire's brothers, Markie and Bobby, born Mark and Robert. Their friends followed awkwardly, eyes bloodshot and giggling. One held a set of drumsticks, the other, who bore an alligator roach clip on his pocket, swayed on his feet. Not everyone had practiced abstinence this morning.

Claire received bear hugs from her brothers, the second of whom lifted her feet completely off the floor in a crushing embrace. Guy was tempted to step in until he saw that Bobby, apparently unaware of his own strength, hugged his older sister with real affection.

The pounding of feet and rambunctious behavior had set Charlie to barking.

"Markie, put Charlie out," his mother commanded.

Danny. Markie. Bobby. Charlie. It appeared Hannah reduced every name to a diminutive. Claire had escaped the downgrade by virtue of her unyielding name. Guy would, too, he realized with relief, for the same reason.

Mr. Roach-Clip was closest to the front door and leaned on it to steady himself, giving Charlie just enough room to dash out. Another caterwaul escaped Hannah's lungs, and all four young men followed the animal outside. The door slammed behind them.

"I told you to be careful with that damned door!" Hannah bellowed through the screen at the boys' backs. "And I also told you a million times, you can't let Charlie loose!" She turned back to Claire, Guy and Daniel. "I could spit nails. He won't be back for days now. You know how he is, Claire. I'll have the neighbors at my door next."

"Charlie is a ladies' man," Claire explained to Guy. "We've seen little Charlies all over the place, proof of his escapades. He even crosses the bay when it's frozen in winter to find females on that side."

Guy opened his mouth to comment, but Hannah had already disappeared into the kitchen. He, Claire and Daniel followed.

"How can we help?" Claire asked.

"Damn that Markie. I told him to take this garbage out for pick up. We're going to miss the truck again," complained Hannah. Saying this, she drew her apron over her head and turned immediately to the stove.

Daniel took the cue and carried the trash bag out to the garbage can and the can to the roadside. When he returned, Claire and Guy were setting flatware and plates around the table. Hannah clapped her hands together again at the sight of them.

"Oh, I just love a man in the kitchen," she squeaked and tweaked Guy's cheek.

He stepped back for a moment, stunned.

Claire turned puce.

"Just roll with it," Daniel whispered so only they could hear.

A phone rang. There were a few moments of confusion while Hannah searched frantically among the piles on the counter for the device.

"Claire, I made your favorite," she announced before she took the call. "Oh, hi, Dorie! Claire's here with her new boyfriend." Hannah dropped the phone a few inches from her face and looked at Claire. "You remember your Aunt Dorie? Here's Claire, Dorie."

Hannah held the phone up to Claire's mouth.

"Hi, Aunt Dorie," Claire spoke obediently.

Hannah didn't wait for Dorie to answer. She stuffed the phone between her ear and shoulder and began gabbing to Dorie at high volume, all the while vigorously stirring the contents of a huge pot.

Guy felt sure Hannah's sharp pinch had left a mark but, in view of Claire's embarrassment, resisted the urge to massage his cheek. He had a sudden urge to laugh out loud, a nervous reaction, he was sure, definitely not suited to the occasion. He didn't regret having Hannah's attention turned elsewhere while he regained his composure. Claire's flushed cheeks hadn't yet faded, and Daniel was watching him closely.

"What, exactly, is your favorite?" Guy asked Claire.

"Looks like it's spaghetti and meatballs. My favorite when I was five, if I recall."

"At least it's not Spam," said Daniel, "or cow's tongue. Remember that?"

This produced a giggle.

The four young men stormed back into the house. Bobby called out, "We didn't catch Charlie", then they all made for the stairs with a second pounding of feet.

"You shouldn't have let him loose!" Hannah hollered at

them and straight into Dorie's ear. "They let Charlie loose again, Dorie!"

As if the decibel level wasn't loud enough, the beat of heavy rock music sounded through the ceiling. Claire looked apologetically at Guy and shrugged dismally at Daniel. Sign language, Guy realized, had a valuable role in this household.

"Roll with it," Daniel mouthed silently.

And lip-reading, thought Guy.

Claire turned from the table to her mother's houseplants near the window. Guy stayed right by her side and watched as she loosened soil with a fork, clipped dried leaves and gave the plants a generous watering. He had come to understand a great deal about Claire in their months together. It was her nature, he knew, to release tension through action. Growing up in a house like this, he reflected, she must never have sat still.

"I always rescue Mom's plants when I come," she said close to his ear. "I've never been here when they haven't been right on the edge."

Guy felt he understood. There was a lot on the edge in this house.

"Hannah!" a man's deep voice called from the front door.

Claire swung around and threw a panicked look at Daniel.

"Oh, God."

Daniel quickly positioned himself next to Claire, which told Guy all he needed to know.

"Could be worse," Daniel whispered. "We managed to escape the freeloading tyrant she picked up this summer. Your father is probably the reason for that. Be grateful for little things."

"Jerry's here. I've got to go, Dorie," said Hannah hastily. She hung up just as her ex-husband darkened the kitchen doorway. "I knew you'd want to see your father, too, Honey," she said to Claire. Pleased with her own prescience, Hannah beamed beneficently despite the halting look on Claire's face.

Gerald Munro was about six feet tall, bald and paunchy, with sky-blue eyes. He had dimples in both cheeks which lent his face a certain charm, even in middle age. He wore a white polo shirt and khakis with a white patent leather belt and matching shoes. Festivities had begun early in the day, judging from his slight sway and glassy eyes.

"Drinking again, I see," Hannah snipped and, her expressive hands being full, she gestured with the stirring spoon and sent a splatter of tomato sauce onto the wall.

"I had a few breakfast mimosas. So what? I've earned the right."

He entered the kitchen, drew his daughter into a tight hug, then released her along with a whiff of alcohol.

"So glad you're home, Bonnie," he slurred.

"Bonnie?" Guy asked from behind Claire.

She was visibly struggling for control.

"Dad favors his Scottish heritage. My real name is Claire, but he's always called me 'Bonnie'."

Claire's brief, matter-of-fact explanation, Guy immediately understood, was meant to trivialize a parental disagreement originated at her birth and very much in play thirty years later.

"'Claire' is short for 'clairvoyant'," explained Hannah with a knowing look and swinging the spoon again. "I was sure Claire was a seer from the day she was born. Gerald never liked the name."

"Voodoo crap," declared Gerald. "She'll always be 'Bonnie' to me."

He grabbed Claire's shoulder and gave her a rough side hug. Guy felt a second, very powerful urge to rescue Claire but quashed it.

"Dad," Claire said, disengaging from his grip and impatient to turn the topic, "this is Guy Gardiner. Guy, this is my father, Gerald Munro."

Guy extended his hand. Gerald seized it and squeezed hard as he looked directly into Guy's eyes. Guy endured the provocation with a perfectly schooled face, knowing Claire was studying him closely.

Gerald let go, tugged his pants higher and pulled himself up tall as he brazenly sized Guy up from head to toe and back again. It was the second time that morning that Guy had to suppress a laugh. From Claire's description of her father, he had prepared himself for a mano-a-mano. Guy stood his ground under the scrutiny, expressionless, hands in his pockets, a picture of nonchalance. Once the testosterone challenge was over, Gerald spun on his heels and headed toward the back room—the "rec" room, as the family called it—as though he still lived there.

"Want a drink?" the man asked Guy over his shoulder.

"No, thank you."

Gerald stopped and turned back.

"One of those, are you? I hear you're an artist. Are you queer?"

"Dad!" Claire blurted and turned red all over.

"Sorry, you're not my type," Guy answered coolly.

Hannah shrieked at this rejoinder, Daniel guffawed, and Claire's mouth threatened to curve into the first smile Guy had seen since their arrival. Her cheeks puckered inward as she bit down to keep her amusement from spreading across her face.

"A smartass, huh? I know your type. No college. My Bonnie has two degrees. I sent her to college to find a doctor or lawyer, not to hook up with some artist pansy."

"You did not send me to college. I sent myself and paid for it myself," Claire corrected him, hands gesturing and voice full of indignation. "And I went for my own reasons, not to hook up with some sugar daddy. Anyway, you never even finished high school, so don't be so nasty." She fired one more shot. "And no more condescension about homosexuals. Just stop."

"Claire has always been great at school," Hannah interjected as if the preceding spat had never occurred. She smiled winningly at Guy as though hawking a family asset. "Always won awards and made the honor roll."

"What'll you have, Claire?" asked her father as he headed again toward the rec room.

"Nothing, thank you."

Guy knew Claire geared her alcohol consumption to the company at hand. Refusing wine altogether proclaimed her expectations for the day.

"Daniel?"

"No, thanks, Uncle Jerry. I'm watching my figure."

A gruff laugh sounded from the rec room.

"I'll have a gin and tonic," yelled Hannah loud enough to be heard above the music throbbing overhead. The bass was now joined with twangs of an accompanying electric guitar. She marched over to the stairwell and hollered, "Boys! Turn that down!"

There was no change.

"Boys!" roared Gerald. "Turn that off!"

Silence suddenly reigned.

"They didn't have to turn it all the way off, Jerry," Hannah challenged her ex-husband.

"I'm not listening to that noise while I'm here, Hannah."

Robert and Mark's friends took Gerald's tone as their cue to leave. They slipped down the stairwell and, while Gerald bent under the bar, waved silently at Mark and Robert and exited without a sound, not even from the broken front door.

"Let's all sit in the living room. I've made some hors

d'oeuvres," invited Hannah.

Claire sank onto the love seat. Guy took the spot next to her. Daniel sat across from them, a protective eye on his cousin. Hannah emerged from the kitchen with a tray, which she set on the coffee table.

"I thought we could nosh until everything's ready," she said gaily as she accepted her cocktail from Gerald. "I planned an afternoon dinner, as you requested, Honey."

"Thanks, Mom."

Hannah gulped half her glass in one go. Gerald drained his and returned immediately to the bar for refills. Guy watched in wonder, having learned in the car that Gerald was known for mixing very strong drinks. A look of panic flitted across Claire's face induced, Guy was sure, by the imminent prospect of both parents under the influence of alcohol. This, Claire had informed him, increased the probability of all hell breaking loose, though Guy suspected hell pretty much always had the run of this place. Claire shrank back, her usual confidence and ebullience under a cloud. No, Guy corrected himself. Not a cloud. It was more like a veil. Right before his eyes, she faded into virtual invisibility, a survival skill and a habit, Guy suspected, of a lifetime. Sad, but remarkably impressive.

Hannah and Gerald, tongues loosened by liquor, shot barbs at one another, oblivious to their company. Hannah gestured animatedly and even more as the decibel level rose, while Gerald threw faces at her. Even when Hannah disappeared into the kitchen, they continued arguing at the top of their lungs between the rooms.

Finally, Hannah appeared in the doorway, threw back the last of her third gin and tonic and called, "Dinner's ready!"

Robert and Mark stormed down the stairs and made their way to the kitchen where seven people squeezed around a table barely large enough for four. In each place, dinner plates were already piled high with pasta and meatballs served by Hannah, much the way Mrs. Gardiner had overfed Guy and Claire with meat and potatoes. There was a battle of elbows until everyone followed Claire's lead and tucked them inward.

Gerald and Hannah's argument had by now escalated to a nauseating pitch. It seemed to Guy like chaos until he realized it was merely drama. Everyone present knew their role, where to position themselves on the stage and how the play would end. When the mixture of acrimony, alcohol and incivility reached its combined climax, the final curtain dropped. Hannah burst into tears, Gerald stormed out, Claire sunk further into silence, and the brothers flew back upstairs.

While Guy and Daniel handled cleanup, Claire worked alongside Hannah to arrange coffee, tea and dessert and listened while her mother slurred out her sorrows. Guy knew it had been thus since Claire was a child, mother unloading to daughter, but hearing it first-hand was illuminating.

"At least your father is gone before Micky arrives," sniffed Hannah, peering out the window. "He should be here soon. I invited him for dessert."

"You did what?"

Claire rounded on her mother, glaring.

"Aunt Hannah!" exclaimed Daniel.

"Who's Micky?" asked Guy.

"Mick is Claire's old boyfriend. They dated for several months," Daniel said. "Claire dumped him for being mean and oppressive."

"He's so handsome." Hannah's voice almost crooned. "He'd like to remain friends."

"Well, I wouldn't," declared Claire, "and you know that. He's a controlling creep and a stalker." She turned to Guy and Daniel. "We're leaving."

Both men followed Claire into the living room, as did Hannah, defending herself all the way and scolding Claire.

"You're so heartless, Claire."

Guy's head jerked toward her, frowning at this unfounded sting.

Daniel exclaimed, "Aunt Hannah!" once again.

Claire took a different tack.

"Yes. Yes, I am, if 'heartless' means I will never, ever cling to undeserving men like you do."

With that shot well slung, she turned her back and stormed out the door, letting it slam.

Guy looked hard at Hannah with a frown and pursed lips before nodding a silent good-bye and shutting the door behind him. He stood on the porch for a moment vacillating between anger and pity for the woman. If she had always been this clueless—or was it intentionally blind?—about her daughter, he doubted the distance between mother and daughter would ever be bridged.

"I warned you," Claire told Guy hoarsely, then crawled onto the back seat and closed her teary eyes.

"I'll drive first," was Guy's only answer.

Daniel bid a half-hearted good-bye to his aunt from the front passenger seat.

They pulled away just as a shiny, silver BMW rounded the corner and pulled into the empty spot in Hannah's driveway.

Bayside Squawker, April 24

Dear Ms. Townsend,

Finally, the townspeople are behind a plan to transform the old canning factory, and you are trying to stop it for no reason except that you and your cronies don't have full control. I don't like some things about the plan, but it will provide needed housing, generate a few jobs, and increase tax revenues, all while maintaining the inviting character of Mayenne Bay's shoreline. It's good for the town economy and the people. Please stop being an obstructionist and let us get on with it.

Name Withheld for Fear of Retaliation

21

The Typewriter

In the days that followed his introduction to the Munros, Guy had little free time as he raced to finalize his paintings for Port Clyde and attended to business and his own family. He spent as much of that free time as possible with Claire in a state of growing agitation. Now that they were on the other side of the dreaded family visit, where did she stand? Did they have a future together? She was oddly quiet on the subject, even aloof, and spoke of everything, anything, but her family. Normally, he could rely on Claire to initiate talk, to face problems head on, especially when goaded by her discomfort of things left unresolved. But he recalled Claire explaining once that, though general anxiety induced babble, real distress shut her down. Perhaps this accounted for her silence. In any case, once again, he found himself wary of forcing an issue before she was ready.

Just one week later, on Saturday, Guy tore himself from his easel early in the afternoon for the promised visit to Sandra Edgecomb. Claire joined him, and they headed over to The Point. When Guy turned off the ignition, they both sat for a moment in the driveway taking in this place so often debated around town. Many felt pride in the Edgecomb house history and Sandra's tasteful restoration, but the admiration was equaled by resentment over the Edgecomb's longstanding proximity to beached treasure at The Point. Sandra's ancestors were thought to have hoarded a disproportionate share of flotsam from the shores. Despite all she had attempted to dispel the notion that she had hidden treasures, she seemed perpetually caught up in this emotional current.

"What a view she must have out back," Claire said.

"An enviable one, which is probably the real source of the scorn directed at Sandra for living here."

"Yes, that plus the gold and jewels in her walls."

Guy stifled his laugh when he saw Sandra step out the front door. He and Claire couldn't help staring. Her hair had been loosed and hung freely around her shoulders. The wind picked it up, and a hand—Louis's hand—reached out from just behind her to tame it.

"Sandra and Louis. I suspected some electricity between them," said Claire under her breath as she exited the car.

"You did? Why am I always the last to see this stuff?"

She cast him a Mona Lisa smile.

Guy opened the car door, swung his feet to the ground, then carefully withdrew his painting, "The Point", from the back seat. He trailed behind Claire up the porch steps.

After greetings were exchanged, Guy asked, "Sandra, where would you like me to put this for viewing?"

She directed him to an empty picture hook on a large wall space at one end of the living room. Once the painting was hung, she signaled toward the couch and coffee table, the latter of which bore a cheese platter, crackers and grapes. There was also a bottled of chilled sauvignon blanc and a pitcher of iced tea.

"Please help yourselves," she invited, then edged closer to the canvas with Louis.

As was his habit, Guy stood back, watching their hosts' body language as they examined his painting up close. Claire planted herself on the couch and poured a glass of wine, all the while studying the mayor in fascination. The recent warm-up of her personality and relaxation of her appearance made Sandra an entirely different creature than just a few months ago, with her tight skirts, red lipstick and French twists. And Louis, whom Claire respected, obviously found much to admire in her. There was a story here. Claire was sure of it as she listened to Sandra's open admiration of Guy's talent and her interest in a painting she hadn't deigned even to acknowledge at the art show last summer. Was the mayor's transformation genuine or some kind of politicking? Claire didn't have an immediate answer.

She was dismayed to discover a large cat lounging on a chairback in front of the sunny window and studying her as intently as Claire herself studied Sandra. She willed the animal to stay where it was and looked quickly away, much like a child who pretends that hiding her eyes will make her invisible. The cat dropped to the floor, stretched its spine in a long curve and headed for Claire's legs. Purrrr. Oh, God. Not again. Claire's body contracted, and she spilled a bit of wine onto her pants. When she reached for a napkin, another, smaller cat appeared from nowhere and leapt directly onto her lap.

"Oh!"

"Let me give you a tour of the…oh, I'm so sorry," Sandra said with what sounded like sincere sympathy. She grabbed the cat from Claire's lap, scooped up the second and shooed both out the front door. "I really can't stand cats, but I had to get them in this old house to keep out the mice. Now, I'm stuck with these two for the duration. I take it you wouldn't like to give one a new home, Claire?"

"I'll pass."

"Did you ever notice they seem drawn to people who

can't stand them?"

"It's been hard to miss, actually."

All four of them laughed aloud.

"Now, how about that tour?" Sandra asked, brushing her arms and shirt free of cat hair.

"Great," Claire said. She stood up and likewise brushed the cat hair from her pants. "We were kind of hoping to get a glimpse of the gold bricks in your walls."

Guy's eyebrows shot up, but he saw that Claire's eyes shone with mischief. That plus the huge grin on her face made certain Sandra understood it was Claire's turn to tease. Sandra laughed sportingly.

"The people of this town have no idea how much I wish it were true!" Sandra raised her hands into the air. "The only gold in the walls is the money I earned on the job and spent to fix them. Restoration of this place can only be called a work of love, it was so costly. Not that I'm sorry to have done it, but had I found treasure, I'd have sold it to fund the project. I gutted this house top to bottom and found absolutely nothing but rot and mouse nests. This doesn't mean my forebears were innocent, though. Flotsam definitely reaches The Point and La Palourde first, and my people had the luxury of being very close to the shores. But whatever was found was not preserved for future generations." She shrugged. "At least, I don't have it."

Sandra proudly escorted them through all the rooms of the house. After many "oohs" and "ahs" from Claire, in particular, the tour ended at the large kitchen window overlooking the bay. Here, the foursome stopped and stood in hushed appreciation of the view.

Sandra broke the silence.

"I want to buy your painting, Guy, and I'd also like to commission another of this very view. I've spent years on all the necessary work to make this house livable. Now, I'd like to furnish it in a way that makes me happy. That begins with artwork."

Claire and Guy both looked into Sandra's face and read earnestness there. This new version of their mayor, Claire decided then and there, was on the level.

They all chatted for a while over drinks and hors d'oeuvres. Sandra was keen to gather their opinions of Mayenne Bay, the "Better Idea" proposal and anything else she could glean from this captive audience. Guy and Claire didn't mind; they appreciated having their mayor's ear.

They departed, leaving "The Point" on Sandra's wall where Guy had first hung it, and carrying a sizeable check.

"I really enjoyed those two," Claire said. "I wasn't sure what to expect."

"Me, too, and Sandra's patronage is huge," Guy said, unable to contain his excitement. "What a turnaround from last year's letdown. And now a commission to paint the bay from her private lookout. I could paint that view from about five different angles."

"What a great start to this season. A purchase and a commission from the mayor and an exhibit in Port Clyde. Your family will be so excited to hear your news."

"My father excepted. He's angry with me right now. And he's never had had much faith in my art as a career."

"You're already proving him wrong."

"Don't expect him to see that. Anyway, with Anna and Asad fresh in his mind, my art isn't even on his radar."

There was a note of sadness as he spoke these last words, sadness about his family that co-mingled with his heavy heart about Claire. He kept to his plan of silence on the subject and returned to the loft to paint, leaving Claire to herself for the rest of the weekend. Perhaps she would regain her usual strength and clarity after some time alone.

Back at home, Claire poured a glass of red, reheated the last of Guy's homemade lasagna and settled at the table with her tablet to the right and Ellie's Smith Corona to the left.

While she ate, she brought up on YouTube video after video about the workings and maintenance of manual typewriters. Tomorrow, she planned to finally put her new acquisition to use.

Over Christmas, when she had researched Annabelle's handwriting, Claire had come across articles about the cognitive complexities of writing by hand as compared to computer keyboarding. Handwriting involves the senses, the body and the brain. There is the smell of paper and ink, the soft scratch of the pen against a fluttery sheet of paper and the alignment of hand muscles to thought. There is the essential coordination required to achieve legibility. Her new fountain pen had amplified this existential experience and slowed her down to fully appreciate it.

Typing on an old manual machine would require a similar mind-body connection. Fingers arch, pound and "clack", as Jay had described it, to a "ding" of the bell at the end of a line. The carriage return lever is manually pushed across with a grind-thunk to reposition the paper. The finished sheet is rolled by hand from the machine. Zzzzzzip. There are odors of paper, carbon, ink and oil.

Having grown up on a computer keyboard, the non-electric typewriter held a bit of mystique for Claire, and Ellie's had a seductive aura of times gone by. Retyping a mere grocery list had been a revelation. It had required unexpected finger strength and dexterity and delivered a gratifying auditory punch with each stroke, a far cry from soft-tapping the electronic equivalent. And its characters had a permanence that made them difficult to alter, forcing her to slow her pace for better accuracy. She had found her focus sharper and her mind more regulated during that brief exercise and was keen to see if and how her brain might be rewired by the Smith Corona over time. She planned to keep the experiment to herself. Guy would award it nothing more than his usual eye roll.

After breakfast on Sunday morning, Claire donned an old shirt and jeans. She spread newspaper sheets topped with an old towel onto the kitchen table and set out bottles of rubbing alcohol, detergent and Rem-Oil along with an old toothbrush, Q-tips and rags. She rolled her vacuum cleaner out from the hall closet and fitted the hose with an attachment meant for close and tiny spaces. She opened her tablet to the YouTube site she had visited last evening. Finally, she transferred the Smith Corona onto the towel and lifted the cover.

For a few moments, Claire stood back and stared at the internal components in utter dismay. She had geared up for a major maintenance session, a gratifying removal of dust and grime that would bring to light the wonder of this old machine. But the components were dirt-free; they practically gleamed. Ellie had obviously taken pride in this writing tool. That, in itself, gave Claire greater pleasure for having acquired it. She determined to go through the cleaning process anyway as a training exercise. It would make the typewriter feel more her own.

She removed the two ribbon spools and set them to one side, then vacuumed imaginary dust from the inside. She went over the keys, joints and moving parts with a Q-tip dipped in alcohol then sprayed them with Rem-Oil. She popped the ribbon back in, snapped the cover back on, and wiped down the outside with a damp rag. Once the cleaning supplies were removed, Claire stepped back again to admire the shining Smith Corona, then carried it and the stationery box to her desk and positioned herself in the chair to type.

She reached in for a sheet of typing paper from the box. Her fingertips were too clumsy to pluck a single sheet from the top of the stack, so she overturned the box contents onto the desk. A used, double-spooled ribbon spilled out. One spool separated from its mate, dropped onto the floor and rolled until stopped by the bookcase. As she rose to retrieve it, the incongruity of a used ribbon among the pristine typing tools of the fastidious Ellie struck her as odd.

She scooped up the spool, so far from its mate now that exposed ribbon, black as pitch, dangled in the air. The ribbon looked in good shape. Any words it had once produced had been lost in the texture of the cloth or, perhaps, Ellie had re-inked her ribbons as Claire had seen done on the videos. That would answer. Disappointed, Claire re-rolled it and tossed it back into the empty stationary box. As she did so, she spied a used sheet peeking out from the pile of paper she had dumped. She slid it out to read the text. She read it again, then rose, ran for her bag and jacket and, with the sheet in hand, headed out the door.

She arrived at the Fish House out of breath and sought Patty, who, seeing the urgent expression on Claire's face, instantly ushered her into the back office. Patty left briefly to arrange for someone else to take over the cash register, then joined Claire and shut the door. The room was small and packed to the gills, but tidy, and held one guest chair. Claire dropped into it, visibly bursting with what she had to say but glad to confine her words to the safe space within these four walls.

"Claire, what's wrong?"

"I bought Ellie Brown's manual typewriter and a box of paper supplies from Jay at his garage sale in March. I haven't had time to try it out until this morning. This infinished letter fell out of the stationery box."

She handed the typed sheet to Patty.

```
To the Mayor and Town Council,

    All this talk of economic development,
and yet rent rates are still unaffordable to
most, if a rental can be found at all. The
```

trailer park slumlords are shameful. Faulty
plumbing, no heat. We need a town
representative devoted to the issue of
housing. How else can we

"This reads like one of the Captain's letters," Patty said, unprompted. "It sounds like a topic he'd choose. But it's not finished, dated or signed, nor is it one I published." Her head jerked up, her face incredulous. "You can't think Ellie Brown was the Captain, Claire."

"Why not? It seems like a huge coincidence that the Captain stopped writing just after Ellie died."

"It would be so out of character for Ellie. She never complained in her life. I'd swear keeping her pain to herself is what killed her."

"This letter was in a box that belonged to Ellie. She might have felt sufficiently protected by the Captain's anonymity to be more vocal in his name. A closeted critic." Claire fell back against her chair. "Want a laugh? For some time now, I've suspected you to be the Captain. I thought you just got tired of writing letters."

Patty's cheeks tinged pink. She shook her head.

"As you've no doubt seen from recent letters to the editor, the *Squawker*'s public would never let the Captain go that easily. If I were he, I wouldn't just drop the ball. The paper relies on him for sales."

"Look, I obviously haven't fully thought this through," Claire resumed. "I just had to talk to someone after finding this letter, and that person had to be you since this involves the Captain's identity. What I can't reconcile with my theory, though, are the several letters from the Captain printed in the *Squawker* after Ellie died, the letters of January 24 and March 6."

"It isn't unusual for the Captain to mail letters early. I recall the January 24 letter was postmarked January 15,"

Patty told her. "I published it on the 24th as the Captain directed."

"And the letter on March 6, the one suggesting that Gloria should be voted off the mainland?"

Patty's eyes dropped to her lap, a reaction Claire personally used as a means to hide her true feelings. She watched as Patty struggled, jaw grinding, then raised her head.

"If I tell you, Claire, it has to remain between us. No one else, even Guy, can know."

Claire was taken aback.

"Wow. Not sure what I was expecting, but it wasn't having to take an oath. Okay, for now, I agree, but I don't like holding things back from Guy and can't do it forever."

Patty released a long breath, and her voice lowered almost to a whisper.

"The *Squawker* has been inundated with letters, emails and calls wondering what's happened to the Captain. He's been completely uncommunicative, off-the-grid or something. So, I wrote the March 6th letter myself, out of desperation and panic, as a stop-gap."

Patty reddened. Claire's eyes grew wide as she contemplated Patty's deception and the extent of her panic.

"I'm not going to cast stones. I have no idea what I'd do in your place. I can understand what could drive you to that, knowing the slim profit margin of a small-town paper. But fake letters aren't a permanent solution."

"No."

"Since the January 24th letter, have you received communication of any kind from anyone claiming to be the Captain?"

"No."

"Do you have any idea why?"

"No."

Claire shook the unsigned letter for emphasis.

"Then surely this has possible implications for the paper. Don't you want to get to the bottom of his absence? Patty, nobody believes he's just on break."

"Surely, you can understand that his continued anonymity is vital to the *Squawker*."

Claire leaned forward.

"I do understand. I don't want to expose the Captain. I just want to find out what happened to him. Are his letters usually typed?"

"Yes."

"Signed?"

"Yes, but the signature is also typewritten."

"Did you edit his letters or were they clean as written?"

"Clean as written."

"So, an English teacher might have been the author. That brings us back to Ellie, who may have both written and typed them. This could be hers."

She shook the paper again.

"Yes, it's possible."

"Who else saw the Captain's letters?"

"No one but me. I pick up the *Squawker* mail from the post office box every day and open it myself. Always have, all these years. I don't want his delivery method or any other details discovered for fear they can be linked to the man."

Claire sat back in her seat.

"Or woman."

"Or woman. But, Claire, don't forget Jay had access to Ellie's typewriter."

"But if he was the Captain, he wouldn't have sold it."

"Unless he was calling it quits."

"That doesn't explain why he'd hand over the stationery box with an unfinished letter in it. I don't think he knew what was in there. And though he's a crank, he isn't much of a grammarian, judging from his speech."

"No, but if Ellie was the Captain, wouldn't Jay have

realized it, after living close together as they did in a small bungalow all these years?"

"If outward appearances were any indication, Jay and Ellie led very separate lives," said Claire.

She stood up, shook herself out and attempted to pace in the confines of the tiny office.

"I've been reading through all the Captain's letters chronologically. Judging from the writing, the Captain's first successor, the one who took over in the 1930's, must also have passed the baton. I think there's a marked change in the letters' language and style around the mid-1970's. Solid English. Good punctuation. Ellie was born in 1946—it was on her funeral announcement—so would have been the right age to be the second successor. And she had the right skills. So, why not Ellie? There's no way to trace the original Captain's or first successor's lineages, as we don't know their real names, but a successor wouldn't have had to be related. Maybe Ellie just fitted the purpose, like the Dread Pirate Roberts in *Princess Bride*."

Patty laughed.

"I love that movie. But, Claire, Ellie was smart and responsible. As she aged, she would have identified a successor. None has come forward after months of silence." Patty slumped in her chair. "I'm at a loss. Without the Captain, I'm sunk."

For both women, Claire's discovery was as vexatious and inconclusive as it was fascinating.

22

La Palourde

"Ready?" Guy asked.

It was an odd question to put to Claire, the Queen of Preparation, but he asked it because he didn't feel quite ready himself. This morning, he had overcome a growing sense of panic when he set down his paintbrushes for a hike with Claire to La Palourde. It was already the first Saturday in May, and it was going to be a squeeze to be ready for the Port Clyde show opening on Memorial Day weekend. But his struggle involved more than just time; it involved focus. The gnawing uncertainty about his future with Claire had, since their trip to the Munros two weeks ago, by now intensified into a debilitating distraction. Everything hung on the success or failure, as seen through her eyes, of that family visit. If she didn't broach the subject herself sometime during the day, he decided, they would have a frank reckoning over dinner tonight. By the time the sun set, he would know where he stood.

"All set," answered Claire.

She drew the door closed.

It was 11:00 a.m. as they headed out in rubber boots

and windbreakers to visit La Palourde Island. Guy had attached his metal detector to a support harness fitted over his left shoulder and slung his camera over his right. He also carried the usual backpack of detecting tools. All the talk of flotsam had led him to believe there might be some unearthed valuables buried out there. Claire carried a larger-than-usual backpack stuffed with necessities like tissues, protein bars, water bottles and a small towel.

They planned to meet Sandra, Louis, Meilin, Roxie and Ben, their guide, on the beach at The Point for an organized trek across the sandbar to La Palourde's three square miles of rock, gritty sand and overgrown brush. Claire had triple-checked the tide chart. Low tide was expected at 12:56 p.m., and the next high tide at 7:17 p.m. She wore her wristwatch, timer set for five-thirty, leaving plenty of time for exploration and a margin for a safe return. A ten-to-twelve-foot tide rise was nothing to take lightly, though Ben was sure to be far more casual about it.

"Heard from Anna lately?" Claire asked Guy as they walked.

"She's settled into her new place near the U-Maine campus. I talked to Joy this week and, as Dad has not relented, she's thinking of joining Anna."

"I'm really sorry, Guy."

Their conversation about the Gardiners ended only as they reached the spot where the others stood waiting. After greetings were exchanged, Ben turned and marched onto the sandbar, trailed by the others. They waded through tide pools and sank here and there into the spongy sand but managed to reach the island dry and unscathed. Ben led the group along a trail that dissected the island and opened up onto a long, rocky beach facing the greater bay.

Once at the beach, Guy had the detector running in seconds. While the other men took turns detecting, he took photos to use for art reference, and the women spread out looking for shells and driftwood. Claire broke away to climb up onto a flat rock expanse high enough to be unaffected by the tide.

"Over here!" she waved and called to Meilin, Roxie and Sandra, who came running.

They clambered up after Claire to the top. Around the perimeter of the flat bed were rocks, some placed there by nature, others piled by human hands. Snugly tucked inside the protective rock piles, atop driftwood logs stacked like Lincoln Logs, was an overturned rowboat. Together, the logs and boat formed a structure tall enough to sit under and gain protection from the rain and wind. The remains of a fire sat inside a ring of stones just outside this shelter.

Claire bent over to peer underneath the boat before slipping beneath it. Three pairs of boots appeared alongside, and Roxie's face poked underneath. Claire spoke from inside.

"There's a tarp stuffed up under the seat and a blanket and this hat," she called to them and slid the hat outside. "Also, there are cans of food in here." Claire pulled one from the bow of the boat and stuck it out into the sunlight. "The date hasn't expired." She slid back out into the open. "Somebody's been living here recently."

"Sandra, we're not trespassing on private grounds here, are we?" asked Meilin.

"No, La Palourde is owned by the town of Mayenne Bay. It's technically part of the town park."

"Camping is okay, but lighting a fire on park land requires a permit," said Roxie as she bent down to sniff the charred remains. "This is recent."

Sandra stepped over to the edge of the rock outcropping, called to the men and waved them up. When they arrived, Guy set aside the metal detector in light of the solid rock surface, and they all wandered the place looking for clues about the camper. Ben took Claire's place beneath the boat. He shoved all the remaining contents to the outside. Four food cans, a can opener, a bowl and spoon, a tarp and blanket and a canvas grocery sack.

"Organic canned goods," remarked Claire, "mangoes and beans and wild-caught tuna. Seems our camper has expensive taste. I don't think I've seen this brand of tuna anywhere locally but at Grace Grocery."

Ben slid out holding the final item, a hurricane lamp. He stretched his back and brushed off.

"The Graces have reported missing goods of late," he said, "always small. Same at the hardware store. The items taken have been trifling, almost not worth reporting."

"It would be tough to haul large quantities of anything across the sandbar without being seen," remarked Louis.

"Ben," said Claire, picking up the ski hat, "the guy who climbed out of the boat cover in the boatyard wore a hat like this. It was the same color blue and had the full-face mask."

"So, you think our drydock boat squatter has more than one home?"

Claire shrugged.

"A squatter, you say?" asked Louis as he glanced around. "He couldn't live out here all year."

"But judging from the lingering smell of that fire pit, he's made a recent stay," said Roxie. "Maybe he's shifting to the island now that the weather has warmed."

Meilin shivered and drew her windbreaker closed.

"If you call this warm."

Roxie put her arm around Meilin and rubbed her back for warmth.

"I have a huge window looking out over the sandbar and have never seen a person in a bright blue hat with a grocery bag crossing onto the island," said Sandra, "nor have I spotted the glow of a fire. I don't think I'd make a very good Harriet the Spy."

"Who?" asked Ben and Louis.

The women, and surprisingly, Guy, laughed.

"Harriet the Spy, from Louise Fitzhugh's book," answered Sandra in a tone that told them it should be obvious.

"My sisters read those books," said Guy. "They were always spying on me."

Claire clapped her hands together.

"I snuck all over the neighborhood wearing sunglasses and an inside-out white sailor hat for disguise. Like no one would notice a skinny, barefoot girl in that goofy hat. I watched people through binoculars and scribbled notes in my black-and-white composition notebook, just like Harriet. She set me up for guiltless people-watching, very important for a person born with an immoderate interest in human behavior as it is. I ditched the hat and glasses and am wise enough now to no longer put my observations in writing."

"I won't scoff if it's thanks to Harriet that you were keen enough to find Denise and notice someone living inside that drydock boat," Ben answered.

"Did you find any evidence there?" Claire asked.

"We found a blanket and a silver St. Jude medallion in the boat."

"The Saint of Lost Causes," Claire reflected aloud. "So, the squatter is likely Catholic. Perhaps of French descent?"

"In Maine, that's most probable, I think," agreed Ben. "It's a place to start, anyway." He pulled an item from his pocket for the others to view. "This crucifix was tacked to the underside of this dory. Between the hat and the religious pieces, it seems quite possible that the boatyard squatter and this one are the same person."

Ben photographed all the other items they had found and put them into the canvas bag.

"I'm going to finger print these and check for DNA, then return them, just in case the person is really hungry or cold," he explained.

As the metal detector had yielded nothing on the beach, it was the dory mystery that preoccupied the group as they made their way back to the mainland that afternoon. All of them had more questions than answers about the squatter.

After the hike, Claire stopped at home to change while Guy headed for the loft to make dinner. It took a lot of willpower to keep himself confined to the loft kitchenette when so much work demanded attention from just 15 feet away. He turned his back to it. Tonight was reserved for him and Claire. After popping a chicken into the oven to roast, he sank into the loveseat in thought to find the words he would need.

The Munros visit had been, ostensibly, to introduce Guy to Claire's family. Hannah had embraced him and pronounced him a Pisces. Gerald had verbally jousted with him and called him queer. No other attention had been paid to Guy aside from a loud invitation to drink and a stinging pinch on the cheek. What, in the end, had Guy expected? Admittedly, a little interest in himself as the purported reason for the gathering and a chance to get to know Claire better through her family. The latter had been accomplished less in spite of the Munros' neglect than because of it.

And what about Claire? No one had expressed curiosity that day about her new life and job in Maine. Nor had she had a single opportunity to inquire into her family. They had talked or yelled at one another or simply escaped from view. Claire had wordlessly withdrawn into herself, a skillful demonstration of emotional distancing in the very midst of chaos. When the worst was over, she had re-emerged to comfort her mother only to be met with accusations of insensitivity. Over and over these past few weeks, Guy had run the visit through his mind and wondered how this woman he loved and admired could possibly be the product of the Gerald-Hannah union.

Guy had taken the first shift behind the wheel on the drive home. Through the rearview mirror, he saw Claire stretched across the back seat, eyes closed. He was sure he heard her crying. Daniel had slumped in the front passenger seat, hair askew, head leaning against the window, eyes staring. Familiarity with the family was, apparently, not enough to shield even Daniel from its numbing effects. For about an hour, they rode in silence.

"Daniel," Guy whispered, "Is Claire sleeping?"

Daniel turned around to look.

"Yeah."

"Was today pretty typical of the Munros?"

"You got a good dose of reality, yeah."

"Pretty intense. Hard to imagine growing up in all that." He paused to pull his thoughts together. "Did I just witness an abridged version of Claire's childhood in the space of a few hours or did I see the tip of the iceberg?"

Daniel released a tense laugh.

"You saw the day-to-day, but they didn't take you over to the dark side."

"Come on, Daniel. This isn't Star Wars."

Daniel grunted.

"You heard my uncle's bigotry. It's prevalent among both his and Aunt Hannah's relatives. As a homosexual, I'm either under attack, the butt of a joke or summarily ignored, as I was today, except for a jibe or two. Marital infidelity is commonplace among the family. It's what broke up Aunt Hannah and Uncle Jerry. He started it. Also, alcoholism, drug use, domestic abuse and even incest run on both sides." He turned fully in his seat to look at Guy. "Dark enough for you?"

At the word "abuse", Guy's head had jerked toward Daniel, then his eyes flicked to the rearview mirror to look at Claire.

"No, not Claire, thank God," Daniel reassured Guy

quickly and placed a hand on his arm. "Gerald is an ass and a drunk but keeps his hands off his daughter. Some of her aunts and cousins were not so lucky. Molested by fathers and brothers."

It took a while for Guy to digest Daniel's repugnant disclosures. Finally, very sobered, he spoke again.

"Is it strange that, after only a single day, I feel like I know the family?"

"Well, they didn't try to hide from you, did they?" Daniel sniggered. "You handled Uncle Jerry well, by the way. Non-resistance. He doesn't know what to do with that. That tough guy routine is his knee-jerk to anything threatening, which you are, by the way, as a contender for his only daughter's affection. He's got a pretty conservative view of his paternal role that galls Claire to distraction. Yet, she can tell you stories of the emotions just under his skin and the countless times he's cried on her shoulder."

Guy shook his head.

"Layers of the onion, as Claire says. So, she's been a consoler to both parents."

"Yes, for years. It's ironic, but I think the role gave her home life some meaning amidst all the insanity, a way to channel the negative energy into something constructive."

"And it spilled over to helping strangers with their problems."

"Exactly."

"That's falling into place better now. I almost walked away from our relationship because of that."

"I know. I advised Claire to dump you after you two split over that last summer. I'm glad she didn't listen to me but I wasn't on your side back then."

"And now?"

"Don't get an overblown ego but you're good for her. Not many men would have handled things as well as you did today, nor would they work so hard to understand. The other guys, like Mick the Prick, just added to the pressure."

"Glad to hear you approve. Since we're confessing, I thought you were an idiot when you showed up at Claire's unannounced, on the verge of financial ruin, and hijacked our romantic evening, our pizza, wine, and dessert without an apology."

Daniel grinned.

"And now?"

"Now I see what a pillar you are to Claire, which means I'm a fan."

"God, would you listen to us both? We sound like one of Claire's support sessions."

They both laughed. At the sound of her name, Claire stirred in her seat. Guy glanced again in the rearview mirror.

"Time to wake up, Bonnie," he teased.

Daniel chuckled.

Claire's eyes opened, and she sat up.

"Very funny."

"That was just to loosen you up because there's something serious to follow."

This roused her, and she leaned forward between the two front seats.

"I have a confession to make," Guy told her. "I called Daniel a few months back to find out more about you and your family. I couldn't understand your prolonged hesitation to introduce me. You weren't giving me much to go on, and I was afraid to press you directly having already been introduced to your inner pit bull last summer. I'm still partially deaf from your yelling and slamming of car doors." He threw her a grin. "And assuming I eventually did reach your mother's doorstep, I didn't want to make things worse. I've been waiting for the right time to tell you."

"And you think this is it?" Her tone was snarky.

"There would never be an easy time, but, yes, now is best. You can't punch me when I'm driving, and waiting any longer would feel dishonest."

Daniel's head bobbed in agreement.

"Now do you see?" Claire asked Guy.

The sharpness in her voice had gone, leaving only the pain. Guy winced, but reached a hand back between the seats to squeeze hers.

"What I see is that you're a remarkable woman."

Claire accepted his hand and stared at him for a few moments before regaining her sauciness.

"How many times have you two got together to talk about me?"

"Knew that was coming," Daniel said, then twisted around to look at Claire. "Just the once, Claire. Honest."

"Except for the talk we just had while you were sleeping," Guy added.

Claire dropped Guy's hand and looked demandingly at both men.

"I told him the worst stuff, Claire," admitted Daniel. "The prejudice and drunkenness, he's seen, but the abuse and incest…" His voice choked off at the end.

Claire looked mortified.

"It was with good intentions, Claire, so I can understand." Guy said. "The same way you want to understand about my family."

This allusion to reciprocity in family matters mollified her. They had left it at that for the remainder of the drive home.

Now, after Claire had had several weeks to stew, Guy feared his clandestine tête-à-tête with Daniel would resurface as a matter of contention. And she might be paralyzed with mortification and even resent him for having seen her family's dirty laundry in the light of day, much the way people did to Claire after they confided their problems to her. He didn't want a resurgence of the pit bull but, more than that, he didn't want to lose her.

He rose to baste the chicken, shifted the oven temperature to warm and closed the oven door just as a knock sounded. Pulling his shirt away from his chest a few times—was he sweating from the oven heat or from anxiety?—he approached the door.

Claire hesitantly poked her head in.

"Guy?"

She stepped in timidly, evidently as nervous as he was, which told him she had intuited his intention tonight.

"Right here."

He pulled her to him and rocked her from one foot to the other. Claire left her head on his shoulder for some time before pulling away to speak in a choked voice, leaving Guy's shirt damp from tears. Her wet eyes were pleading.

"I know I should have spoken sooner but I've been so overwrought and really afraid. Thank you for visiting my family. It's so unfair you had to endure their neglect and rudeness. They do have a better side that surfaces on rare occasions, but it's not everyday wear. I'm really, really sorry, Guy."

Of all the things he had anticipated from Claire tonight, an apology hadn't been one.

"Claire, you've met my Aunt Helen. You've been given a taste of my sisters' histrionics and now my father's ignorant prejudice. No family is without blemish. Mine is quiet about it; yours isn't. That's all."

"You're telling me that the transgressions of our families are equal, but for the noise?"

"I honestly couldn't say with a tight-lipped family like mine. I have no idea what other offenses lay uncovered. But making this kind of comparison doesn't get us anywhere."

"You're right."

He took her gently by both shoulders and directed his eyes into hers.

"Claire, my love for you is greater having met your

family. When I look at the brave and compassionate person you are, despite all that, I'm filled with respect. You are just the woman for me."

The chicken roast would keep a little longer.

23

Written Proof

Guy's preoccupations with work deprived Claire of his company for yet another Sunday. It was just as well. She had promised to tell him nothing, for the time being, of her theory about Captain Crabbish. That promise was far harder to keep in Guy's presence. Yesterday's preoccupations with La Palourde and the Munros had kept the subject at bay. Today, she was free to give the Captain all her attention and resume the research begun so light-heartedly months ago. She spent all day revisiting her microfiche notes and studying several recent Crabbish letters she had wheedled from Patty. All the while, she kept one eye glued to the clock.

At 6:00 p.m., Claire stood before the door to the Fish House and knocked. Patty opened it and secured it behind her with a snap that rang loudly in the eerie silence. Claire had never been in the place when it wasn't bustling with people. Now at rest, its long history seemed to resound from its walls, despite the stillness of the place. Overturned chairs clung to the tabletops. The floor shone wet in the dim light. A sour mix of cleaning solutions hung in the air.

She wiped her feet and followed Patty into the office where a bottle of red Bordeaux sat on the desk next to two glasses and a cheese plate. Patty poured while Claire stretched her sweater over the back of the chair, slung her sack over one corner and withdrew a handful of papers. Then the two sat down and faced one another.

"Patty," Claire began, "I've been trying to determine, one way or the other, if the Captain's letters were typed on Ellie's machine. That unfinished housing letter I found amongst her stationery increased the probability, but without checking against a few of the Captain's recently published letters, I couldn't be certain."

"Until you asked to view several of his latest submissions, it never occurred to me to look more critically," said Patty. "I tend to look the other way where the Captain's identity is concerned." She read the question in Claire's eyes. "Yes, I do want to know what you've discovered."

"I compared the text in the housing letter against the samples you provided. Offhand, I couldn't see a difference in the type but wanted to be more scientific about it. First, I tried online typewriter simulators. Some come complete with sound effects to mimic the experience of a manual. Great fun. But when you print computer-generated text, neither an ink nor a laser printer leaves a tangible imprint on the back of the paper. Here's the January 26 original letter you loaned me, and here's a version I retyped and printed from the computer." She pulled these from the pile on her lap and handed them to Patty. "Feel the backs."

Patty did so.

"That circles us back to a manual typewriter. The heads or slugs…" Claire stopped and giggled at Patty's confused expression. "You see what a nerd I am. The head or slug is the end of the typebar that holds the letter form and strikes the paper rolled around the platen. It can leave an impression on the paper or even punch through, especially the period key. That's what you're feeling on the back of the housing and the recent letters, like Braille, proof it was typed manually."

Patty leaned forward.

"Okay, Claire, I'll give you that. The Captain used a manual typewriter. Now, let me play devil's advocate. Many people use manuals. There's even been a resurgence of their popularity in recent years."

"I had the same thought. That begs the question, did the originals come from Ellie's particular machine? Look again at the computer sheet. The online simulator replicates old fonts and the most common idiosyncrasies of old monotype machines, like uneven lines, uneven ink, overtyping and incomplete letters." She waited for Patty to examine the type. "What it can't do is recreate the idiosyncrasies unique to one particular typewriter."

Patty looked up, eyebrows raised. Claire shrugged.

"I've obviously read too much Sir Arthur Conan Doyle. His Sherlock innovated typewriting analysis."

Next to the January 26 original and its computer-printed counterpart, Claire slid a third sample to Patty.

"Just this morning, I typed this, a reproduction of the January 26 original in front of you, word for word, using Ellie's machine and stationery. It was uphill work to complete an identical and flawless duplicate. I'm not yet trained to this."

Patty set aside the computer-generated sheet to focus on the original and the reproduction from Ellie's machine.

"Compare them," urged Claire. "You'll find the typeface anomalies are the same. The 'y's' are elevated. The 'c's' and 'r's' hang low. And the 'o's' are incomplete. The head of the 'o' typebar on Ellie's machine is worn and needs to be replaced. And the period, in particular, pokes through. It's the same for the other originals you loaned me and for the housing letter as well."

Claire pulled them out, coupled with duplicates she had created on Ellie's machine, and spread them before Patty. Then, she grabbed some cheese and sipped wine to curb her impatience while Patty minutely studied the text.

Finally, Patty looked up.

"Yes, they appear to be the same."

"There's also the matter of the stationery," Claire went on. "Judging from the two recent originals, the Captain's letters were produced on the same paper as that in Ellie's stationery box." She waited while Patty fingered the sheets and checked the watermarks. "Add to that the fact that the Captain's language is grammatically correct, something Ellie was particularly qualified to produce. Someone used Ellie's machine to produce the Captain's letters. Who, if not Ellie?"

"I have no idea."

"Patty, we have to accept that all evidence supports Ellie being Captain Crabbish, assuming no one else has come forward."

Patty shook her head.

"No. No one has. I can't think of an argument against your theory, Claire, but if this is true, it puts me in a tight spot. I need time to think."

Claire departed soon after and left all the evidence with Patty. As she made her way home, she mulled over Patty's dilemma. The *Squawker* owner had two choices: reveal to *Squawker* readers that the Captain was no more or discreetly find a successor. The first threatened to doom the paper. The second, in a town where gossip spread like wildfire, was hard to imagine. How could a successor be kept under wraps enough to maintain the Captain's mystery? Almost three months had already passed since the Captain's last letter, aside from the March letter ghostwritten by the publisher in his name. If no one voluntarily came forward soon, Patty would be forced to take action.

Claire returned to work on Monday full of nothing but the Captain. Her co-workers, she found, were consumed with the subject as well. In the coffee room, they speculated openly about his long absence from the *Squawker*. As their theories got wilder, there was a great deal of laughter, but Claire sensed an underlying dispiritedness over the loss of their local crank. Captain Crabbish was, indeed, a bit of a crab. Claire chuckled to herself at the aptness of his name, for which her searches had yielded nothing. But he was their crab. In a town where tourists, businesses, and even natives came and went like the tide, the Captain had demonstrated staying power of more than a hundred years. His otherwise ordinary complaint letters to the editor of a small, local press had achieved an elevated status. Captain Crabbish had come to symbolize Mayenne Bay's resilient people and their belief in the popular voice. If coffee-room chat was any indication of town sentiment, his disappearance bordered on a personal affront.

Alone in her living room after work on Monday, Claire decided to pull out one of the books from the garage sale. She chose a 1911 first edition of *The Secret Garden*, by Frances Hodgson Burnett, a story she had read and cherished in childhood. She ran her hand over the crafted leather cover and examined the color plate centered on its face. Inside, there were captioned illustration plates, also in color. The book was in perfect condition. There wasn't a fold or stain or the slightest hint of a dog ear throughout. Judging from the ridiculously low prices at his garage sale, Jay couldn't have known the value of this pristine volume when he sold it, though monetary gain had not seemed foremost on his mind at the time. This book, like many others, had been a vestige of his life with Ellie that Jay could no longer bear to be around. As strongly today as the day she had acquired it, Claire felt more its custodian than its owner.

She leafed gently through the first few pages, taking time to fully appreciate their history and artistry before finally splaying the book to read. As it opened wide, a folded sheet of stationery slipped from the back pages. Claire opened it and read, in evenly spaced lines of elegant longhand, a well-written statement of support for a new town ordinance.

The lobster is an important source of food and a boon to our economy, a wild creature that should not be confined to a water tank. Leave it where God intended. Support the new ordinance to ban lobster pets.

No date. No signature.

Intrigued, she moved to her desk to run an internet search. With so little historical material digitized, she was surprised, thanks to a large out-of-state newspaper that had taken interest, to find a faded and wrinkled online photo of a boy and his pet lobster with a caption referring to the ordinance passed in Mayenne Bay in 1925. Claire looked again at the statement in her hand. It referred to the ordinance as "new", new as of 1925. Her eyes widened. This scrawl had to be nearly 100 years old. She held it close to the light to examine it more closely. The writer had used a fountain pen. Was Claire staring at a letter by Captain Crabbish, perhaps the very first, the original Captain? It was possible. The Captain had begun addressing letters to the editor in 1900. The writing in Claire's hand was created 25 years later. But if it was the work of the original Captain, what was it doing in Ellie's book? Was this further evidence of a connection between Ellie and the Captain? Was she correct that Ellie had been the original Captain's successor, once removed?

It niggled Claire at first that a 1925 letter to the editor, which she judged to be fairly formal correspondence for the time, hadn't been typed. Home and portable typewriters were already popular by then, but it didn't follow that every household had one. Perhaps the writer was simply in the habit of using longhand, as were many in the day. Perhaps his cursive, so clear and even—"a good hand", such skilled writing had been called—made typing unnecessary. Handwriting had gradually yielded over generations to a predominance of type which endured to this day. Cursive had dwindled, even more in recent years, to the extent of being removed from school curricula. Claire wondered just how many people today would be able to read "a good hand", let alone scratch like Annabelle's. But the unsigned missive before her had been drafted while handwriting was still in its heyday.

Interesting as they were, she brushed aside these tangential lines of thought as unproductive. What mattered was not the mechanics so much as the authenticity of the letter in her hand as further proof of the Ellie-Captain connection. She closed her eyes and mentally reviewed her perusals of old *Squawker* issues but couldn't recall a letter about pet lobsters, a topic she was sure would have raised a laugh and stuck in her mind. But the microfiche had been tedious, even hypnotic at times. Her eyes had blurred even with the aid of reading glasses. Maybe she had bypassed it in her befuddlement.

She bit off a chunk of dark chocolate and chewed while she thought about what to do.

Here she was, unwittingly drawn back to her theory because an old letter had been stuffed in Ellie's book. She went to the bookshelf, pulled Ellie's other books out one by one and gently flipped through the pages. Nothing slipped from among them except a single, folded sheet of carbon paper that descended to the floor at Claire's feet. She picked it up and carefully unfolded it. It, too, was written through in longhand, though not in the same good hand as the lobster letter. The carbon had undergone multiple uses, resulting in a confusion of overlaid cursive letters difficult to decipher.

Again, Claire resorted to the internet for information. Carbon paper was available in the early 20th century, though wax-based carbon was replaced by a polymer base in the 1950's. From the familiar feel of the carbon in her hand, Claire guessed the sheet was formed of the latter. The letter strokes on it were firm, the work of a strong pen, a manifold-nib fountain pen, known to work with carbon paper and available since the 1930's, or a ballpoint, introduced in 1945. Using Ellie's stationery, Claire tested her own vintage, Parker duo-fold fountain pen on a tiny, clear spot of the carbon sheet and immediately ruled it out. The pressure applied to the carbon was far more likely the product of a ballpoint.

But what did all this mean? Was it at all important? She didn't want to get lost down some rabbit hole born of her own imagination.

She dug out her reading glasses, flicked on the LED desk lamp-magnifier and bent the goose-neck to position the light and glass over the carbon. Then, she opened The Secret Garden book cover to the "ex libris" bookplate Ellie had affixed bearing her name in longhand. Claire compared the plate to the letters she could decipher on the carbon. That they were nothing alike made perfect sense. Why would Ellie crank out writing with a ballpoint pen when she had the comparative ease of her beloved Smith Corona? Claire worked until past midnight, bent over the hovering magnifier, trying to extract words of meaning from the carbon. Ellie Brown, in death, had turned out to be quite an enigma.

Next morning, despite her tired eyes, there was no avoiding the office. She blinked away the fatigue as she crunched numbers, chafing to get to the library every minute she sat at her desk, until Ricky stopped by. There was still no news of Valentina. His depression and exhaustion were manifest in his face and dropped shoulders. When he left, Claire suddenly felt ridiculous. She had no right to be in a fever over a worn-out carbon paper or a local crab in the face of this man's troubles. What was a little town newspaper intrigue compared to the loss of a daughter? She spent the rest of the day chastened, with a laser-like focus on her accounting work.

Guy continued to be unavailable that week, so Claire spent her Tuesday evening hours at the library. First, she asked Peggy for permission to rifle through the box of yet uncatalogued books Peggy had taken from the Brown garage sale. She found no more letters or carbons. Then, she scanned 1925 microfiche issues of the *Squawker* for a letter about the lobster pet ordinance. She found none, though she did find a short feature on the boy, probably the one in the photo, whose clandestine collection had ignited the controversy behind the new law. He had been discovered with a zinc bathtub full of the creatures at a time when sensitivities about the lobster population, after several years of cold Augusts had taken a toll on lobster larvae, had been high.

Interesting as the story was, it didn't prove the lobster

letter's authenticity, nor did it offer any clue to the name or whereabouts of the present-day Captain. After this anti-climactic conclusion, Claire turned again to the carbon but concluded the tangle of overwriting had reduced its content to useless gibberish.

Red herrings, just as she had feared.

Mind awhirl with disjointed information, she felt muddled. What Sherlock needed was Watson. She had to see Patty again if only to clear her head.

24

Memento Mori

Gloria shut the car door and ascended the front steps of the Mayenne Bay Historical Society building on Crest Street next to the library. The place consisted of a single, spacious room, formerly a used bookstore, that had been overhauled thanks to monetary and in-kind donations from supportive townspeople. The society itself subsisted on funding from membership fees, grants and ongoing generosity. Gloria had neither donated to its cause nor graced the museum with her presence before today but felt no qualm over these omissions. She gave more than enough to this town.

She had intentionally chosen a Friday afternoon for her errand, knowing Peggy Cyr would be working at the library and, consequently, absent from the museum. Gloria would rather suffer the ineptitude of a half-witted intern than deal with Peggy's smugness. Peggy, who had softened the blow for Nicky, the art fraudster. Peggy, who threw her influence behind the flawed "A Better Idea" project. Peggy, who had somehow figured out how to be content as a single, middle-aged woman in this suffocating town.

Gloria opened the glass door and stepped inside. To her

left hung a huge honor roll plaque listing the town's war dead. To her right was the work area reserved for administration and artifact curation, where Peggy's minion was rising from her computer station in answer to the old bell that had rung over the door. Along the side walls, extending to the far back, were permanent exhibits dedicated to Mayenne Bay's maritime history, French emigrés, the Wabanaki, the early frontier and daily life in general as once was. Framed maps, photos, documents, art and needlework of old were fitted in wherever space allowed. Three-dimensional pieces lined the floor below. Through the middle of the great room ran a row of table displays of old farm and fishing tools, basketry, textiles, pottery and antique housewares. The recently uncovered artist studio artifacts from the Rainwater shed were spread on the first of these. Had Gloria been inclined to appreciate what was, primarily, Peggy's handiwork, she would have marveled at such a sizeable and cross-representative collection of treasures in a town so small.

On the far back wall, on either side of a large, annotated town map, were pictures of the town's registered historic places. It was for this that Gloria had come, and she headed immediately in that direction. She had applied to the National Register of Historic Places to have the Town's End B&B designated as a historic site, constructed as it had been in 1819 by one of Mayenne Bay's early sea captains. Captain Campbell Adams had been an esteemed person, a town dignitary. He had commanded ships and invested in the town shipyard. He had been an authentic, enterprising personage quite distinct from the phony Captain Crabbish, whose impudent use of maritime rank was an insult, in her mind, to real seafaring heroes. The State Historic Preservation Officer had notified Gloria by email that the B&B would be evaluated at the next regular State Review Board meeting. She didn't doubt the outcome, despite the fact that Captain Adams had, like his compatriots of the time, transported goods—cotton, tobacco, sugar cane—produced by enslaved people down South and even slaves themselves. Adams was objectionable by today's standards but had been a significant player in Mayenne Bay's maritime past.

With the application process almost behind her, Gloria now sought a means to publicly advertise the B&B's historic status. The National Register offered no official recognition program, but the Mayenne Bay Historical Society had established conformities for recognition of historic sites within the town's borders. Gloria sought the sourcing details to purchase a commemorative plaque. She also wanted assurance that the B&B would be incorporated into the museum display and the map of historic places, once the property was formally registered, in time for the upcoming tourist season.

She examined the back wall thoroughly and helped herself to a free historic site map before making her way to the maritime exhibit to satisfy herself that Captain Adams occupied a sufficiently distinguished place there. She took a photo of the display to blow up for the wall of her B&B, then headed for Peggy's underling, who stood in expectation at the front counter.

The young woman was pretty, overweight, oddly coifed and bespectacled. Her bright expression didn't dim as Gloria insolently scrutinized her from the top buttons of her mandala-patterned dress and brown leather bomber jacket right down to her black army boots. Gloria suppressed a snort at the sight and prepared for a dearth of intelligence, another of Peggy's pathetic charity cases. The woman's name tag read "Quince Greene, Intern".

Quince stood, smiling, and gripped the pendant hanging from a ribbon on her neck while she discreetly regulated her breathing. At the sound of Gloria's entry, she had immediately flipped off her New Age music and risen from her chair to greet the first, perhaps the only, visitor of the day. Gloria had ignored her and headed straight to the back of the museum. Quince knew of the B&B owner by reputation and would not, under any circumstances, allow Gloria's arrogance to disrupt the free flow of chi she had achieved in her morning meditation. Nor would she sully her own karma by responding to the negative woman in-kind.

"Good morning," Quince greeted Gloria, her hand tightly clasping the pendant. "I'm Quince Greene, the society's intern. How can I help?"

"Gloria Townsend," Gloria introduced herself curtly in return, "owner of the Town's End B&B. I'm here for information on historic building plaques and to apply for inclusion on the back wall and the historic site map." She slapped the free map onto the counter. "I'm expecting approval of my registration any day now."

Quince recited a calming chant in her head as, with quiet efficiency, she supplied Gloria with the necessary assistance. The transaction took place so quickly and smoothly that Gloria was out the door before she understood it was over.

"Have a wonderful day, Ms. Townsend," Quince sang melodically to Gloria's back, well aware that she had just dumbfounded the woman Captain Crabbish wanted to vote off the mainland.

In the wake of Gloria's visit, Quince wandered the place, repeating the chant aloud this time to clear Gloria's disruptive vibrations. Once satisfied, she made a cup of chocolate peppermint tea, resumed her seat in front of the computer and clicked on some soothing native American flute music.

Despite the game face she had maintained in Gloria's presence, Quince felt painfully conscious that Gloria had judged her a simpleton among other uncomplimentary things. She was accustomed to being underestimated. Something about her appearance—her cherubic face, her weight, her unconventional style—immediately threw her IQ into question. Few hung around to discover the substance beneath. Most simply gawked and gave her up as an airhead. The mystery to Quince was why people didn't look past the obvious to the underlying person, as she did.

She again grabbed hold of the St. Jude medallion that hung from her neck. She had chosen this symbol without regard to any religion, not because St. Jude was patron saint of impossible causes but because he was also a symbol of choosing faith when all seemed lost. It was to this charm that she clung to maintain her faith in humanity and to guard herself from the dispiriting effects of others' judgment, like Gloria's.

All this left Quince feeling lonely and apart. Somewhere, she was sure, awaited her soulmate. The one who would caress her face and cuddle her soft body. The one who would appreciate her style, brains and kindness. The one who would share her music and laugh at her jokes. Her split-apart, her match on the Zodiac. Every day during morning yoga meditation, Quince raised imaginary antennae to signal through the ethers for her true mate. She spent the rest of her waking hours in a state of constant expectation. She had reached her twenty-fifth year with no results, but time, as Einstein had told the world, was relative. Maybe her mate's arrival wasn't late; maybe Quince's anticipation was just premature.

Quince held in reserve a secret for the day her soulmate arrived. She had been told by a very reliable psychic—the best two hundred dollars she had ever spent—that she was a reincarnated victim of the French revolutionary guillotine and, before that, had been forced to contribute her skull to the Aztec Tenochtitlan's display dedicated to the gods of war and rain. Knowledge of these two past lives, experiences when head had been ceremoniously separated from body, had led to Quince's fascination with skulls. She regarded them as sacred former receptacles of the living and was continually amazed that something so plainly dead could provoke such deep contemplation of life. She privately looked forward to celebrations like All Souls Day and Día de Muertos, the Day of the Dead, with its elegant skull, La Calavera Catrina.

Her affinity for skulls had led her to sketch and paint them. As she rendered their contours and cavities on paper and canvas, she meditated deeply on human life and its brevity. In this, she had much company among artists, so many of whom embraced the skull in their work. The Dutch masters. Cezanne. Van Gogh. Picasso. Indigenous peoples. The Hindu. The skull was a constant reminder of human mortality and, at the same time, an ironic souvenir of life, a symbol of passing and an affirmation of having existed.

Experience had taught Quince to keep her enchantment with skulls low key. She never raised the subject. She had yet to display her art. She occasionally wore skull jewelry or images on her clothing, but not as a rule. The only regular hint of her captivation was a black memento mori ring, inlaid with gold skulls, on her right-hand ring finger.

Quince had another secret that had stopped being secret just a few months ago: she was an over-the-top, all-out, self-taught computer geek, a fact she had learned to hide to avoid unending requests for free help. Her particular interests were the digital reconstruction of faces from skulls and their identification through facial recognition software. It was a narrow specialization, one she had intended to conceal from the historical society. But when she had learned these very skills were sought by the local police in connection with the skull found on Louis Rainwater's property, Quince had been too intrigued to hold back. She relished the chance, however remote, to breathe life back into a bodiless skull by giving it a name and a past. Even now, she was experimenting with open-source facial recognition apps to identify the facial image provided by Officer Tripp's forensics colleague.

Despite her aptitude and affinity for technology, Quince didn't rely on it alone. In a town where the grapevine was vibrant and many didn't have home computers, she had found that a hard copy image circulated fast. She had posted the unidentified face in the *Bayside Squawker* captioned "Do you know this person?", thinking it would be a long shot. Almost every day since, she had received responses suggesting the face resembled someone's ancestor or a historical personage hereabouts. It was a slow process, but better than shoving the image in a file for eternity without any attempt to learn its name.

In Mayenne Bay itself, speculation about the skull's identity had reached an intensity equaled only by the impassioned theories about the Captain's whereabouts. And Quince's outreach had given her an unexpected connection to the community, a sense of belonging that, to a remarkable extent, offset her loneliness. She aligned daily with the universe but also tuned into the lifeline of Mayenne Bay.

She returned to her desk, where she found another email about the photo. A shiver ran up her spine. It was thrilling how a single skull could generate so much liveliness. She sensed that people were digging through their attics this very minute.

25

Port Clyde

The second half of May passed by in a blur of paint and canvases, frustrating Claire's further progress on the Captain. Guy, increasingly uptight about the Port Clyde exhibit, fell into a state of complete disorganization. Claire stepped in to keep up the loft, do laundry and make meals during her off-hours. She ran errands and gathered together business cards, price tags, picture-hanging hardware and other miscellany for the show. She even helped title paintings when Guy struggled to find words enough.

On the Thursday preceding Memorial Day weekend, Claire took the afternoon off and accompanied Guy to the Port Clyde House where they were met at the door by Georgia Wilson.

"As you can see," Georgia said, with a broad sweep of her arm toward the exhibit room, "all we need now is your art on the walls."

Though Guy and Claire had seen photos of the original house and occasional renovation progress shots posted on the PortClydeHouseReboot website, nothing had prepared them for the full effect of the restorations. The ceilings were a warm white, and the walls ivory, to amplify reflective light without overpowering the eye. Streamlined track lighting ran across each wall above a system of gallery rails and adjustable hanging rods. The large windows had been replaced in keeping with the historical status of the house. The polished wood floor creaked beneath a huge, nautically-themed area carpet in muted blues, greys and greens. The combined effect was a calm and inviting openness and an underlying, renaissance vitality, the same energies radiating from Georgia's eyes.

Madeline Littlefield, Georgia's daughter, and Nicky Littlefield, Georgia's granddaughter, emerged from the kitchen.

"Maddy and Nicky, how nice to see you again. You made quite a drive all the way from Fort Kent," said Claire.

"The revival of this house has historical and sentimental meaning for the whole Littlefield family," Maddy gushed.

"Wouldn't miss it," Nicky said. "This is a family legacy. One day, I want to put my own work on these walls."

Nicky was a promising artist herself, as she had proven to them all last summer when she had doctored a few paintings not her own under the pseudonym of Monique LaBelle. Today, in her T-shirt and worn jeans, she looked a far cry from the diva-like artist she had once pretended to be. Nicky had long since made amends for her deceptions accepted by everyone in Mayenne Bay with the obstinate exception of Gloria Townsend.

Under Georgia's watchful eye, the other four unloaded Guy's paintings from the car, unboxed them and set them on the floor along the walls. Claire pulled the entrance door closed just as Guy gingerly added the last painting to the lineup. There were a few minutes of silence while they all stood back to view the twenty canvases of varied sizes, each portraying a Maine seascape or landscape in Guy's signature style.

"Guy, these are fabulous," Georgia exclaimed, pressing her palms together.

Her reaction was echoed by the others.

He acknowledged their enthusiasm with a slight nod and a weak smile, entirely lost for words. Though grateful for the four fans before him, looming self-doubt took the shine from their seals of approval. He flushed. He could barely breathe. At this, his debut solo exhibit, where he hoped to exude professional confidence, he felt less like an accomplished man of 31 years than a little boy at his first piano recital. How did other artists do it? Impatient to siphon the nervous energy from his frame, a technique he learned from Claire, he reached for the first painting and lifted it to the wall with a glance at Georgia for approval of its placement.

The team spent the next several hours arranging, hanging and labeling the exhibit. Maddy and Nicky, in turn, handed Guy his paintings. Georgia, increasingly excited with every addition to the walls, wielded the measuring tape. Guy adjusted the length of the rods to fit and hang the work. Claire followed behind straightening the paintings, affixing name and price tags and cleaning up packaging materials as she went. By five o'clock, the full collection was up. They all stood back to enjoy it while they helped themselves to drinks and snacks.

The reception for Guy's Port Clyde House exhibit was scheduled for Saturday evening, just two days later, starting at four o'clock. Guy and Claire returned early that afternoon to assist Georgia, Maddie and Nicky with last minute arrangements. When they all slipped upstairs to wash and change, Claire hung back, fussing with the flower bouquet on the entranceway table. Guy looked at her questioningly.

"I want to take a minute by myself while everything's quiet," she told him. "I'll be right up."

From her position near the front door, Claire took in the entryway, where huge colorful tributes to Creative Agenda and to Roxie's Frames advertised their businesses' sponsorships of this premier event. These, along with other posters and guides, had been produced by Guy's hand as fully as the paintings in the adjacent exhibit room. Claire perceived the stark difference between the striking, illustrative designs and the artistic sensibility on the canvases and marveled that these could be the work of the same man.

She strode forward to take in the collective body of Guy's paintings. Until this event, Claire had viewed his works singly or a few at a time. Twenty paintings gathered in one space revealed so much more about the artist. She roved from canvas to canvas, then planted herself in the center of the room and cast around for an overall sense of the art. At the Mayenne Bay Art Show last summer, she had claimed to detect the influence of artists' personalities in their work. This evening, she felt all the more that her observation had merit.

Like the artist himself, Guy's paintings were plain to see and understand without the need for interpretation or trendy art-speak. There was a comfortable allure about them, a gentleness infused in each canvas that marked each as Guy's own. Even the nocturne of the Bash bonfire, with its stark contrasts of flickering flames and pitch darkness, had a quality that didn't emanate from the scene alone. Honest but not overconfident. Soulful but not sappy. Inviting but not overwhelming. Guy's talent lit the room pianissimo, and Claire basked in it. She headed for the stairwell, unable to suppress a giggle. Even in her own head, she sounded like a pretentious gallery owner. Guy, she was sure, would roll his eyes.

Georgia and Maddie returned downstairs in classic black pants and white blouses. Georgia had added a multi-colored scarf for flair. Nicky appeared in a simple, green A-line dress that offset her red hair, now in a braided updo. Guy wore the black polo shirt and black slacks Claire had purchased for him after looking into his woefully deficient wardrobe, dressy, by Guy's standards, without sacrificing comfort. Anything more formal had been out of the question. Claire returned last in black capris and an elegant, silk turquoise top that ruffled at the sleeves and bottom.

"Where did this come from?" Guy asked.

She frowned.

"Too much?"

"It's a good look for you."

Her shoulders relaxed.

"I bought it special. I thought the partner of an artist should look the part, you know, show some creativity and color in her presentation. The boring tones of the accountant take a back seat tonight."

Before Guy had a chance to pursue her use of the word "partner", the voices of Meilin and Roxie called from the doorway. There were greetings and hugs all around.

"Guy," said Meilin as her eyes roved the room, "this opening has you all over it, starting right at the front door. Graphics work, setup, paintings. Very impressive."

Coming from a former gallery owner with a keen eye for optics, this was a high compliment.

"You can't get away from him tonight," joked Claire to cover for Guy's lockjaw. "He wanted to make the hors d'oeuvres, too, but we needed to draw the line somewhere."

The laughter was interrupted by more arrivals.

"Here comes the rest of the Mayenne Bay invasion," remarked Claire.

Guy froze in the center of the exhibit room and stared

at the parade pouring through the entrance.

Sandra and Louis. Peggy, Quince and Patty. Ben and Rhonda with Annabelle in tow, a special request from Claire. Celeste with Jerome, Denise and newborn Lilou. Thomas and Beatrice. Christy and Ken. Ricky and Celia. Morrie and Mary Bouchard. Bruce Raymond. Even John Mills, aka Pierre Cliché, showed up in mismatched, but clean, attire, free of paint.

A few minutes later, Geoffrey Bristolwaite appeared in the doorway followed by other artists from up and down the Maine coast and even Monhegan Island. There were dignitaries invited by Georgia—officials, teachers, professors, gallery owners and art collectors—and several journalists who got right to work snapping photos for features on the Port Clyde House opening and its first exhibitor, Guy Gardiner.

Anna Gardiner appeared, hand in hand with Asad and accompanied by Joy. Minutes later, Mr. and Mrs. Gardiner followed, the time lapse between their respective arrivals a telling sign of the chasm between parents and daughters. Claire, marveling that Mrs. Gardiner had convinced her husband to come, greeted them all warmly but turned away from the family's saga. This was Guy's night, and she meant to keep it that way.

Guy's feet remained cemented to the floor in the face of the oncoming tide of people, overly conscious of his "Featured Artist" name tag and in a state of complete confusion. Should he stand at the door like a Walmart greeter? Usher guests to view paintings? Pitch sales? He reflexively smiled and shook hands. The faces swirling around him left him dizzy, so he anchored his gaze onto one of his paintings. This proved more a torment than a salvation; he suddenly saw nothing but flaws, enough to feel the urge to pull it down from the wall.

"Here," Claire whispered and handed over a glass of

iced tea.

Guy gripped the glass so hard he jostled the liquid, which spilled onto his shoe. Claire laid a comforting hand on his lower back.

"Catch your breath and try to get rid of the deer-in-the-headlights look. The work is done, Guy, and well done at that. All you have to do tonight is coast. Remember that we're here about art and Georgia's Port Clyde House. You can talk about those until the cows come home."

She waited until he made eye contact with her and held her gaze for a few moments to steady himself before she advanced to the door to greet Daniel and his new flame, Paul. Claire returned again to Guy's side and took his arm.

Georgia tapped the mic and called for quiet.

"You can't imagine how heartened I am to see such a gathering at the revival of my grandmother's Port Clyde House and to spotlight, as our opening and inaugural exhibit, the beautiful art of Guy Gardiner."

Applause followed, and a few calls of "Hear, hear".

Guy turned beet red and pasted the requisite look of gracious acknowledgment on his face, praying Georgia would not, God forbid, ask him to speak. His prayer was answered. From the hint of a smile on Claire's lips, he guessed he needn't have worried. Claire, his angel, his partner, had made sure of it. With her next to him as co-pilot, Guy managed to get through the rest of the evening with a reasonable degree of poise.

By the time he awoke the next morning, his body was clear of rigidity but felt like the aftermath of a mad workout at the gym. He laid there, immobile, and soaked in the quiet of Claire's apartment for some time before rising. Faces and conversations from last night's reception flooded back to him, oddly much clearer the morning after. Two of his paintings had sold. He could hardly believe it. He had met gallery owners interested in representing him. And he had connected with so many Maine artists formerly unknown to him, he had lost count. His eyes flicked to the pile of business cards on the bedside table.

From the kitchen, he could hear the tell-tale sounds of a breakfast underway. No matter how late she retired the night before, Claire didn't like to miss the morning. She was probably already dressed and well into her agenda for the day. Before joining her, he would grab a shower to ready his head for the barrage of thoughts she had accumulated since she first opened her eyes.

At the sound of the shower, Claire set Guy's teapot to brew, then pulled out the blueberry popovers warming in the oven, wrapped them in a cloth and set them in a basket on the table. Butter, jam and lemon curd followed. She was glad he had overslept. After months of build-up to the show and the surfeit of people and talk, he had returned home exhausted. The limelight had conflicted with his natural introversion and humility, and the inner battle had drained him. It was one of life's incongruities, this tug-of-war between his unassuming personality and the public exposure of his talent, but Guy would eventually find his balance. Claire took heart that, no matter what his success, he would never be spoiled by artistic egotism.

It was just past noon when, rested and fed, they reached the loft to clean the mess left in the wake of packing for the exhibit. Guy brought out a few LPs to play and, in between clean-up, twirled Claire to Sinatra Swings tunes. It took more than an hour to restore the tiny living space to rights, then Guy turned to organize the work area.

"I'm not much help there. I'm going to pop over to Annabelle's with these extra popovers," Claire said, then shook her head. "Did I really just say that?"

"You did."

They both laughed.

"What would a neuro-linguist say about unpremeditated

puns?"

"What would a psychologist say? Add that to your cookie addiction and compulsive people-watching and you're probably in a classification by yourself. They'll need to update the diagnostic manual."

Claire threw him a face and left.

Annabelle was the ultimate test for Claire's attempts at authentic Maine dishes. She had approved Claire's homemade baked beans, New England clam chowder and haddock tacos. She had devoured her ployes and fish pot pie. Claire felt she was passing an important test by winning the culinary blessing of this old Maine native. As she approached the landlady's door with the basket of popovers, she could already hear the whistle of the tea kettle. As usual, Annabelle had anticipated her.

"Oh, I do love blueberry popovers," Annabelle exclaimed, palms together in glee.

Claire helped prepare a tray of plates, napkins, butter and jams and carried it into the living room. Each woman sank into a worn armchair, Claire with a mug of strong, black coffee and Annabelle with a teacup and saucer. Annabelle dug into the popovers, chattering between swallows, energized by the company. Claire listened to the pent-up news she had collected since the last visit. The years hadn't sapped this old woman of the strength of her opinions, nor had her isolation on this rural spot off Union Road stopped her from keeping close tabs on Mayenne Bay. Claire let her talk until she tired, then found her opening.

"Annabelle, since you told me your maiden name is Boisvert," she said, the images of Annabelle with Kitty at the Christmas party and Ellie's funeral resurfacing in her mind, "I've been curious about it. 'Greenwood' is 'Boisvert', anglicized. That's Kitty's last name. Is that just by chance?"

Annabelle, who had flowed freely about herself and her history during all of Claire's visits, squinted her eyes with a wariness Claire had never seen before.

"Why are you asking that?"

She set down her cup with a demonstrative clack and scrutinized Claire. Seeing she had struck a nerve, Claire proceeded carefully.

"After we talked, I researched the difficult history of the French in Maine. I can't imagine what you and your family went through back then. The names Boisvert and Greenwood came back to me. I wondered when and how names like that might have diverged into the two languages, or if they came from different sources altogether. I didn't get very far on that score but I did stumble on Kitty's property in the town tax records. It's listed under the name of Katherine Boisvert, not Kitty Greenwood. But let's talk no more about it if the subject upsets you, Annabelle."

Claire leaned back into the chair and sipped her coffee, awaiting the verdict.

"Kitty said you was nosy."

"She's right. I'm very interested in people but only to understand them better, not for nefarious reasons or to gossip or anything."

She endured more of Annabelle's scrutiny without speaking another word. Annabelle broke the silence.

"Kitty is my cousin. Her real name is Katherine Boisvert, but people hereabouts know her only as Kitty Greenwood. She don't want that to change."

Annabelle glared at Claire, who crossed her heart with her finger to signal her secrecy. Annabelle sipped tea for some time in silence in an obvious struggle over how much more to reveal. She decided to trust Claire.

"Poor Kitty came here from Washington County after a wicked brush with fire," Annabelle said, tears forming in her eyes. "She was just ten and home alone when the old woodstove caught on. Katherine—Kitty—got out with burns on her face and head, and the house was heavily damaged. Her parents blamed her, accused her of playing with fire, even though the fire chief said that the stove was very unsafe. The burns was bright red and really painful for a long time and made her look freakish. Her hair wouldn't grow right. Kids teased her. People stared and hounded her all over town. As soon as she was old enough—well, she was still a kid, really—she came here and started over as Kitty Greenwood. That's why she wears the wig and make-up. Keeps her real name quiet."

Annabelle's face was sadder now than Claire had ever seen it except at Ellie's funeral.

"How awful. And she worked at the Fish House all these years in that wig and make-up."

"Ayup. Worked hard. Turned bitter. Stayed a loner, except for Ellie and me."

"Ellie Brown?"

"Ellie Boisvert Brown, Kitty's older sister. They kept that pretty secret, too, to protect Kitty's identity. Ellie was meant to be home the night of the fire but she left Kitty alone to step out with Jay. Never forgave herself."

Claire covered her mouth with her hand.

"Ellie took care of Kitty the rest of her life. Bought her that house on Bayberry Lane. Paid the mortgage and taxes all these years. Her life insurance covered the balance plus an allowance for Kitty's old age. That's when Kitty decided to retire."

Staring over her coffee mug at the far wall, Claire thought through all she had just heard. The odd and exclusive coterie of the three women, Annabelle, Ellie and Kitty, at the Whispering Seabreeze Christmas party came into focus, as did Kitty's standoffishness at the Fish House in light of her terrible scars. No doubt she endured unwanted commentary on her wig and makeup, not to mention speculation about her origins and age. No wonder Kitty filled her home with cats instead of people.

Claire herself had shared in perverse speculation about Kitty, conduct she now sorely regretted. She had been repulsed by Kitty's cat-filled house, that life-saving gift of shelter provided by penitent and generous Ellie, set back as it was from the beaten path to protect her sister from oglers. Its condition was, Claire decided, less a commentary on Kitty's slovenliness or negligence than a reflection of how she must have viewed life all these years. And now, Kitty was more alone than ever, bereft of her sister and benefactor, with only Jay, Annabelle and her mangy cats for company. Claire felt overwhelming shame over her judgments and filled with sadness for this brave and outcast woman.

"Annabelle, thank you. What you just told me is heartbreaking. No matter what Kitty thinks of me, I'll be a better neighbor to her knowing her history. I promise to tell no one but Guy."

Annabelle saw Claire to the door, where the women hugged affectionately. Claire left behind the remaining popovers and rejoined Guy at the loft. He had cleared the final clutter and just brewed a steaming cup of chamomile. He listened and yawned through Claire's repetition of Kitty's story, then swearing himself to secrecy, stretched himself out on the love seat for a much-needed nap.

26

Rumors

The Monday following the Port Clyde reception was Memorial Day. Claire had kept the day clear just in case the art exhibit proved a disappointment. Happily, Guy had been pleased as a clam at high tide over the show and had needed nothing more the day after than a cleaning assistant and some sleep. Today, he would tackle his backlog of graphics arts projects. Claire had the day to herself.

She rose at sunrise, 4:59 a.m. on this morning so close to the summer solstice, and took a leisurely walk along the waterside, then relaxed on a bench watching the bay until the Fish House opened its doors. Not many stirred at this hour. Blue Bickford, the harbormaster, was among the exceptions, though she wasn't yet on the job. Claire watched her climb aboard her red boat with two large takeout coffees from the Main Street Coffeehouse.

Once inside the Fish House, she found Ricky and Celia already seated at a front table. They signaled to her to join them. Before she dropped into the chair, Celeste had already arrived with the coffee pot.

"I keep hearing that false rumor about you, Claire," she said in a voice unusually loud and clear. "It makes me so angry. I'm one of the people you helped in confidence. I've never met a more trustworthy person."

Claire looked astounded at this formal speech but caught the waitress's sideways glance toward one of the booths. There sat Erin, clearly picking up every word which, Claire guessed, had been Celeste's aim. Ricky and Celia looked nonplussed after Celeste sped away to the kitchen.

"Remember I told you I revealed Valentina's health condition to Officer Tripp?" Claire quietly said to Ricky and Celia, who both nodded. "Well, I was apparently overheard stressing that the information was confidential, and it got about that I was spilling a secret. Two people were within earshot." She jerked her head toward Erin. "The other was Kitty, who's been telling whoever will listen that I'm not to be trusted."

Celia took Claire's hand.

"We understand exactly what you did and why, Claire," she said in a volume meant to be heard. "We don't have a single reservation about your integrity."

"None at all," said Ricky, even louder.

After Erin rose to leave, Celia spoke again.

"Ricky has had to correct this slander more than once at work."

"Thank you, Ricky," Claire said, as they all watched Erin exit.

"Claire, I'll repeat again, beware of that woman," Ricky said, his voice now returned to a more conversational level. "She has a grudge against you and will use anything to diminish your standing at work. She's aware not only that you wanted her job, but that you disapproved her hire."

"Believe me, she's done nothing to mask her dislike. What makes you think that's the basis for it?"

Ricky shrugged.

"IT people are like servants. People forget we're in the room when they're talking."

After breakfast, which featured lengthy speculation about Valentina's whereabouts, Claire headed home, where she packed up leftover Manhattan clam chowder and homemade cheddar-and-bacon biscuits from yesterday's supper to bring to Guy and Annabelle. Manhattan-style was Claire's preferred chowder, though she was careful not to broadcast the fact too widely. It was blasphemy in Maine to make anything other than the creamy, New England version. She had gone so far as to dare Annabelle to try the Manhattan version, and Annabelle had accepted the challenge.

She stopped first at Guy's loft to make sure he was getting along. He was immersed in work and had little time for anything other than a hug and kiss, so she left him some soup and biscuits and headed for Annabelle's.

Annabelle didn't appear at the door as she usually did. This minor alteration in the behavior of an elderly woman with regular habits alarmed Claire. She held her breath, knocked again and cracked open the door, fearful of what she might find inside. Annabelle sat in her favorite armchair with a cup of tea and box of tissues on the TV tray in front of her.

"Annabelle?" Claire said softly, not wanting to startle her. "Annabelle?"

She turned her head toward Claire. Her face was blotchy, and she sniffled and dabbed her nose with an over-used tissue.

Claire unloaded the items she carried onto the floor and approached.

"What's wrong?"

Annabelle shook her head but wasn't inclined to explain. Large tears filled her eyes, though they didn't obscure her vision. She pointed at the insulated bag Claire had set down.

"What have you brought?"

"I have biscuits and some Manhattan clam chowder for you to try."

Claire's tone was taunting, and the corner of her mouth turned up into a devilish half-smile. Annabelle snorted.

"That ain't real chow-duh."

"Let's see what you think after you taste it. But first, I brought this over to talk to you about it."

She reached for Ellie's typewriter case, set it on a corner of the dining room table and removed the cover. Judging from the state of the table, the old woman had been spending a good deal of time immersed in nostalgia. Photo albums were piled, some splayed, atop old newspaper clippings and letters written in Annabelle's almost illegible longhand. The clean freak in Claire threatened to impulsively scoop everything up and restore order, but she held it in check and tucked her hands in her pockets for good measure.

"This machine was Ellie's. Jay sold it to me. He couldn't stand looking at it, he said. I feel uncomfortable keeping it without first offering it to you now that I know you and Ellie were related. Kitty has her own typewriter. I saw it on the desk in her house. Judging from how well Ellie kept this one, it had to be one of her prized possessions. It should be with family, if they want it. I also bought a number of Ellie's books. Some are first editions and worth something. If you're interested in looking those over, I can get them from the car."

While Claire arranged servings of soup and biscuits on the TV trays, Annabelle rose to inspect the machine. She stroked its sides tenderly and began to cry again, then replaced the cover with a negative shake of her head. As with Jay, it seemed the presence of Ellie's typewriter brought only pain. Ellie had passed almost six months ago, but Claire felt she should have realized Annabelle would still be grieving.

"You keep it," Annabelle said. "I can't type. I write by hand."

"I've seen your writing. I'm still trying to read that cookie recipe," Claire joked, hoping to tease Annabelle into a better state of mind.

At this, the old woman looked at Claire through watery eyes, then began to rummage through the memorabilia on the table. She carefully selected some photos before she sat down to soup and biscuits. As they ate, she passed the photos to Claire, who recognized younger versions of Annabelle, Ellie and Kitty at a time preceding the terrible fire that had so disfigured Kitty.

"This is how I like to remember them…us," Annabelle said. "We was so close back then. That fire changed everything. We wasn't so carefree after that."

They ate in silence for a while. Annabelle downed several biscuits and heartily ate Claire's soup. She refused to call it chowder, though she gave it a grudging nod of approval. Then, she rose again, this time to pick through the piles for some letters, and began to talk at length about Ellie. Claire became so absorbed, she let Annabelle spout for over an hour before she realized the time.

Far later than planned, Claire raced home with her head full of all she had just heard from Annabelle. It took a real act of will to push all that aside for now. Today was the final day to register for the art show. In fact, barely two hours remained until the deadline and, as registrar, she was going to have to scramble. Her phone buzzed with texts alerting her to the stragglers whose submissions had come through just this afternoon. She had to process their applications before five o'clock, then shut down registrations.

At home, she opened her tablet and accepted submissions by several artists unknown to her before turning to an entry from Quince Greene, the latest art club member. Claire almost jumped back when the image of Quince's "Forget-Me-Not" popped open to full-screen size. She hadn't suspected Quince had this kind of artistic talent. She had used colored pencils to render a realistic skull, with a third eye on its forehead. It looked almost alien. The eye and two empty sockets stared out from a foundling-type basket lined in a green cloth and adorned with a small bunch of forget-me-not flowers. Around the skull and basket floated artifacts: a compass, an old key, a magnifying glass and a puzzle piece. A three-eyed skull in a basket seemed an odd choice of subject matter for a seaside art show, but Claire's place was to enroll, not to judge. She clicked "accept".

Claire turned to the last entry and the second surprise among the latecomers: a submission from Gloria Townsend. Gloria had not participated in last year's art show, so Claire had never before seen evidence of her talent. She had painted a realistic watercolor of the B&B, with sunlight illuminating the yellow clapboard siding and white porch. It was quite well done. A plaque next to the front door distinctly read "1819". The digital image of the painting was, Claire noted, the first among all she had processed to bear a watermark. In a note in the comments section of the application, Gloria indicated that only prints, not the original painting, would be offered for sale at the show.

Though the clock was rapidly ticking toward the five o'clock deadline, Claire had no choice but to delay and defer this deviation to the art show committee. She texted Meilin, Roxie and Peggy a request to view the submission, then immediately made her way to Creative Agenda to meet them. The doorbell sounded as Claire entered the store where she found the three already in conference around Gloria's image on Meilin's tablet.

"So, you've seen it," said Claire.

"Leave it to Gloria to muck up the proceedings with a

last-minute wrench in the works," Roxie grumbled.

Meilin, who had been scrolling through the art show rules, looked up and sighed.

"The rules say all submissions must be original work, but they don't explicitly state the original must be offered for sale, though it seems to me that is implicit in the arrangement."

"Yes," Roxie said. "One would think entrants would take that for granted, as the show is a fundraiser. But this is Gloria."

"The rule is arguably ambiguous. We'll have to accept the submission as is this year and edit the rule for next year's show. It's too late to issue a clarification this year," Peggy said.

"Agreed," answered Meilin. "No other artist made this stipulation, so Gloria's entry is the only one in question. We have an irritant, not a mutiny, on our hands."

"We could tag her painting 'Original not for sale' and offer one print, displayed by its side," Roxie suggested. "Keeps the committee from acting as her print broker."

Claire intervened.

"I understand the reluctance to act as broker, but if the goal is to raise money, wouldn't the sale of multiple prints be more advantageous to the show? She'd have to share the same fifty-percent commission. And it's only for this year. The committee won't be setting a precedent if the rule is later clarified."

"A reasonable argument," Meilin said, brow furrowed.

"I didn't approve her entry," Claire told them, with a quick glance at the clock, "pending your approval."

Meilin's face changed. She seemed to have come to a decision.

"Gloria submitted her entry at 3:47 p.m. knowing full well the deadline was 5:00 p.m. today, and we would have little to no time to object. The app isn't set up for meaningful back and forth in any case, but we're out of time. Even if we mean to accept this, I don't think we should do so without first putting Gloria through a few hoops. We shouldn't allow a sneaky, last-minute strike to be an easy win."

She grabbed her phone and texted a request to Gloria to meet with the committee immediately at Creative Agenda or risk having her entry rejected.

"Let's see if she can manage the same tight squeeze she handed to us."

Meilin's phone buzzed.

"She's on her way, almost as if she was expecting to be summoned."

"Of course, she was," said Peggy.

"A setup," groaned Roxie. "This'll be fun."

"The by-laws include the caveat that any entry can be rejected at the sole discretion of the committee," Meilin reminded them, "but I don't want to invoke that rule arbitrarily or just because Gloria is behaving like…well, a brat. Our decision has to make sense not just today, but for future shows."

"That loophole may be the only thing that saves us if she makes a fuss," Peggy said.

"Count on it," muttered Roxie.

"Claire, do you mind staying?" asked Meilin. "As you're the registrar, I think it's appropriate. And the more heads in the room, the better."

"Okay, if you want, but you heard her the night I was voted into the art club. She's not my greatest fan. My presence may not help."

Twenty minutes later, Gloria entered the store with a half smirk and a defiant posture, clearly surprised to find the full committee assembled and in qualified agreement to her proposal. She must, they insisted, submit an ample supply of prints for sale at the show in order to gain their approval.

Gloria hesitated at first but finally agreed to their terms and departed in a triumphant swagger to her car.

"She showed up loaded for bear, expecting a battle," Roxie observed. "We surprised her with a ready compromise."

"She got exactly what she wanted," said Meilin, waving a hand toward the window, "and caught us fair and square. We can't deny she's clever."

"You mean devious."

Meilin turned to her tablet to add the committee's caveat to the comments section before approving Gloria's entry and shutting down registration. Then, she pulled up the upcoming art show committee agenda and added a new topic, a proposal to modify the show's by-laws for next season.

Gloria pulled away from Creative Agenda delighted at having rocked the boat and perturbed Meilin and her holier-than-thou cronies. She had submitted her painting solely to advertise her B&B, with the secondary motive of drawing attention to prints for sale. Both would be achieved, even bolstered, by the committee's acquiescence to her entry terms. She also had ambitious hopes that her excellent painting—she knew her own talent—would place this year, especially as the committee had engaged an unbiased outsider as judge, Geoffrey Bristlewaite. For the first time in a long time, Gloria felt things had shifted somewhat in her favor.

Bayside Squawker, June 5

Readers,

Once again, the geese are overtaking the park and leaving droppings all over the walking trail and wharf. This is unhygienic and unattractive. Where is our park maintenance crew?

Captain Crabbish

27

Together

"Look at this, Claire. Captain Crabbish has returned," Guy said. He slid his copy of the *Squawker*, folded to the Letters to the Editor page, onto her lap. "And for once, I agree with the crank." He bent down from the rock where they sat to scrape goose droppings from his shoes.

"Everybody at the office was blathering about it in the coffee room yesterday. You'd think the messiah had returned," answered Claire.

"You're the one who called him an institution. Hailing his return goes with the territory. He chose a lofty topic for his comeback letter, though. Goose poop."

"After a hundred years of running commentary, I think he's entitled to any topic he wants, as long as its civil."

"There I was hoping he'd retired."

"Admit the truth. You only started to buy the *Squawker* because you wanted to comment on his letters, like just about everybody else in town. Patty's right about the draw he creates. I don't always agree with him but I'm glad he's back."

"After all that research you did, you never did figure him

out. It would have been quite a coup if you had."

Claire stood up abruptly at this, rolled the paper tight and handed it to Louis to add to the kindling in the sand pit. He set it afire just as Sandra emptied her arms of the last logs from the wheelbarrow. There was a slight breeze, not too strong for a Friday evening beach bonfire, but just enough to hold most bugs at bay.

Sandra reached out her fingers to catch the warmth of the budding flames.

"I can't remember the last time I did this, Louis," Claire heard her say. "When I was a kid, I think. My parents loved fires on the beach."

"I don't know how you resist, living here on The Point." He slung an affectionate arm around her shoulder. "You're one of those driven people who needs to be taught how to relax. I can help with that."

Sandra nuzzled into his shoulder.

Claire looked away from this intimate exchange and saw Meilin and Roxie approaching, followed by Ben with four others in tow. She drew in a sharp breath when she recognized Ricky with two, almost identical, women at his side. One was Celia. The younger had to be their long-lost daughter, Valentina. Behind them came Blue.

"We wanted to share our news," Ricky told Claire, beaming. "Valentina has come home."

Tears welled in Claire's eyes as Celia drew Valentina toward her.

"Valentina, this is Claire Munro. She worked to help us find you."

"What a pleasure to finally meet you," Claire told the young woman and gently took both of her hands. "You were very much missed. I'm so glad you're home safe."

Valentina looked awkward and pleased at the same time. Claire studied the young woman's eyes and face. Her spirit— the one that had dared to plunge into the wide world on her own and survive—wasn't evident there. It was hidden, Claire guessed, under a mask of complacency induced by a return to medication. Blue stood behind the Diazes and, reading Claire's face, reflected back a sorrowful expression that told Claire this was probably true. Ricky and Celia, by contrast, looked at peace with their hard-won reunion and their tenuous truce with their daughter. Valentina was a painful example of the collision of imperfect medical intervention with human nature. How long would it be before she tired of the oppressive chemicals and struck out again on her own? How long would she comply with a drug program that flatlined emotions, even if the alternative meant another round of instability and worsening psychiatric symptoms?

When the Diazes approached the fire, Ben pulled Claire and Guy aside with Blue.

"Claire, I owe you an explanation after your considerable help. The religious medallion from the drydock boat and the cross from under the dory are both Valentina's. Latin Catholic, not French Catholic, as we originally guessed."

"I can't believe I didn't think of that."

"Valentina has been the town thief and squatter all along, wandering from Louis's shed to the boatyard to the dory on La Palourde. It was Blue, here, who really rescued her and secretly kept her aboard her boat through the cold months."

Blue's and Claire's eyes met.

"It wasn't a secret from my point of view. She was homeless but of age," Blue told them. "She said her name was Tina, so I didn't make the connection to the missing Diaz woman. I don't leave the waterside much. I missed your posters until recently. Then, I had to convince her to come forward."

"I've seen the long hours you work here, Blue, so it's no wonder you didn't see the posters. You showed such kindness to a stranger, but then, it's what I've come to expect from most Mainers."

Blue's head dropped almost imperceptibly in acknowledgment before she wandered over to the fire.

"So, Valentina never truly left home," observed Guy.

"Somehow," said Ben, "that seems to be a comfort to her parents." He looked over at the Diazes with both compassion and puzzlement. "At least for now. She stayed aboard Blue's boat for a large part of the winter, with brief excursions outside when the weather warmed. Never thought Blue had it in her. The woman is as gruff as Jay Brown and a loner. Somehow Valentina got to the heart under all that sea-weathered skin."

"What about the shed fire? Did Valentina start it?" Guy asked quietly.

"She was definitely there. The earrings you found in the rubble, Claire—the ones crafted by Denise—those are Valentina's. She confirmed this. But we have no evidence to implicate her other than the earrings. And she left behind trinkets at every place she stayed. So many people traversed Louis's property, it could have been anyone or no one who started that fire. Even if Valentina did it, I suspect it was accidental, not arson. I sense nothing sinister about her. I've held off further questioning until she settles in. I need to move carefully so I don't spook her."

"I doubt Louis will want charges pressed one way or the other, knowing her circumstances," Claire said, her voice trailing off as she looked over at the group collecting around the fire.

"I expect the boatyard will be similarly forbearing," Ben said, "as there was no damage to the boat."

He returned to his beat, leaving Claire and Guy to themselves. Claire dipped her toes in the shallow water.

"While the tide's low, want to walk along the beach? I have a few things to tell you."

Guy took her hand, and they set off along the waterside.
"Should I be worried?"

"Remember the confidentiality rumor spread by Kitty?"

"I'm glad that's resolved." He squeezed her hand.

"Me, too, but the whole thing set me to thinking about receiving confidences. I'm worried one day I might be given one I can't share with you."

"Are you saying you're conflicted over maintaining honesty between us and divulging someone else's information to me?"

"In a nutshell, yes. The way people tend to confide in me, it might be necessary to withhold something from you someday."

"I can't say the thought is a surprise or even that I'm unsettled by it."

Claire studied him.

"But would you want to know I'm carrying a secret, at the very minimum, even if I don't divulge the details?"

"Only if it serves our mutual interest for me to know."

"If a secret ever threatened to come between us, I would tell you."

"I trust you completely, Claire."

He leaned over and kissed her head tenderly.

Guy's absolute trust, so plainly spoken, was a relief, but they made their way back to the beach fire and their friends in unequal equanimity. Guy seemed content to let things lie. Claire, less so. She came from a family bedeviled by secrets and lies and understood too well their punishing effect on relationships. She feared that, with her promise to Patty about the Captain, she had instigated the first fissure in her connection with Guy, a hairline fracture, but one that might not withstand the insidious forces of uncertainty and time. Though she chatted readily around the fire, inside, Claire remained deeply conflicted.

Once back at home, despite the late hour, she drew on

an old shirt and jeans and pulled rubber gloves onto her hands. She would either find something to scrub or scour the already clean. The action, not the outcome, mattered just now. She desperately needed to offload the torment. It was well after 1:00 a.m. when she finally fell onto her bed.

Guy arrived earlier than usual on Saturday morning. Claire answered the door wearing her cleaning clothes, rumpled from a restless sleep. Her hair was askew, and she hadn't yet splashed her face. The usual order of things by this time of the morning—fresh appearance, brewed coffee, breakfast underway—were not in evidence. She threw a sideways glance at the tell-tale bucket on the floor and the rags hanging over the sink, all too aware that Guy could read the signs of last night's mania. Her cheeks turned hot, and she dropped her gaze to the floor.

He shut the kitchen door and remained on the floor mat taking in the kitchen, so clean, Claire realized, it was almost blinding in the morning sunshine.

"You worked like a demon last night, didn't you?" he asked without needing an answer. "Claire, what's going on?"

She sank onto the nearest kitchen chair, tears streaming from her eyes. He kneeled down in front of her and pulled her head onto his shoulder.

"What is it?" he whispered and stroked her hair.

Claire kept her face hidden, uncertain how to answer. Her distress was all about honesty, impeccable honesty, the mainstay of any strong relationship. She had seen the lack of it in her parents' marriage and the damage it had done.

"I don't want to withhold things from you. I'm petrified of being the ruin of our future, all in the name of a loose connection to a near stranger. I've seen secrecy work on couples like undetected cancers, eating away at the bond between them."

"Is that what this is all about? You're torturing yourself for not betraying a confidence? That makes no sense, Claire.

You keep confidences all the time."

"Not from you." She looked into his eyes. "It's just that, for the first time, I was expressly asked to say nothing, and I promised out loud to say nothing, even to you. I wouldn't have done it if I'd thought it had any bearing on us, but I have felt increasingly uneasy ever since."

Guy rose, pulled her up to him and regarded her carefully.

"I trust us both not to let it come between us."

But the onion had another layer. Claire started crying again.

"The thing is, you're going to uncover this confidence I'm holding even if I don't say a word about it. You know me. You watch me. You read me."

"If that's how I discover it—and I won't be trying, mind you—you won't have broken your promise, and I'll keep mum about it."

Claire continued as if he hadn't spoken.

"Once we're living together, you'll intuit everything no matter how deep in my chest I've buried it."

Guy froze.

"Claire."

She wiped her eyes with her sleeve, then caught the intensity of his gaze.

"Are you saying you'll move in with me?"

"Absolutely not," she replied firmly.

Guy's intake of breath was audible, and Claire caught the pain that flicked across his face.

"We cannot," she quickly resumed, "squeeze two people comfortably into a 600-square-foot loft with all your business and art stuff and that awful, lumpy twin bed. You have to move in here."

He lifted her into an embrace that left her feet swinging over the floor and twirled her several times.

"When?"

"Today, now, if you'll risk it."

They didn't surface from Claire's bedroom for more than an hour. Afterward, Guy brewed tea and coffee and started a panful of bacon while she showered. When she emerged, he grinned like a little boy.

"I'll keep the loft for my business office and art studio. My rent there is low. What do you think?"

"Perfect. The rent here is low, too. I got a deal because the previous tenant was found floating face down in the bay."

She made a screwed-up face.

"I remember that horrible story but didn't realize yours was the place. So that's how, with housing in such short supply, you were able to find a place so quickly."

"Yeah. Nobody wanted to come near the building after that, so they rented it for a pittance to someone 'from away' who didn't know its history. But I scrubbed it so hard, there can't be a dust particle left of that sad history."

Guy gazed around at the blinding clean.

"No argument there."

She pulled some mugs from the cupboard and sat down, her mind already onto reorganizing for a housemate.

"We'll need to rearrange a bit around here and make room for an easel in the spare bedroom. You won't always want to paint in the loft."

"I love when you say 'we'."

He poured coffee for Claire, removed the finished bacon from the pan and cracked a few eggs into the remaining grease.

"Toast?" he asked.

"One slice, please."

When they were finally seated in front of their breakfast plates, Guy said, "Look, Claire, as much as I appreciate a clean home, can we try to avoid resurgence of the sterilization tornado that blew through here last night? Too much hygiene is just not healthy."

Claire laughed and promised to do her best.

They spent the rest of the day making Claire's place fit for two and shifting Guy's meager personal possessions from the loft to Harborview Street. Claire took charge of food while Guy collected clothes, toiletries and personal items. Before leaving the loft, they stepped over to Annabelle's house to inform her of the change.

"Don't worry," Guy assured his landlady. "I'll be here most work days and will be available to help you as usual."

"I'll bet you'll be even later with your rent," Annabelle teased.

"I'll remind him, Annabelle. And I'll come over to visit you every Sunday just as I have been," Claire promised.

Back at Claire's, Guy arranged his clothing in the dresser drawers and closet spaces Claire had cleared and set up a small painting corner in the spare bedroom, careful to protect the floor and walls from splatter. Claire stored the food from the loft in her—their—pantry and refrigerator. She couldn't stop grinning. In spite of all her reservations, she had finally taken the third plunge toward overcoming her fear of commitment. Gamophobia, psychologists termed it, a disorder that could lead to everything from heart palpitations to debilitating depression or to fanatical cleaning, in Claire's case. The first step had been dating Guy. The second introducing him to her family. The third, living together. With all her compulsions—psychology, cookie-binging, wardrobe decisions, people-watching—she thought it best to avoid a full-blown disorder if she could. She had enough to be getting on with.

Full credit for her strength this morning went to Guy, a man like no other she had met, a man who was master of how to leave space in a relationship. No one else could have convinced her to take this step. Daniel would be thrilled when she called him later this evening. The Gardiners would approve as well, once everyone was talking again. Hannah, whenever she resurfaced, probably around the holidays next year as she inevitably did, would screech.

But the qualms Claire held in her heart about withholding things from Guy lingered beneath her euphoria.

28

The Captain

By Sunday morning, Guy and Claire had settled into her apartment together as though their co-habitation was nothing new, which, as a practical matter, it wasn't. Claire had clung to that distinction, that fine line between serious dating and living together, to keep her fear in check. Now that she had crossed over and thrown caution to the wind, she felt a bit giddy and, at the same time, immensely content. That feral creature deep in her breast, the phobia born of misuse and neglect, occasionally stirred and rumbled. She could only hope that, with time and with Guy, it would finally be tamed.

After breakfast, Guy headed for the loft to collect his art gear. He planned to meet with Sandra over composition concepts for the painting she had commissioned, then to create a few color studies. While she waited for him to leave, Claire tapped away on the Smith Corona, now officially her own since Annabelle had refused its return. As soon as he pulled out, she grabbed her bag and headed for the Fish House, where she and Patty sequestered themselves once again, this time with coffee and fresh croissants.

Claire had been bursting for some time to meet with Patty again about the Captain. They had last parted in a quandary about how to handle his silence and how to interpret the clues that indicated Ellie Brown and he were the same person. Since then, Claire had learned much, and the *Squawker* had published the Captain's first comeback letter.

"You've seen the Captain's letter in the paper," Patty began. "It was delivered in the usual way, by regular mail, posted in Mayenne Bay, no return address, but I vacillated for several days before publishing." She reached into her desk drawer for the letter and handed it to Claire. "The paper isn't Ellie's. This letter was printed from a computer, not a manual typewriter." She laughed. "You see, I'm getting kind of nerdish myself."

"There's no reason the Captain or his successor shouldn't change his method to keep up with the times," Claire replied.

"True, but his sudden return combined with this change seems suspicious. It could mean that he passed the baton, and the successor has different methods, or that the same Captain decided to upgrade his devices, or else it's an exploitive fraudster. The writer enclosed no note to explain himself, which leads me to fear the third possibility."

"But you decided to print it anyway."

"Yes. The letter had the ring of the Captain, regardless of the mechanics. I took a chance. I haven't heard any objection from the Captain, whoever that is, so I'm hopeful."

Claire looked as if deciding where to begin.

"I'd like to back up a bit. I made a few more discoveries, including a red herring, but you should be aware of everything." She handed a sheet to Patty. "Here's a letter I found in one of Ellie's books from the garage sale. It expresses opposition to a 1925 town ordinance against pet lobsters." Patty threw her head back in laughter. "I revisited the *Squawker* microfiche for that year and didn't see it published. That's why I asked you for a few specimens from around that time. Did you bring them?"

Patty pulled out the writings Claire had requested and spread them on the desk. The two women leaned over to compare the penmanship to the lobster letter.

"It appears the handwriting is…or was…the Captain's of the time," Claire said, "so the lobster letter is probably authentic but not very useful to our present case. You can keep it for your archives. Now look at this, found in another of Ellie's books."

She placed the heavily used carbon in front of Patty.

"I can only decipher individual words or small letter strings from it, some misspelled. And since a digital word search is impossible on the microfiche, I can't match words to anything published. I think a ballpoint pen was used, which dates it 1945 or after. Any idea when he shifted from longhand to typing? I ask more out of curiosity than anything else."

"Not offhand. I'd have to go through the files to find the precise date. He's been typing his letters for decades now, since well before I bought the newspaper."

Claire leaned in.

"I think this particular carbon is a red herring, but its discovery sparked an idea that I was able to confirm. The latest Captain wrote his letter draft in longhand using a carbon to make a duplicate. He gave the original to Ellie to clean up, type and deliver to the paper and kept a carbon copy, plus the carbon itself, for his own record."

"What? That's sounds awfully convoluted, even contrived. You think there have been two parties in the business?"

"Yes. In fact, I'm sure of it."

Patty shook the computer-printed letter in the air.

"But if this came from the Captain, and Ellie is gone, someone else is doing the editing and typing now."

"Correct."

"How can you know this?"

"Because I have met the Captain."

"Oh, my God!" Patty jumped to her feet, spilling coffee from her mug. "You've actually identified him?"

Claire answered with a nod. Patty blotted the spillage with a tissue.

"But how?"

"Pure coincidence. One of those serendipitous moments when you're in the right place at the right time. I have those often. It's kind of my lot in life."

"Wait, back up a bit." Patty held up both palms. "You know the person who wrote the handwritten version of the comeback letter?"

"I do."

"And he and the Captain are one and the same?"

"They are."

Patty didn't hide her skepticism.

"How do you know this, Claire?"

"He showed me evidence, handwritten carbons and duplicate letters going back decades to the year he took over. He always kept records for himself. All of them were edited before delivery to the *Squawker*. I was able to match them up with the letters published in the *Squawker*."

Claire fell silent and waited for Patty to catch up, to realize what this all meant.

"So, the Captain was never Ellie."

"No, but Ellie was his secret editor and typist."

Another long pause.

"Does he want to keep writing?" Patty asked, eyes wide.

"He does. He's been anxious about missing issues of the *Squawker*. That March 6 letter about Gloria that you wrote in his name confused him. He agreed with the message but was worried an imposter was trying to take his place. The Captain has a strong sense of duty about his legacy. He sees his public statements as a service to the community, performed for generations, to keep Mayenne Bay on its toes."

Claire tilted her head to one side.

"You haven't asked who the Captain is."

Patty waved a hand.

"Because I don't want to know. It's better I don't."

"That's a relief," breathed Claire. "I can't share his identity. I was hoping we wouldn't have to battle over that."

"But how is he producing new letters now that Ellie has passed away?"

Claire reached once more into her sack to withdraw a cleanly typed letter, again printed on computer paper.

"This is the next installment from the Captain, edited and typed by me, on a tablet, not the Smith Corona, and laser-printed. I'm far too clumsy with the typewriter and see no reason not to use a computer. You will continue, though, to receive all letters in the traditional way after this one."

Patty once more rose to her feet.

"You're kidding. You don't mean…" When she next spoke, her voice was almost breathless. "Claire, are you sure you want this responsibility?"

"I am. If I don't, either the Captain stops writing, or his identity becomes known to yet another person. This is cleaner. And it's not like I'm typing a dissertation here." She lifted the newest letter. "This took me five minutes, tops."

"And the Captain has agreed to this?"

"Yes. He was relieved, in fact. Since Ellie's death, he's been in a panic, afraid his voice would die with her." Claire looked thoughtful. "Patty, I can't promise this arrangement will last forever, but it solves the immediate problem for the Captain, who wants to be heard, the *Squawker*, which needs him, and the Mayenne Bay gossip mill, always itching for more."

Patty came around her desk and hugged Claire.

"One more thing. I promised I would come to you first with whatever I learned, and I have. So far, I've told no one this information but you. Only the Captain and I know his identity. Only the Captain and you know I'm the typist and editor. And the day will come soon when I disclose everything to Guy. I'll tell you when I do."

"Got it," agreed Patty.

"And I don't want my involvement known to anyone outside the three of you…ever."

"You have my word."

Claire headed for the door acutely aware that she, who valued forthrightness and candor, had just committed to perpetuate a grand subterfuge on the populace of Mayenne Bay. She had already felt the adverse impact of unfavorable judgment in this little town. If her involvement with the Captain was found out, she had no doubt things could get much worse. She would be accused of influencing the Captain, disrupting the status quo, deceiving the populace. She, a newcomer, an immigrant from away, a foreign threat who had already been suspected of being untrustworthy. Then, the fat would really be in the fire. The sneering faces of Gloria, Erin and Kitty, for starters, floated before her eyes. But these faded behind others: Renée, Patty, Meilin, Morrie, Ricky, Celia, Celeste, Ben, Peggy, Annabelle and, especially, Guy, on whom she could count as allies. Because of them, there was a very real chance she would manage this little conspiracy with the Captain and keep her head above water.

Epilogue

It started in the late evening on the west side. Since it was early June, daylight hung on, so the early flames, small yellow and orange licks of air, were washed out in the brilliance of the unrelenting sun. The first indication that all was not well was a rising spiral of black smoke against the bright sky. Mayenne Bay's unsightly canning factory, as though it could face the town's disownment no longer, was about to self-destruct by fire.

The first to spot the smoke trail was Blue as she brought the tugboat into dock. Within minutes of her 911 call, sirens wailed and firetrucks roared by. Mayenne Bay's own firefighters were joined soon afterward by fire brigades from adjacent towns. Even their combined response would be hard-pressed to contain the fire within the grounds if the whole factory erupted into a full-blown conflagration, which looked probable.

A crowd gathered just outside the bustle of emergency responders, muttering amongst themselves their collective surprise that the place hadn't caught fire before this. The factory's wooden structure was old and quite dry, aside from airborne moisture off the bay, and there had been no rain for some time. Various inspections conducted last year in preparation for the doomed condominium complex on the site had revealed greasy floors and leaky cans of food-grade and machinery oil all around the factory's ground level. There was enough fat in this fire to light up the place like a tinder box.

The county Emergency Management Agency promptly issued an evacuation order for buildings surrounding the site and advised a shelter-in-place order for all within a half mile's circumference, anticipating the ballooning smoke and stench would pose respiratory problems. Though the factory had been cleared of toxic materials late last summer, the odor was nevertheless noxious, and the hazmat team was summoned, just in case. The harbor and sidewalks of Mayenne Bay emptied quickly. Windows slammed shut. Ventilators and air conditioners that drew in outside air were closed off. Residents dug out respiratory masks from their closets. The emergency room prepared for an uptick.

At the sound of the siren and roaring trucks so close by, Mayor Edgecomb stepped outside the office to identify the firetrucks' destination. At the same time, Chief Manning jogged past and breathlessly called out the news. Sandra raced back to the office and grabbed the protective gear she kept stored there, then followed him down to the waterside and along the wharf that ended at the factory site. What had begun as a flicker had fanned into a full blaze by the time she arrived. She stepped back a bit to avoid the radiating heat and adjusted her goggles and face mask. As the flames quickly intensified, a billowing, black cloud of smoke began to drift toward US Route 1, threatening visibility for highway traffic. Police sirens could be heard heading for the bridge.

Claire and Guy closed up the apartment on Harborview Street, gathered some food, valuables and a change of clothes and made their way to the loft to wait out the fire a few miles away from ground zero. Annabelle climbed the stairs to the loft to watch through the second story windows. With the height advantage, it was easy to see the sizeable glow of the fire in the sky, even before sunset. When night fell, the high, arced streams of water from the army of firetrucks sparkled in the light of the flames and floodlights. Even from a distance, there was no doubt that, by morning, the old factory would be nothing but a pile of blackened bones.

Curious as she was about the origin of the fire, Sandra didn't dare disturb Louis or the other responders while they were in the thick of it all. She made her way to the Fish House where she was sure many townspeople had gathered in defiance of the evacuation advice. Sure enough, the place was packed. Patty was keeping the doors open for the duration of the fire, unless the situation dictated otherwise, and had the police scanner turned to full volume on the checkout counter. So far, Sandra learned, no evidence had been found of persons in the burning building, and no one had been injured. Relieved, she milled about the place among the crowd hoping to pick up information from the chatter that might be useful to the inevitable fire investigation. The competing speculation bounced from mischievous kids to a desperate homeless person to deliberate arson. In other words, no one had a clue.

She ordered a cup of coffee and drank it standing at the window with a view of the blaze. Already, she worried about the fire's impact on her constituents and reflexively began to prepare her mind for the blowback on the mayor's office. Assuming no direct injuries or deaths at the site, prolonged exposure to smoke was the greatest potential risk, especially smoke from burning oil and plastics that could release dangerous substances and trigger respiratory, even cognitive issues. Children, the sick and the elderly would be particularly vulnerable. No doubt her phone would ring nonstop with overblown complaints about the disruption to homes and businesses caused by the temporary evacuation and shelter-in-place orders. It had amazed her, since taking office, how quickly real injury could be overshadowed by minor incommodiousness in people's minds. She gritted her teeth and determined not to allow these distractions to hijack energy and resources required for the truly needy. She would not permit real injury or loss to be dwarfed by the inconvenience factor.

Even now, with the fire roaring, smoke spreading and terror among the populace, Sandra knew things could have been much worse. Emergency teams had arrived in record time. No persons had been killed, injured or even found on site, so far. No workers would be displaced by the factory loss; the town would not be forced to contend with a sudden and considerable increase in unemployment. And, as plans were already underway to clear the old building, one could argue the fire was doing the town a favor, as long as everyone stayed safe. Bulldozing a pile of ashes to make way for the "Better Idea" project would be cheaper and easier than demolition of a standing factory.

All this, Sandra kept to herself for the time being, knowing full well her present optimism might not be shared. The gossipmongers of Mayenne Bay would feast for weeks, maybe months, on this incident, and even Captain Crabbish would have a field day, but she had every confidence Mayenne Bay would bounce back once the smoke cleared.

PERCY A. SANBORN

Percy Sanborn was a real Maine artist, born in 1849 in Waldo, Maine, who lived most of his life in Belfast, Maine, where he was struck by a car and killed in 1929. Percy worked in both watercolors and oils and painted seascapes, landscapes, still lifes and animal portraits. He is particularly known for his paintings of ships. He began his career as a sign painter and window shade decorator and also worked as an illustrator, theater backdrop painter, potter, wood engraver and violinist.

DOLLY SMITH

Dolly Smith was a real Maine artist, born in 1824 in the seafaring community of Prospect (later named Searsport), Maine. She painted landscapes, portraits and animals and painted so prolifically, she was the premier artist in the upper Penobscot area until she died in 1891. Her large landscape featuring Hiawatha currently hangs in the Carver Memorial Library in Searsport.

Note from the Author

Quite unexpectedly, writing has become a mission for me. Not a day goes by when I can't wait to get to my desk. Ironically, I find it hard to put the reason for this compulsion into words. My goal is to create an alternative to sensational story-telling, so prevalent on bookshelves, that kindles appreciation for all that is captivating in everyday life.

Brush with Fire is my second Mayenne Bay novel. By now, I've fallen so much in love with the place and the characters of my own invention that I can understand why authors write series that run into many volumes.

I have the usual family and friends to thank for this book, though there is nothing at all usual about their contributions to my life and work. They correct my mistakes, broaden my perspective and fan my imagination while making sure I don't lose track of the essential humanity in my stories.

I should also put in a word of thanks to Sir Arthur Ignatius Conan Doyle for his influence on this book.

KIM YESIS lives in Mid Coast Maine with her husband and creative partner, fine artist Peter Yesis.

www.ingramcontent.com/pod-product-compliance
Lightning Source LLC
Chambersburg PA
CBHW021023310726
48969CB00006B/1522